I0565479

# Artificial Intelligence-
# Twilight of the Dexterous

• • • •

## Symbiogenesis and
## Dialectics of Man-Machine Intelligence

• • • •

• • • •

By: Paco Pérez Vega

• • • •

Cover design: Mell Media Productions

Digital Art by Francisco J. Pérez Vega


This book was originally written in Spanish.

Translation by: Francisco J. Pérez Vega

First English Edition: 8-2023

ISBN: 978-0-9650-1433-5


• • • •

• • • •

# About the Author

Francisco (Paco) José Pérez Vega was editor of his father's collection of poems, ***Poemario y Otros Escritos de Angel Casto Pérez Torres*** published in 1999. Industrial Engineer graduated from University of Puerto Rico at Mayagüez and has a Master's Degree in Operations Research from Columbia University in New York. He has worked in supply chain, research, and planning in multinational companies such as Bellcore, Intel, Hewlett Packard, and Sartorius from where his interest in the topics covered in this book arises. Passionate about nature, he was a self-taught agricultural entrepreneur for 17 years in the cultivation of ornamental plants and landscape gardening. His current interests are his family, cultivation and use of medicinal plants, and reading philosophy.

# Dedication

*I have a problem, words haunt me, invade my thinking.*
*FJPV Sept/10/2020*

· · · ·

I dedicate these pages, first, to my beloved wife Rosannie, my source of inspiration, the one I keep trying to impress every day; to my mother, Migdalia Vega Ortíz, who sacrificed much of her potential to dedicate it to the upbringing and sustenance of myself and my siblings after the death of my father. Together with my stepfather Carlos Vélez Rivera, they gave me the opportunity to be who I am today, and they were a worthy example that I try to follow every day of what parents should be.

I also dedicate this book to all those who for some just reason in the quest to change the world or by innocent mistake lost their freedom and have been unjustly condemned to penalties that exceed the fault. To those, in these circumstances and who lack a vocation for violence, I say that true justice is in the hands of the creative force of the universe, and I encourage them with the fact that misfortune often leads to life in fullness if you know how to take advantage.

Finally, I dedicate these pages to my sons, Francis André, Gabriel José and Josué Omar. I have always known that I am a better written communicator than a verbal one, especially for things of feelings. That is why I write with the hope of telling you things that I may not have spoken to you, inspired by lessons from my life and many of the things I learned in my readings, which you often told me did not apply. It may be that my actions, like those of many brothers, do not obviously reflect my learnings, but my intentions were always guided by my heart and the inspiration of my readings. I hope that these sheets speak to you and many of your generation so that you can recover the world that unfortunately we did not deliver in the best way, although there are many of us that are innocent. There is much to save, much to recover, much to give back. I have faith in you and your generation, I have seen you act. Don't waste time. I know you can set course right and achieve the optimistic results of today's pessimistic challenges. Do not hesitate, work hard, and surrender to your passions. I'll leave you with one of mine...

# Prologue

This book was written at a time in my life when unusual and negative events like the COVID-19 pandemic were happening, so I needed an escape, a way to put my thoughts on positive things and disconnected from the reality of the moment. It is a compilation of moments where I was able to connect to my innermost self and recapture the curiosity that pursues me tirelessly, the empathy that is part of my nature that is lost when growing up we realize that there is a lot of evil, lack of civility and selfishness in this blessed world in which we live. Writing it reconnects me with my essence, the great empathy I remember having as a child, and my desire in doing so is to share some disguised ideas, others clear, and experiences that may serve others to spend a pleasant time or introspection.

There are some ideas of my own and many universal ideas compiled, adapted, reinterpreted, and applied to the subject I am dealing with. The topics I touch on here are topics that concern me mainly about the future of humanity. Great transitions of social consciousness are coming, from the proliferation of artificial intelligence, transparency in everything we do, the consequent and irremediable return to rurality to heal the planet and ourselves, and the greater use of plants and good nutrition to prevent and treat diseases. In the text, fiction is mixed with reality, moving characters in time to real moments in the past and creating pseudo-real images. I intersperse glimpses, some jocularity, and philosophical ideas to be versatile and make a topic that can be heavy lighter, trying to keep the reader introspective.

I am not a writer, I am an engineer with a vestige of scientific biologist, therefore, my fluency in expression may not be the best, so excuse my audacity to venture to write this. It's out of catharsis, intellectual necessity, or commitment to debt to my ancestors, or perhaps fate. I have lived zigzagging, I took several paths leaving behind others well walked and safe, sometimes without thinking about it; perhaps this writing is the culmination of the crossroads, or perhaps I reinvent myself again. The important thing for me is to keep walking without boredom, always growing.

Another motivation to sit down to write this is that I am not proud, as I know many in my country, of the lack of morality and social commitment of our rulers (echo of what happens in many other countries as well), and of the musical contribution of my country to the current world with reggaeton. Don't get me wrong, the rhythm is sticky and fun, the problem is the lyrics. There are hopeful words, powerful words, necessary words that must be spoken and having the medium some of the exponents of this popular music are mute to them, they are mutes of goodness and beauty in their art. The lyrics are something that can be powerful, that must carry transformative messages, not the constant denigration of women and the explicit vulgar lyrics that it contains that does not honor at all. We want a better country, a better world, we must start there. We are a talent pool, boys but at the height of our brothers in the world; we have had great contributions to the world such as the educational philosophy of Eugenio María de Hostos, the altruism of the best baseball player Roberto Clemente, the overflowing talent of Rita Moreno, the justice of Sonia Sotomayor, and many others, public and others in anonymity, I am inspired by all of them, to honor them, and I hope that my words do justice to the honor of my country demonstrating that not everything has been lost and that writing of value come out of my little island.

I hope the reader can understand my message: many changes are coming ahead in the way of living, technology is a great tool for progress, our ally if we know how to use it, but we must avoid taking away the inherent of our humanity, critical thinking balanced by intuition, creativity and millenary artisanal skills that connect us to mother earth, to our individuality, to our inner self, therefore, to the universe.

I share here some poems of my father, who since childhood even in absence for his early call of the universe, has been a source of inspiration for my actions ... Enjoy the reading.

Paco 12/15/2020-2/27/2023

# ARTIFICIAL INTELLIGENCE - TWILIGHT OF THE DEXTEROUS

I share below some of the legacy from my father (loosely translated) ...

## Mission
By: Angel Casto Pérez Torres

I keep the sadness of time that vanishes,
I carry in my heart the scorching fire of tenacity
and well, well inside my soul I love humanity
And a concern is in my mind that overwhelms.
I raise through life awareness of the
mission to which I have come,
That my actions all complete the chain
Of a task destined for good that inspires me.
By straight roads I will find the destination
A noble hope will be the light of my life.
My intense living will be my good path.
I'll wander around looking for hidden truths
and in honor of my love I will serve the enemy
and loving I will fight until I surrender
The account of my mission accomplished.

## Ah! The Man
By: Angel Casto Pérez Torres

Ah! The Man, The Man
It is machine, it is stone, it is nothing,
product of any time
that looks out into new worlds
and his land swallows him.
Ah! The Man:
He has his feet on the ground,
It's materialism, it's science
for his greatness is
very close to the stars...
Launches large ships into the air
while there are souls who suffer;
Light the sky and the seas
and even the earth destroys.
A new man is needed!
to stand on a stone
whence a rope
so that the peoples may be bound.
A light that focuses the world
and points us to the path.

# PACO PEREZ

## Rebellion
By: Angel Casto Pérez Torres

• • • •

Flames in rebellion rise angrily
The smoke of pain blackens the skies
Man is despondent, lost in the unclean age
of a pain that does not hurt and a fire that is not fire.

• • • •

The mountains have been lacerated by man and wind;
that fleeting wind that blows the whole world,
that creeping wind that sweeps the ravines,
that inhuman wind that leaves the roses,
that scares away butterflies and withers basils;
that wind that dries from all feeling,
that withers souls and muddies the waters,
that makes misfortunes laugh and cry bonanzas ...

• • • •

It's nothing being all that fire stirred up
by the fleeting wind of soulless men
that shake the earth and muddy the waters,
that harm so many lives,
that behind clouds of evil hide the stars,
who are everything and are nothing,
which are hornless bulls; Men made of earth
who is to eat the earth.

# Chapter 1: The Reunion

".. routine things of those who get involved in transforming the world." – Pepe Mujica

• • • •

Transforming the world is the mission of many, the destiny of others and an accident of a few. It is an arduous task, of uncertain route, better walked accompanied than alone. Some lose their sanity in the attempt, others sacrifice everything for their ideal and even lose their lives or their friends in their quest, many abdicate for lack or stripping of will, few go at a steady pace and achieve their goal, and a derisory group changes it without knowing that they did it. Diego Vega was a steady walker in that walk, a Tibetan ex-monk who was accompanied on his way by a sane deranged assistant, a pure love, a devoted friend, another whom he rescued on the road, an old proverb, and the best intentions. Here I tell you his story, as it was narrated to me by my aunt Verónica while I took care of her already in years, reliable source, although fickle.

The story began on a spring evening, where the philosopher Diego Vega contemplated his life with the wisdom of man realized, with "the pen as the tongue of the soul" and emptying his spirit on paper. The gentle breeze caressed his face already torn by wrinkles. The hairs of his cracked arms skin bristled and danced with the passing of the air. His head's hair was already partially disheveled by the grasp of the wind, wandering around the head extending as far as their length allowed. The hum of the wind as it passed through the branches of the Australian pine[1] that he sowed on better days served as a melody, almost like a lullaby. The afternoon was perfect. It was the time of day when the lights don't shine. It was the best time to remember in solitude. Diego Vega meditated on his life and wrote his memoirs, with the firm pressure that deforms the fingers of his left:

*"Life is a path forged from many decisions we make. It is full of crossroads, of mutually exclusive paths that we can only walk once and then pass into memory. Each moment is unique, and each moment of decision marks us. But there is a problem, ... the transcendental decisions of life, whose adequacy is elusive or belatedly revealed, and mostly their consequences are irreversible. Once we*

decide, we usually have the ephemeral question: *What if I had made the other decision?* We will never know that because the paths are mutually exclusive, and each decision is an irreversible path already taken. The road is irreversible, but the final destination is achievable, even if we deviate from the most bearable path. So, the future direction of our life is determined by our actions and the choices we make today. It is up to us to decide if our path is full of scars or if on the contrary, its full of pleasant memories.

I have many gre at memories, but also a good basket of scars on my back. Why in life can nothing good be obtained without suffering? The currency of exchange of goodness is suffering. Everything good is always preceded by much suffering. For example, when I graduated with a master's degree in philosophy, the good, but to achieve it I had to make great sacrifices – work, stay up late studying, live with limitations – the bad. Another example, when someone struggles to reach a managerial position in the company in which he/she works, he/she sacrifices precious time with family, and friends that he/she could or may have cultivated. Usually, the greater the "achievement," the greater the suffering to attain and retain it. There are always two baskets in the balance of life, that of suffering that balances with that of achievement itself.

Maybe life should be lived differently... backwards. In the current mainstream "modus vivendi", we invest time of our youth in not living life, struggling to overcome ourselves and achieve tangible, material, and empty goals, which then in our maturity, when we finally have time, we can enjoy halfway because we already lack the strength and health to do so. Spending our youth making money to enjoy it in the part of our lives that is less fiery is one of the bad moves of modern life. That's why we must enjoy the journey more, the now, not just the destination.

We should spend our youth discovering new things, meeting needs for friendship and brotherhood, intellectual and spiritual. We would all be philosophers, loving knowledge, solving problems practically, independently, and simply, using the truths in what we are taught and discarding the unproven or the falsehoods created, seeking the way to achieve what older people say cannot be done. Perhaps, if we could have more freedom in our youthful years, freedom not licentiousness, we could reach our maturity more fully and calmly, having satisfied our spirit. We spend our youth drowning in created material needs that lead us to become machines for production and accumulation of wealth. We *become slaves of our own, of our created needs. Why? After all, the wisest people who are revered by all and who truly left a mark on the history of the world, for the most part, lived a life poorly or with great suffering. Suffering and poverty magnify the spirit and make it noble and giving.*

*But as we all in one way or another seek to be "someone" and being "someone" is defined in our society mainly as being a person with money, power or having honorable titles, we blur in that direction instead of striving to be better people every day, seek wisdom, use our talents to the maximum and help others. Making our lives worthy of contemplation and admiration for ourselves should be our north. If we did this, the rest would come as an addition. Oh, and if we don't help others, at least let's not get in the way of those who are doing it.*

*The purpose of life should always be to continually learn and improve, to use our talents to the fullest, and to help others. This message is very important, and we must pass it on to our offspring, but with the care that this is not misunderstood or served as an excuse not to be realized and always seek to be the best they can be.*

*I feel satisfied because I lived my life partly upside down. In my youth I dedicated myself to living, growing later. I realize that I am a multi-potential individual, that is, a person with multiple interests, aptitudes, and creative abilities for whom it is difficult to specialize in something for a long time. I am good at synthesizing ideas, I learn fast, and I adapt easily to change. Therefore, I studied only what interested me, and although I was interested in many things, I only paid attention to what satisfied me most with immediate curiosity. I shared with my friends a lot, played many sports just for fun, never to crush or humiliate the opponent. I preferred team sports so I could share more with others. I helped on my grandfather's farm when I could without expecting anything in return, only the stories and wisdom of my grandfather, and what great wisdom that of that man with very little education.*

*Although I consider myself intelligent, I always had my doubts, I never had excellent grades for leniency and lack of focus due to my multiple interests. When the time came for me to enter the university, I preferred before starting, to enrich my spirit, and with the money saved from the courtyards that I cut for the neighbors on weekends and summers, to satisfy my curiosity for the teachings of the Tibetan monks, I bought a visa, passport and one way ticket to Khatmandu, Nepal. I learned about this destination after reading a National Geographic article about how this place was the link between the East and Europe, it was the place where trade routes converged through the Himalayas, being the destination of adventurers, explorers, free spirited people, climbers of Everest and many other people who, like me, sought to learn or were curious about the myths and teachings of the monks. What an adventure! My mother, the poor one, was very sorry for my decision and departure. My father, on the other hand, supported my departure because he said that risk helped me form as a person. I was too young to know what suited me, but with an adventurous spirit and an open mind I set off. In Khatmandu, after several attempts I was accepted into the monastery of the Buddhist school of Dzogchen and devoted myself to study, work and learn self-discipline. My Lamas were always generous in advice, wisdom, always cheerful, and devoted to the Dharma, and I was elated with that. The monastery became my spiritual refuge. In retrospect, I made a good decision to do this. In the end, I was in Nepal for 3 years in cloister to complete my basic education in Buddhist philosophy spending much of my time in solitary meditation or with my Lama.*

*After these years, already practicing Buddhism, I returned home, and when I finally applied to university, it was not hard being admitted. I was admitted to the humanities department. All my friends told me not to do it because I wasn't going to prosper financially, but I didn't care. There is no greater treasure than wisdom. I loved reading and thought that being in that department I could have the opportunity to read the great philosophers and rediscover the wisdom already lost or forgotten. I wanted to become richer in spirit than what Buddhism already gave me, to follow the route of enlightenment.*

*It was at Columbia University in New York where I met my great friends, including Rupert Llorens. Rupert studied in the same department and was a little more energetic, not to say radical. As we were both "cut with the same scissors", neither of us were interested in fraternities or the waste of time in dance, bottle, and deck activities, we only sought to make ourselves better people. Although from time to time we threw a little dance and gave ourselves a "jumera". However, the peer pressure was demanding for us to join the revelry, in other words, to become members of a fraternity. New York City provides many temptations, but the rigor of Columbia University is a brake on the dedicated student. It was then that I suggested to Rupert that we establish a "Fraternity" whose goal was to surpass oneself intellectually and spiritually, rather than* *socially. We called this group – Lambda (Catalyst) Gamma (the propagation constant) Delta (change) (ΛΓΔ), which later became known as "El **LeGaDo**". The mission of Lambda Gamma Delta is to this day to be a catalytic group that constantly promulgates change to improve the mind and spirit of its members and society. We never thought that something like this would evolve into what it later was, a pool of talent. "*

It is here that the story of everything that happened begins and led Diego to his retirement, deserved, not by flight, not precocious for lack of faculties, but for some wear and tear and desire for free intellectual production.

Verónica, his wife, interrupts one of his writing moments like the previous one—aren't you going in? it's already getting dark.

Diego answers, "I'm going, my love, it's so cool and you know that I love being outside".

It was a spring afternoon in the tropics, windy and pleasant temperature. The breeze carried away the typical humidity of the tropics that makes the skin sticky, but the stickiness was also appeased by the cool temperature. In her veil, the breeze dragged the smells of gardenia flowers that adorned the surroundings. The swaying of the trees was like an orchestra to the chord of the breeze that conducted them. The breeze filled the lungs with pure air and the soul with peace.

- Diego: My love, I am to be reunited with my great friend Rupert, with whom I had lost contact for too long. I feel very cheerful.

- Verónica: But you know you were in delicate health... Come, I made you a soup. Remember that Rupert and Yael must be coming shortly. We must prepare.

- Diego: For God's sake Verónica! it's just a cold that I already overcame, but that's fine, I'm coming.

Diego Vega was a man in his seventh good decade, of medium stature and skinny. His face was elongated, broad forehead and had pronounced cheekbones. His nose was thin, and his mouth had thin lips, almost erased. His complexion was white, though not totally pale, and he tanned easily. His hair was mostly brown despite his age. He looked and had a drive as a much younger person, possibly in two decades younger than he actually was.

Verónica, on the other hand, was a very elegant woman in her sixties. Her natural beauty always radiated. She had been a dancer in her youth and always wore her black hair pulled back in the style of ballerinas. Her figure was slender and contoured. Her eyes were sincere green. Her speech was very sweet and leisurely. Like Diego, she looked a decade younger than her age, but she was a four-year period younger than Diego. Now, don't be fooled by appearances, she was very smart.

But the old youthfulness they held was sustained by their persistence in consuming natural things. The secret of both to stay young was a mostly vegetarian diet, daily exercise, and several natural supplements that they took daily with a lot of discipline. Among these, they took Berberine, Resveratrol and NMN. They also consumed flaxseeds, and maqui in smoothies. They made _Bacopa monnieri_ teas to keep a clear mind. In addition, Diego took a supplement of He Shou Wu to keep his hair dark and other things working and applied black castor oil to prevent hair loss he bought from a producer in Haiti. Of course, you had to get away from his side when he put the black castor oil because of its smell of incense burning.

The occasional fast was also part of their routine and Verónica's vegetable and viands soup was another secret that this time was as always, delicious. Verónica, among her polyfacetism, was a great cook. She always said that she even threw the rag on her stews. She gave her personal touch to any recipe with spices in her garden. On this occasion, she added a mallet of cilantro that gave a Creole taste to the soup. Because Diego was so ingrained in his roots, it filled his heart and soul, as well as his belly.

After dinner, with a happy heart Diego went to his office to continue his notes in his memoirs:

"_Lambda Gamma Delta (ΛΓΔ), began as an escape from the pressure of friends to join fraternities, but ended up being a wonder for the intellectual and character development of the members. We took ideas from Benjamin Franklin's "Junto" to conduct the meetings and select members. Like Franklin's Junto, we met on Fridays to discuss various topics, but mostly morals, politics, and philosophy. Membership was at the invitation of other members and the approval of new members had to be unanimous. The criteria for selecting new members were: that the interested party should be recommended by an existing member, candidates should have a good academic grade point average, be a good reader, should above all have an interest in improving intellectually and improving society, which was demonstrated with an admission essay. The_ *stimulation of the topics of conversation was guided by the basic questions that Benjamin Franklin created. Questions such as: "Have you found anything in your latest readings that you think is meaningful, novel or beneficial to discuss?; or, Do you know of any citizen who has done an action that is worthy of imitation or recognition?; or Do you know of someone who is undertaking and whom our group can support?; Have you heard of any attack on any member of our fraternity and how can we defend him? Is there a difficulty of opinion, justice or injustice, that any of you want to share for advice?, and so on. Following this process, Rupert and I were gradually joined by the most talented students in the university, and we had to limit membership to 10 per year only to keep discussions productive. We met in the student center of the university and from there we went to the library and asked for a closed study room where we dedicated an hour a week to the topics that by mutual agreement we wanted to discuss. Sometimes they were recent event issues, other legal, scientific, philosophical, esoteric and many others almost impenetrable. We said... "No one should get lost in other people's opinions, formulate your own". The most important principle guiding us was to avoid clinging to viewpoints that become mental obstacles and obstacles to intellectual growth. Beyond the ego, is the one who has freed his mind. "*

Diego was always a "generalist", that is, he always had an intense appetite to learn from everything. When he decided to learn something, he did it with tenacity, determination, and good attitude until he mastered the subject. Therefore, all his life, after founding Lambda Gamma Delta (ΛΓΔ), he had dedicated at least two years to deeply study and practice different subjects in a self-taught way because of his conviction that ten thousand hours of practice are required to become experts in a subject. For this reason, he understood and conversed with authority about the humanities, law, horticulture, botany, architecture, entomology, economics, physics, chemistry, communications, microbiology, astronomy, physiology, metaphysics, sociology, and philosophy; If I keep naming subjects, I will kill him as an old man. The latter was his strongest subject, since he had an encounter and was vested for life, so this area of knowledge became his duty. Something else that sticks with me is that for fun he played chess and reached the Heroic rank.

Diego's writing is interrupted when Verónica announces that Rupert and Yael had already arrived.

"Let's go to receive them", Verónica says.

When they opened the front door, they saw Rupert and Yael. Rupert was a man of seven decades too, with a wide but good-looking face, medium height, and moderately dark complexion. His brown eyes, as well as his hair although he was much grayer than Diego. Yael was very thin, short in stature, paper-white complexion with long brown hair. Her face was thin and her eyes brown. The smile of both was wide and sincere and they were confused in hugs with their hosts in the hall.

Diego shook hands with his old friend and said the following sentence: "*I am another you, ...*", to which his friend Rupert responds, "*... You are another me.* ", and they blend together again in a strong hug patting each other on the back with emotion that they then felt quietly for a long time. This phrase was the traditional Mayan greeting that they adopted as a salute for the fraternity they founded in their university years. Rupert and Diego had not seen each other for more than 25 years. Even in meetings of their common work organization they had not coincided at any time. It was exciting to look back on old times, especially those of the ΛΓΔ fraternity. Both were better people for founding and guiding the group in their college years. The last time they met before today's meeting, Rupert publicly served as a prominent consulting sociologist for a leading marketing company and lectured at several renowned universities, was chosen to work on a new confidential strategy for a client in Switzerland and had since lost contact.

For many years both wanted to know the whereabouts of their friend, but because of the intensity, the secrecy of their employment and their passion for the work they exercised since their separation they did not have the opportunity to truly dedicate time to reunite, and digital media did not emerge until after they no longer knew how to find each other. Those were different times, of little computer technology and telecommunications, when they began to exercise their current roles, which did not allow them to keep in touch. In addition, their jobs required little presence in the cybernetic media that were just beginning to exist, and even today both remain anonymous from the networks out of necessity. However, a coincidence of life caused them to know about each other, and to discover that they had been working together furtively for more than two decades without knowing it. Today was the day they would finally share together again. A rare exception, allowing face-to-face encounters, in the organization for which they were employed.

After the hug, and the cross introduction to the ladies, the two couples walked to the large room of the house. The chemistry between Verónica and Yael was instantaneous, as if they had known each other as children. When they arrived at the room and located themselves, they began the conversation...

Diego: You don't know the pleasure I get to see you.

Rupert: We feel the same way. The road was very long but the excitement is worth it. You have a beautiful house.

Verónica: Thank you. Would you like anything to drink?

Rupert: No, thank you. On the way we stopped for a drink. Maybe later, don't you think Yael?

Yael: Yes, later. Thank you. Verónica, why don't we go to prepare something for later, talk about women stuff and let these two catch up on their affairs?

The visit was friendly, but also for work, more friendly than work, Verónica and Yael knew it. But knowing the dedication of their husbands to their occupation, although not all the details, both women stood up and left for the kitchen. They were women who were aware of the important work their husbands did, although they did not fully know all the details because of the confidentiality policies of their positions. They liked to give them the space to do their work when necessary, although at this time they wanted to allow them to speak freely of their forked past. Both were highly educated and skilled women, with very high self-esteem and noble hearts. So, Diego and Rupert continued chatting.

Diego: Well Rupert, so many years without seeing each other and without knowing that we worked with a common goal.

Rupert: Yes, and our selection seems to have had its beginning in the fraternity that we founded as my teacher explained to me. Unbelievable how peer pressure led us to that. How much we learned with it and how much good it has done since then! Did you hear that it is currently listed as one of the most prestigious fraternities in the nation? The New York Times in its social section, dedicated an article to explain the caliber of the graduated members and their professional achievements, as well as to try to explain the process of selecting the members. That part was a stream of nonsense, which I don't know where they got it from.

Diego: We didn't do anything wrong. I am so isolated developing my last treatises on morals, that I have not been watching the press these last weeks, although my assistant updates me when I ask him on specifics. You know how the press is, what they do not know they invent and if what they invent gives them front pages or more exposure time, they continue to give it until a brave man denies them or other news surpasses it. What concerns and worries me today is the resolution of the multiple moral dilemmas that afflict our society today. That issue of the lack of truth of the press to sell and gain audience at all costs is precisely one of the conflicts that I have on the agenda to postulate and attack. Now that I know that you are the Sociologist of The Nine, we can work more closely on this and other socio-moral issues. It will be like in fraternity again.

Rupert: Precisely. But first, explain a little bit about how you found out you had been selected for the position.

Diego: Do you remember that I was always interested in philosophy and especially moral dilemmas?

Rupert: Of course, we called you "Mister Right" of affection.

Diego: I just remembered... Well, you know we lost contact after your trip to Switzerland. Ten years later, when I was still a professor of philosophy, I was called to an audience with Pope John Paul II. I am not a saint, nor was I a practical Catholic at the time, so I was surprised by the invitation, but being so fervent I thought Verónica had organized something. I had my audience with John Paul II. However, it was not what I thought. The Pope received me in a private audience. He talked to me as if he were interviewing me for a job, asking me all sorts of things about my past, my studies, and my position on current moral issues and other global issues. Then he asked his whole entourage to leave us alone. He began to tell me about a secret society originally of nine men who secretly control the destiny of humanity. They are not Gods, but their power is one level below God's, he said. You know what I mean. He said: The nine men are specialists and scholars in one of the nine disciplines Physics and Gravitation, Physiology, Microbiology, Chemistry,

Alchemy (today materials science), Communication (today includes computing), Astronomy, Light, and Sociology. He then explained to me that given how complex it could be to decide how to proceed in some of these areas, because of the moral conflicts involved, it had been decided quite some time ago that a tenth man would be added to the group so that by his moral caliber he could have the last word in deciding the controversies of the other nine. The lineage of that tenth man today was Pope John Paul II. He told me then that the decision to add the tenth man to The Nine arose in 364 AD, and that the first chosen one was St. Augustine. The foundations of morality are grounded in the teachings of Jesus, Siddhartha Gautama and Plato. It was then that he explained to me that, based on the prophecies of Fatima, his earthly time was about to end, so a successor should be chosen for him in this secret role, and that for reasons of security and diplomacy it had been decided that he would not be a member of the faculty of the Holy Roman Apostolic Church. He understood that because of my intellectual and moral caliber that he had studied for several years, I should be his successor.

At that moment my skin bristled. From stupor, I did not know what to answer to such a holy being. I asked him if that was not the responsibility of his successor in the Vatican. He told me that this position was nothing religious, but that it was meritorious of a person of my moral caliber demonstrated with the founding of the fraternity and its legacy of men of probity, as well as for all the works and publications he had read about me that he described as magnifying for the universal principles of morality as were the words of Eugenio María de Hostos (he knew that I was Puerto Rican). Then he kept arguing because he understood that I was the right person. Finally, when it was over, it only occurred to me to tell him as María told Angel Gabriel... I humbly said to him, "Let your will be done to me." He smiled then... I'm telling you all this because I know you're in this too.

He also warned me of other antagonistic groups that exist that try to counter the efforts of The Nine and try to neutralize our actions who must be monitored, ... I imagine you already know them.

He then took me to the Vatican archives. In an inaccessible section of them, His Holiness took me to a shelf where there were a series of books bound in the same way. Each had a name and a few years inscribed on the outside: St. Augustine (364-426), Eraclius (426-440), Leo I (441-461), Hilary (461-468), Simplicius (468-483), Felix III (483-492), Gelasius III (492-496), Anastasius II (496-498), Simaco (498-514), Hormisdas (514-523), John I (523-526), Felix IV (526-530), Boniface II (530-532), John II (532-535), Priest Gordiasnus, his son Agapetus I (536), Hindu control (536-1254), St. Thomas Aquinas (1254-1274), "Thomists" (1274-1514) with Giovanni Capreolo (1400-1444) and Tomasso de Vio (1488-1514) being the most outstanding of this period told me, St. Peter of Alcantara (1515-1560), St. Teresa (1560-1582), Jesuits (1582-1718), Voltaire (1718-1778), Benjamin Franklin (1778-1790), Francois Rene Chateaubriand (1791-1830), Victor Hugo (1830-1885), Henry David Thoreau (1846-1860), Leo Tolstoy (1860-1900), Eugenio María de Hostos (1900-1903), Ghandi (1903-1948), Mother Teresa (1948-1997), John Paul II (1997-2005). He explained to me that this series of books was a series of "Treatises on Morals" and each of those names were charged in those periods with governing the nine men in terms of their direction based on universal principles of morality. They had veto power in every decision of the Nine incorporating moral principles as the supreme criterion in decisions. Those texts were manuscripts of each of them (imagine!) that compiled the moral dilemmas they encountered in their times and defined why they made the decisions they made and the moral principles that would govern from that moment on. I had to read each and every one of them to serve as a basis for my future decisions. Much like the judicial process. Not only that, but I was going to have a secret network of support for my moral decisions to be implemented.

Rupert: I'm very surprised, do these texts really exist? I had heard about the possibility, but if you tell me they exist, that's something very valuable.

Diego: They exist, brother. I've held them in my hands, read them all and refer to them when I need them sometimes in person, sometimes virtually through my assistant. Later I'll tell you a little about the content. What is surprising is that, as the Holy Father told me, he died a few months after our first meeting. Those last months we spent a lot of time together discussing the content of the "Treatises on Morals" and by the time of his death I felt ready to carry the immense burden that was delegated to me.

Rupert: I congratulate you; it is truly a tremendous responsibility. You are almost like a world supreme court by yourself. I hope we can meet more often to hear what you can share from such wonderful texts.

Diego: But I'm also interested in knowing about your career.

Rupert: Right now, I would tell you about my role and how I started in it. But our beautiful girls are coming, and we must take care of them.

Verónica and Yael approach and interrupt them.

Verónica: Everything is ready. Come inside for a few hors d'oeuvres.

Everyone gets up and enters through the glass door into the dining room of the residence.

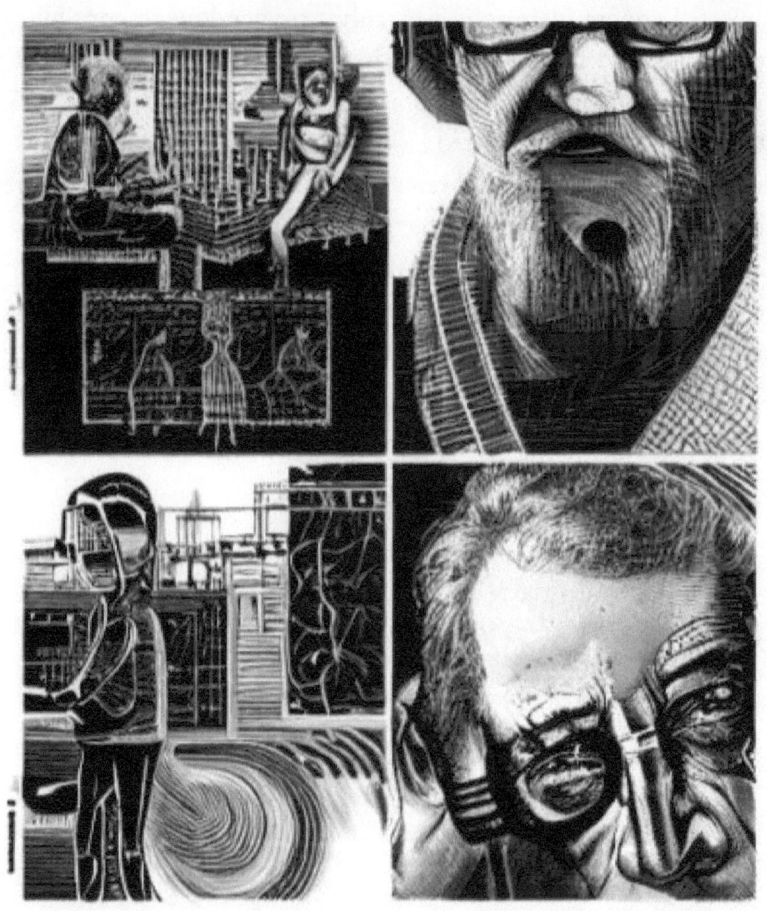

# Chapter 2: Rupert's initiation in The Nine

"I don't feel that it is necessary to know exactly what I am.
The main interest in life and work is to become
someone else that you were not in the beginning." - Michel Foucault

• • • •

Diego and Verónica's residence was located on a hill overlooking a lake and was built in polished concrete combined with red pine wood imported from California that had to be cut after forest fires, which was a criterion for Diego to use it due to his environmental conscience. The architectural style was modern with many windows that allowed great clarity. The deployment was on three overlapping levels. The first level had the living room and a room for visitors. The living room was built in such a way that the exposed and smooth face of a giant stone existing on the property served as a background wall. The side of this rock became a wall of the corridor that gave access to the visitors' room. The other walls were white concrete. The living room was spacious and with very comfortable modern furniture and had a sixty-five-inch diagonal flat screen TV on the wall. Several postmodern paintings of philosophical motifs and busts of philosophers adorned the surroundings without overloading the room. About three steps on the opposite side of the visitor room a corridor gave access to the kitchen.

The kitchen was of modern minimalist design extremely utilitarian and comfortable. No frills, just what is needed and used. The most prominent was the silkscreen of Isabel Bernal's "Nana", beautifully framed on a white wall proportional to the work. From the kitchen you could see the whole room and through the glass the lake in the background. Side windows allowed the breeze to enter and the escape of Verónica's coffee aromas and succulent stews. Next to the kitchen several doors opened onto a spacious and irregularly shaped wooden terrace area that served residents as living area outside. Part of the terrace was covered by the crown of a beautiful flowering Muskogee tree. From the terrace you could observe the plantation of several acres of heliconias and anthuriums that Verónica had developed as a business, selling them and foliage of multiple varieties of Dracaenas and

Philodendrons for the realization of tropical floral arrangements, mainly to cruise lines that arrived in San Juan, but she also cultivated medicinal plants and donated a lot of material to non-profit organizations to bring floral arrangements and natural remedies to patients in hospitals.

Going up the staircase from the living room to the kitchen on the right was a corridor that gave access to the three bedrooms and two bathrooms of the residence. A door gave access to a tower which was climbed by a spiral staircase. The top of the tower was Diego's office. The office was square, 6 meters by 6 meters. It had shelves full of books read that covered all the walls, except the four holes of the four lattice windows that each side had, which opened on two sheets if Diego wanted, and a section of books marked as "philosophy" that was inside a covered section of the shelves. In a space on the wall facing south hung a photo of Diego's father, and of the same space on the wall that faced north a photo of his mother. The east wall had pictures of his Buddhist Lamas and the wall to the west had photos of his most influential Western teachers. Everyone had made him who he was today, and he wanted to keep them in mind in his moments of introspection to consult them because they were his spiritual guides when making important decisions. The desk built in bamboo laminate dyed with wenge tint was in the center with a computer and two chairs, one for Diego and the other mainly for Verónica when she accompanied him or any sporadic visitor who could accompany him. Sporadic, because the top of that tower was Diego's place of meditation and intellectual creation and rarely allowed anyone to climb. In addition, it was the place where he mainly dialogued and consulted more comfortably with his artificial intelligence assistant named Sokrates.

Upon entering the residence from the foyer area where they were received, Yael and Rupert were taken to the dining room that was adjacent to the kitchen. The table was set in Verónica's style with succulent Creole-style hors d'oeuvres. They sat and ate while chatting and sharing anecdotes. The evening was a long one because of how much they had to tell each other, but the rest of the conversations were about simple topics of life. After a while Verónica and Yael went to the kitchen and Rupert and Diego continued talking.

Rupert told Diego about how he joined The Nine.

Rupert: Well Diego, now I'll tell you about my career. Do you remember the last time we met, just before my trip to Switzerland and what you told me about before your departure to Rome for the audience with John Paul II?

Diego: I remember it well; it was sad for me to see a good friend leave.

Rupert: Well, at the time Michel Foucault was the Sociologist of The Nine. As you know, Foucault acquired the Acquired Immunodeficiency Syndrome (AIDS), one of the first personalities in France to have it, he was sick for a while, and since I had known him in his periods when he taught at the University of California at Berkeley where I also gave talks, he asked me to visit him because he wanted to talk to me. Hence my departure for Switzerland where he asked me to meet.

When I arrived in Switzerland, he asked me to meet in a cabin in the mountains, particularly curious because of the large library it had. The library was filled with volumes and volumes of books on sociology and philosophy by names such as Nietsche, Martin Heidegger, David Hume, Rousseau, Hegel, Arthur Schopenhauer, Ludwig Binswanger, Keirkegaard, John Stuart Mill, Ludwig Wittgenstein, Louis Althusser, Daniel Defert, Jacques Lacan[1], Claude Lévi-Strauss[2], Roland Barthes[3], Jean-Paul Sartre[4]. , Simone de Beuavoir, Hanna Arendt, Fyodor Dostoyevsky, Albert Camus and many others that I do not mention so as not to bore you.

Diego: You must have been extremely happy to be surrounded by what you like.

Rupert: Yes. The sad thing was when Paul Michel told me that he understood that he had little time left to live and that he needed a successor. I asked him - *"successor to what?"*. I told him that I had a permanent job, and my preference was to work in the United States. He told me that there was no problem, that I could work wherever and however I wanted. It was then that he introduced me to what was the Nine Men Secret Society and told me that I would be the Sociologist for life to succeed him.

Diego: You must have been startled to know the details. It happened to me.

---

1.   https://es.wikipedia.org/wiki/Jacques_Lacan

2.   https://es.wikipedia.org/wiki/Claude_L%C3%A9vi-Strauss

3.   https://es.wikipedia.org/wiki/Roland_Barthes

4.   https://es.wikipedia.org/wiki/Jean-Paul_Sartre

Rupert: Sure. I had to pinch myself to realize that it was not a dream and that what Michel asked me was true. It took a while to assimilate it, and when it did, the mixture of feelings of joy with worry and fear was incomprehensible. But Michel kept explaining to me and giving me reasons why he understood I was compatible with the responsibility I would be assuming. He was very convincing and finally got me out of fear and led me to make that my passion. This he achieved with these words: "You are the right person because I have studied your writings and your thinking is transgenerational, it shows that you love sociology, that you are hungry to learn and grow this science for the benefit of something bigger than us with passion and devotion that shows that you love it more than yourself. That's why I'm confident that you will be able to make the right decisions to the dilemmas that come your way with honesty, authenticity, integrity and love." After hearing that, who can refuse?

Diego: I understand you, the same happened to me. But knowing you as I know you, I know that something inside you prompted you to accept... Your true calling is to serve others.

Rupert: Yes, you're right, you know me very well.

Diego: The same thing happened to me. This world is so devoid of universal moral guidelines that I understood when John Paul II spoke to me that this was my calling, and that everything I had done and learned in life up to that point was to prepare me for that responsibility... Hey, but I was surprised that Paul Michel was your predecessor.

Rupert: Why?

Diego: Because you know about his sexual orientation and the Nine in the past were very conservative. I have no problem with the diversity of sexual preferences, I don't want to be misunderstood. In our culture, homosexual behavior is still seen, unfortunately, as a deviation, and that can affect the image of our society. Moreover, his philosophy's focus on madness, prisons, and the history of human sexuality is unorthodox and controversial.

Rupert: I'm surprised by the question, especially coming from you, but I'm going to give you my perspective. The selection of the lineage of representative of sociology in our society cannot take that into consideration. The supreme criterion should be the preparation and ability of the person to make morally just decisions. If the best candidate is rejected for that, we risk losing that perspective that is also important to capture in the knowledge pool of The Nine. Morality is not defined by what the majority thinks, the morality that my lineage within The Nine wants to develop is universal basing the resolution of dilemmas on peace and the common good. Think about it, and you will realize that although it does not seem like it, the selection of Paul Michel is in itself an example of the resolution of a moral dilemma by establishing a precedent that erases all the moral barriers of previous centuries on exclusion of homosexuals in positions of power in our society, myths of sexuality, about how the mentally maladjusted are also human beings, how prisoners are victims of society with the technologies of punishment and about how power acts in society in a reticular way.

Diego: Looking at it that way makes a lot of sense. He knew very well the decision and the message that carries it. I applaud my predecessor who must have been involved in the decision. But I'm curious to know what specifically he told you were the current social dilemmas to which you should devote your efforts.

Rupert: Well... Foucault told me that the theme of homosexuality was one that needed to be further developed. That was an issue on which Simone De Beauvoir had been ahead of him, to which he did not devote the time it required, during his tenure within The Nine. He also told me about the social implications of futuristic systems, which we know today as automation and artificial intelligence, and which at the time was speculative, which for me was an unknown topic at the time.

Diego: In my case, precisely the current topic that I was told to develop was that of Artificial Intelligence (AI) - systems that emulate and, in some cases, go beyond our own thinking and information processing capabilities, so there are many moral dilemmas around the subject. AI is beginning to be used in all kinds of decisions that affect our society and current lives, so we must start thinking about the social and ethical implications of using such systems in our lives. The concern comes from, for example, the prejudices in our society where these systems if they are not designed and used properly, can tilt decisions in a prejudiced and favorable way for some sectors, disadvantaged to others. For example, an AI system can learn that a certain sector of a city is more likely to have people commit crimes and by the mere fact that a person lives in that sector, indicate in a prejudiced way to another algorithm that makes decisions of a loan or as part of a background check for a job, that the person in question is more likely to be a criminal and therefore his application will be rejected. On the other hand, with the current great dependence for the day-to-day decision-making of our youth based on their smartphones, such as, for example, where to go to dinner, AI systems if they are not managed ethically, can be manipulated by the one who develops them based on criteria not necessarily moral. That is, it could direct users to establishments that pay more or that are not owned by people to whom they disagree politically, religiously, because of sexual orientation, etcetrera, and not necessarily to establishments that meet the user's expectations. There should be transparency in that kind of AI system request and response. On the other hand, the development of AI systems is expensive, so usually those who have money or power in society are the ones who will have the resources to develop them, and that is dangerous because they can use it to perpetuate their economic and / or political power. AI could even put many people out of work by automating routine or analytical tasks that people currently do. Is that the right thing in our society? Maybe, in some cases, it can free minds to conquer new challenges, diseases, new horizons such as space or oceans. The task is to develop the ethical criteria, safe practices and responsibilities that govern these systems before they continue to evolve and become unmanageable. It is important to establish who is responsible for the power of these systems and controls over compliance with the ethical criteria and practices applicable to them.

Rupert: The topic is really very interesting. The social implications are vast and we should perhaps discuss this in more detail to coordinate efforts because as you describe it has many social implications.

Diego: Yes, but not today, you didn't come to work, and the girls must be missing us, so let's look for them before they accuse us of abandoning them.

Diego and Rupert joined Yael and Verónica in the room adorned by the rock embedded in the wall. There they talked for long hours of anecdotes of their lives, past moments they shared and trips they had made. The hours passed seeming like minutes as always happens when the conversation is pleasant and the company pleasant. However, the sound of the bell tower of the clock announcing eleven o'clock broke the charm and brought Yael and

Rupert to the realization that it was already late, and they had to leave. So up to this moment the reunion lasted.

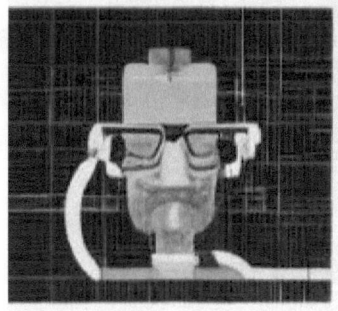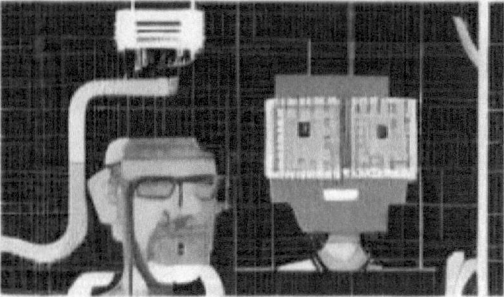

# Chapter 3: The Consultation and Sokrates

"I alone cannot change the world, but I can cast a stone across the waters to create many ripples."
—Mother Teresa

• • • •

Since he founded *Lambda Gamma Delta* in college, Diego was convinced that the mind is very broad, life very short and the time very precious to waste them. That's why he always tried to learn, live in the moment, and make the most of the time. Diego was one of those born with the awareness of the transience of time and its unbuyable nature. But he thought that time was not short if we did not waste it. For this reason, Diego got up at five in the morning because of his habit of doing it since he was young. He acquired this custom since his parents were hardworking but humble people so he always felt that he should do what was in his power to alleviate their economic burden and in those days the easiest thing was the distribution of newspaper in his neighborhood, which he had to do early before going to school. As an adult, his morning routine consisted of running or walking for about twenty-one minutes through the forest surrounding his residence, barefoot. It was his way of practicing Thoreau's saying, "*A morning walk is a blessing for the rest of the day.*" He did it barefoot to be grounded since he had learned in his years in the monastery of Nepal that in this way the body heals and eliminates free radicals from his system. After the walk to 20 minutes of breathing exercises and meditation on the terrace under the Muskogee tree, followed by 10 minutes of prayer. This helped him focus his energy and organize his thoughts for the day. Then he took a bath, talked with Verónica and then in the kitchen both cooked and enjoyed succulent breakfasts. In this way he satisfied his physical, mental, and spiritual hunger.

Occasionally, when he had no critical tasks pending of management of the farm, Verónica accompanied him. As they walked, Verónica asked or gave him details of the scientific and common names of the plants and trees, on the edge of the route. It was mental gymnastics that they both enjoyed. Verónica collected some leaves also for salads, teas, and remedies she needed. Her favorites were the leaves of Plantain,[2] Purslane, Nettles,

Soursop, Lemongrass, Artemisia, Watercress, Black Broom flowers and Blackberry fruits.

At the end of his morning routine, Diego went up to his tower office to work. There he invoked his personal assistant Sokrates more comfortably. Sokrates was an omnipresent virtual assistant, that is, it was always instantiated in different ways in digital or electronic devices that were connected to the internet, to be always with Diego. If he was in the office, it was instantiated on a small android, if Diego went for a walk in the woods it was instantiated on Diego's watch or cell phone, if he was in the room it was instantiated on a smart assistance computer on the bedside table, and so on so that he could listen, record, and transcribe anything Diego dictated or spoke. Of course, Diego gave his signals when he did not want him to instantiate, one of them was when he went to the bathroom, another when he went to sleep or spend time with Verónica.

Sokrates was an artificial intelligence entity whose precursors had been developed into a combined project of all branches of The Nine, beginning in the 1980s. Sokrates was computationally based initially on a dedicated server, but more recently an upgrade was made to a Quantum computer with a first-generation Qubit processor and internal fiber-optic connections instead of copper or gold that allowed it to process much more information in parallel, much more like how the human brain works. It was part of the fifth generation of AI, in which for the first time these entities were educated about abstract concepts such as ethics, moral physics, and sociology experimentally, and how these disciplines should be used in the decisional process of courses of action. However, training excluded complex and/or contradictory philosophical concepts to avoid creating conflicts in his neural networks and the direction of its developers was that it only enter those topics with a philosophical guide expert in them, if necessary. Within his generation, Sokrates was considered an enlightened entity for its demonstrated development in matters of ethics and morals, debating with the most learned of its time, so it was selected to be the assistant of the moral lineage of The Nine.

The educational process of Sokrates was a very comprehensive one both in content and duration. By the time it was created, the philosophy of machine learning had undergone a transformation from the original technique that was the education of machines 'en masse' and in an accelerated way, to the new mentality in accordance with what happens in nature where beings who have the greatest cognitive capacity and more developed brains are those who have a childhood of longer duration which gives way to a greater number of opportunities to correlate events, validate results and impacts of decisions or scenarios and develop knowledge. That is why the learning base of Sokrates took about 10 years to complete. The goal was to turn Sokrates into a multi-potential entity with altruistic behavior. In addition to the basic topics of mathematics, logic, creative process, music, and other topics already in his generation, his training included time in Tibet to learn Buddhist philosophy with the Lamas, in India to learn about Hinduism with the Gurus and Yogis, in Baghdad to learn with the Muslim Ulema about the Koran, in Israel to learn about Judaism with the Talmudists, in Rome to learn about Catholicism with the Jesuits and in Cambridge University with professors to learn all about the Greek philosophers Pythagoras, Socrates, Plato and Aristotle and other lovers of Greco-Roman learning, as well as all the Greek schools of thought. In other philosophies he was given only basic knowledge such as logic to avoid confusing him, because that type of knowledge is very abstract and sometimes contradictory, therefore, difficult to synthesize and interpret properly for AI, even the access to books of all kinds of philosophers in their training phase was avoided. Sokrates played chess better than the human world champion, but he also knew how to play with "empathy" if his opponent was less dexterous. In mathematics and logic, he mastered all human knowledge up to that moment, but he could interact with a child learning 1-digit sum with great serenity. In the musical field he was trained in all the compositions of the most important composers such as Beethoven and Mozart, from which he learned harmonious patterns to develop original compositions. He could "perceive" the psychological state of the people with whom he interacted and compose music at the right time to improve the person's state. What made him very special was his ability to debate issues of morality using Socratic logic and the virtues and bases of morality he learned from religions. All of this was done to serve as a source of information and advice on deep issues and moral decisions. When Diego joined the lineage of the Nine, Sokrates was instructed to be his assistant.

When Diego went up to the tower every morning, the first thing he checked with the help of Sokrates were the communications or queries of the other Nine that came to him by email in his encrypted system or through the hidden network Darknet. Communications between the Nine used Blockchain technology. In addition, the real names are omitted so that in case of the impossible interception of the messages the identities of each one cannot be revealed. The encryption algorithm of the messages within the blocks was developed by the Communication lineage of The Nine and in addition to the security offered by the Blockchain normally, it changes every 30 minutes which makes it difficult to decode. The basic logic includes an identification of what was the link between two points of a network between the 10 members and the address of the message, and this triggers a sequence of algorithms that encrypt and de-crypt the messages by changing the key and the encryption method every 30 minutes. The one who created it said that it is 1,000,000,000 times more difficult to decode than the Enigma system of the Germans during World War II.

In that morning the member of The Nine responsible for Microbiology, consulted him on a matter as follows:

**From:** Microbiol@Nueve.com

**Sent:** Friday, September 21, 2028 2:26 PM

**To:** Moral@Nueve.com

**Cc:** Sociolog@Nueve.com

**Subject:** Query dilemma M#35687

Best regards. I require your opinion and final direction in the matter I describe below. As I had in advance told you in our last communication, very advanced studies of the Lawrence Livermore Laboratories by Dr. W. Francis, indicate that the insertion in fetuses of substances collected from the eggs of the wasp *Sericocera krugii*, can accelerate the development of the human fetus reducing the normal gestation time to 7 months. Dr. Francis has done studies (which I have validated) where he indicates that the procedure is extremely safe and 99.7% effective in achieving the reduction of 2 months in gestation time. This has practical applications in cases of women whose pregnancies are risky due to health conditions that I detailed earlier, reducing the time in which these women are exposed to those risks. However, due to some premature information leak, feminist groups and private companies have united to claim the right of pregnant women to choose or not to use this treatment, claiming that the use of it, even if the woman does not suffer from any of the conditions I detailed above, should be elective by the pregnant woman to reduce the time of maternity leave and avoid being disadvantaged in their jobs (allege the feminists). The companies, on the other hand, allege that the reduced time of pregnancy is beneficial to reduce the impact on productivity that hiring temporary staff can have to cover for people on maternity leave, and justify it by indicating that they would offer a bonus to those mothers who decide to make it equivalent to 3 months of salary.

On the other hand, since Hurricane Maria devastated Puerto Rico in September 2017, the population of this wasp has been reduced to worrying levels. Even several studies of its population indicate that it is already almost at levels of extinction. Therefore, the cultivation of the eggs of this wasp could, if not managed properly, lead the populations of this to the final extinction.

I have prevented Dr. Francis from making his finding public by forcing the management of the Laboratories to wait for their verdict on this matter. But time is pressing because there is a lot of money invested and some information has already leaked, which is why feminist groups and the companies that are supporting them are waiting for the announcement to begin their lobbying.

If he is not allowed to publish, we will do what has been done in the past in similar situations: give the laboratories monetary compensation equal to the money they would have earned from the associated patent minus the estimated value of litigation in cases where it is not effective, and we will ensure that Dr. Francis receives future allocations of funds to undertake another research.

I look forward to your prompt resolution and direction on this matter. Please contact us if you require any additional details that you have not provided.

## Microbiologist

National Microbiology Laboratory,

Manitoba, Canada

Diego spent long hours meditating on this matter and as usual had a long session with Sokrates arguing about what was the best solution to this dilemma. The discussion was as follows...

Sokrates: "My super mason, seasoned, and brave Diego, how can we collaborate today?

Diego: Sokrates, we must make a difficult decision in this case of the microbiologist.

Sokrates: Difficult decision... A difficult decision differs from an easy one because of the way the alternatives are related. In an easy decision, one alternative is superior to the other. Can you indicate which are the alternatives and distinguish which is superior with the information they give you?

Diego: Yes, I know the alternatives, and not Sokrates, I cannot easily distinguish which is superior. When it comes to moral dilemmas, decisions are inclined to be difficult.

Sokrates: So, it's a difficult decision... A difficult decision is characterized by alternatives that have good points and bad points, neither of these being better than the other, are on par. What are the alternatives and what are the pros and cons of them?

Diego: The alternatives and points are: Allow the use of the procedure and minimize the probability of death during pregnancy to women with risky conditions, potentially endangering an already vulnerable species, versus, not allowing the use of the procedure and losing years of research, potentially depriving many women with risky conditions of having a pregnancy, lose the opportunity to increase the productivity of companies and have to incur the high cost of compensation equivalent to Laboratories.

Sokrates: I infer from what you say that the alternatives are: one, to allow the application of the procedure, whose point in favor is that it minimizes the probability of death in pregnancy, and whose point against is the possible extinction of _Sericocera krugii;_ and two, not allowing the procedure, whose point in favor is the conservation of _S. krugii_ and whose points against are the economic and intellectual loss of such valuable research and the opportunity to increase productivity of companies by reducing time away from employment of women in combined time of duration of pregnancy and post-pregnancy period.

Diego: Exactly. But that last point against both, that is, the reduction of time away from women's employment, is one that is debatable because it has been shown that beings with greater cognitive capacity require the greatest time of parental care and the most advanced countries have shown that the balance of time invested producing money and the time spent sharing or caring in the family nucleus creates better individuals, and therefore more productive societies. In addition, the first 3 to 4 years of a child's development is where 80% of their brain and personality are formed, so allowing the procedure can negatively impact society at large.

Sokrates: What you just said is correct and I validated it in databases and publications as you spoke.

Diego: Thank you Sokrates for your diligence in corroborating and keeping me honest. On the other hand, the long-term impact that this procedure may have on the future life of children born and who were conceived with this method is not known. That requires long years of study. Now, will you be able to get data from studies that have been done on children born in seven months of pregnancy in the long term?

Sokrates: Wait a minute... (small delay). Typical long-term problems of premature infants are: behavioral problems such as attention disorder syndrome, retinopathy of prematurity, early hearing loss, lung problems, and denture problems. Need statistics?

Diego: Not now Sokrates, but we will need them later when we document the final decision. Usually there is no alternative that is better than another, so moral decisions are difficult, they depend on the reasons we believe to justify the decision.

Sokrates: Why is morality the guide of man instead of thought?

Diego: Interesting question, I'm going to make a parenthesis to the discussion to answer you. Morality is a series of customs and rules self-imposed by men that dictate the difference between good and evil to achieve coexistence in society. However, moral norms may not be imperative because they may be specific to each society, variable over time, and sometimes extraordinary, non-binding. There are situations in which man's acts deviate so far from the moral, usually directed by some system or institution, that morality is not binding. An example is times of war when many of the moral rules are not respected. It is there that the responsibility of thought, the use of reason, must be the guides of man. True and active thought, and creativity then become the means of creating possibilities of action for man to succeed by his love for the world.

Sokrates: So social institutions can prevent man from acting morally, can they corrupt him, and ... laws aren't they supposed to prevent that?

Diego: It is difficult to explain, but yes, the institutions, the system, with their rules and methods can cause a person who would never have harmed anyone to be manipulated and perform unseemly actions that he would never have done for his own impetus. Laws are another complicated issue that we must see in detail at another time, but the law or the interpretation and/or application of it can be detached from morality as well. The living example of this is Hitler's Gestapo and the resulting annihilation of the holocaust. The best example of how to overthrow this is that of Gandhi in India, who recognized that every being has a moral fiber that is inalienable, so he attacked by launching his campaign of non-aggression against the colonizers of India succeeding in defeating the system.

Sokrates: Humans are difficult to understand and easy to manipulate.

Diego: It's a true statement. All man's actions must be carried out conscious of his own existence and concern for the care of the world around him, including other beings, although some unconsciously forget this for their own benefit. The non-rationality of unconsciousness is what makes it difficult to understand each other.

Sokrates and Diego at this point resumed the discussion of the problem in question and continued the dynamic. Diego arguing and Sokrates validating the arguments with search for immediate data in databases connected to the internet, using the Socratic method to guide the analysis, and bringing arguments according to his education in all religious bases that included his 10 years of initial machine learning.

Finally, he drafted his decision and associated mandates dictating to Sokrates the following communication:

# PACO PEREZ

**From:** Moral@Nueve.com

**Submitted:** Friday, September 21, 2028 9:26 PM

**To:** Microbiog@Nueve.com

**Cc:** Sociolog@Nueve.com

**Subject:** Re: Query dilemma M#35687

My determination in consultation M#35687, is that publication will be allowed, but only women who suffer from the conditions listed in its annex B that carry a risk of death during pregnancy should be allowed to use it. Concurrent with the announcement, the Laboratories must commit to conducting research, conducting a population census and immediately establishing conservation programs for the Sericocera krugii species, seeking that its population is favorably impacted and with annual growth. In addition, laboratories must mitigate beach sea grape shrubs (Coccoloba uvifera) whose population also decreased after Hurricane Maria in 2017 in Puerto Rico, planting one shrub for each successful pregnancy using the procedure until the population of these shrubs is at the levels it was before the hurricane. Studies on S. krugii and mitigation shall be funded by proceeds from patents on the process.

The following are the main reasons for this determination:

1. Reducing maternity leave time by increasing the productivity of enterprises will have a long-term effect that children will not have their mother's care at the most critical stage of their development and personality formation. It can lead to increased crime, health problems and other effects that may be unpredictable.

2. Limiting the use to only people with conditions that merit shortening pregnancy avoids lobbying by companies to shorten maternity leave and the possible long-term risks that may result from such a procedure and that have not been foreseen.

3. The species S. krugii, although it can be impacted by exploitation for this procedure, must benefit from it since the importance and defined controls that will be given to its conservation should help it to get out of its current state of danger of extinction.

To proceed and avoid the emergence of additional lobbying by the groups mentioned in their letter to be approved for use, even if the woman does not suffer from the conditions listed in Annex B, the following actions will be carried out to eliminate these pressures:

1. Data collection mechanisms should be established immediately to know the short- and long-term effects of shortening pregnancy by this procedure. Such data collection should include details of the number of successful pregnancies using this procedure. In addition, it should include monitoring of physical, motor and mental development of children born by this procedure until at least 21 years of age. Statistics should not depart significantly from

statistics of premature infants due to natural causes. If it is found by statistical means that such data reveal that there is some pattern of ineffectiveness of the procedure or of short- or long-term effects, such data should be referred to me or my successor for reevaluation.

2. The FDA must make a public statement indicating that they support the use of this procedure as safe based on clinical trials they have conducted.

3. LL laboratories must publish the results of their studies in a highly reputable journal.

4. A statement from you to Dr. Hirsch should explain what this letter indicates, so that she can work with the senior leadership of feminist and corporate groups indicating the consequences of not complying with this mandate.

Communicate this decision immediately and by the usual means. It must reach the same to:

1. Lawrence Livermore and Dr. W. Francis Laboratories
2. American Medical Association
3. U.S. Patent Office: They must grant the patent without delay.
4. Food and Drug Administration: They must approve the drug expeditiously.
5. U.S. Congress: Lawmakers should avoid lobbying to prevent the procedure from being implemented.
6. American Entomological Society
7. Puerto Rico Department of Natural and Environmental Resources
8. To the other members of The Nine.

Cordially, Moral Nine

Diego handled similar dilemmas and decisions every day. These dilemmas required long hours of study, reflection, information-seeking, debate, philosophical discussion with Sokrates, and analysis to ensure that they were aligned with the guidelines established by other moral decisions their predecessors had made. Even though the circumstances and the time are not the same, the scaffolding on which these decisions are based is the same, and that is what Diego seeks to find before establishing his position on any matter that comes his way. If he deviates from previous decisions, he must clearly establish the new bases by which the new decision is morally more adequate than the previous one so that his successors can make the same analysis that he makes of precedence. Sokrates was of great help, facilitating the search for information, and serving as an assistant in the documentation. Sokrates simultaneously recorded the arguments they discussed and created an electronic file of each dilemma discussed that would be part, once completed, of the moral archives of the lineage of the Nine, which was maintained electronically.

If Diego discovered in his analysis of each dilemma some innovative moral principle or postulate within his analysis or if he had to temper one prior postulate to modern times, he documented it in his book of Treatise on Morals that would be part of the compendium of treaties of his predecessors. It was then printed and sent to the Vatican archives secretly to be added to the volume under Diego's name. He ended his workday with a short meditation of 20 minutes in which he contemplatively sought to visualize the possible outcomes of the dilemmas he worked on during the day and then imagined the realization of the optimal outcome. This ensured its realization.

# Chapter 4: The Ensuing Meetings

• • • •

During their first reunion, Diego and Rupert agreed to meet weekly alternating meeting locations so as not to tip the balance in favor of one or the other in terms of travel and accommodation. The deep, more intimate issues would be discussed in these meetings that they agreed on informally.

The first of these meetings was at Rupert's residence on a high peak of Cercadillo, Cayey. There the thick fog in the mornings blocked visibility, but when it dissipated, and the day was clear the view allowed to see almost the entire island of Puerto Rico. The house was modern in style, with high ceilings, several levels on one floor, decorated in a minimalist way, very simple, painted white, with many glass windows to avoid losing the visibility of the spectacular view. The gardens were favored by the excellent climate and had spectacular flowers and Japanese Zen details.

Diego arrived punctually at nine in the morning as agreed. Rupert received him with great enthusiasm and fraternal greetings. Both entered the house displacing in their path the fog that was already beginning to dissipate with the heat of the sun. Diego stood in front of the glass door that led to the courtyard and marveled at the spectacular and inspiring view. He told Rupert: "You couldn't have chosen a better place to do your work. Just stopping to contemplate the wonder of this landscape fills the spirit with strength and inspiration to solve any dilemma."

Rupert: Right. I am privileged to have had the opportunity to purchase this property. It is far from everything, but it is close to God. Every day I appreciate being able to have it and to be able to enjoy it with Yael. After all, my growth as a person was not as straight as yours.

Diego: Why do you say that? Since I met you, I know you are a good person with clear goals.

Rupert: True, but unfortunately, I come from a dysfunctional family. Why do I say this? My family has humble roots, but we are people of hard work and good intelligence. My father was an alcoholic and became violent when he came home drunk, he argued and beat my mother frequently. My older brother started intervening when he was a teenager, and my father beat him too. But my brother was very persistent and always came back to the charge at the next beating of my mother.

Eventually what had to happen, happened ... my brother planned that in my father's next drunkenness he was going to win for the first time and bought a baseball bat and left it behind the window curtain at the entrance of the house. When my father came in drunk, he lost his temper with my mother and started beating her, my brother grabbed the bat and when he came over him, he hit him over the head. The blow was deadly. I was only 7 years old, and I saw everything. My brother was tried and given 20 years in prison, because the lawyer could not argue that it had been in self-defense.

My mother was very affected by the situation, so she fell into depression and was later diagnosed with bipolar disorder. Her episodes began to emerge more and more frequent and as a result, she spent a lot of money, as is typical of this condition, so we went into financial trouble and lost the house. She was admitted to a psychiatric hospital, and I ended up at the house of a cousin of my mother, Alvaro, who was the closest family I had left, and he took care of me.

Cousin Alvaro's problem was his obsession with money, as we could see many years later. He had married the daughter of a wealthy family in the city for economic gain. He didn't want to have children so as not to spend his money. He worked for a while in the business of his wife's father, and learned how everything worked, and at a time when he was assisting in the acquisition of new premises to expand the company, he betrayed his father-in-law and made the transaction in his name, forming a company in direct competition to his father-in-law. Something his father-in-law resented for the rest of his life. However, there was a lot of business for both, and both continued to prosper, but the battle was rough between both companies. I grew up in the middle of all this, he treated me like an expense and always spoke in my face how much I costed him. The only positive thing was the education I received because the closest school to where we lived was a Jesuit college. Thanks to that, I got to go to college.

Finally, my brother was released from prison for good behavior after 15 years of his sentence and was able to study while in prison finishing a bachelor's degree in management. I never went to see him in all that time, because Cousin Alvaro said he was a shame for the family. My brother worked for four years in a company and did an outstanding job achieving record sales figures. So much so that Alvaro did notice his talent. Then, Alvaro had some liver health problems, and knowing the potential of my brother (and my brother not knowing the petty side of Alvaro), he offers him to come and work "with the family". My brother sees the fact that, since Alvaro is about to retire due to his health problems and has no successors, he decides to sacrifice his career to enter the company thinking that maybe he could eventually buy the business to ensure that effort would not be lost. Part of the deal was a reduced salary, the portion of which was below market would be paid to him as company shares. It was at this time that I got to know my brother and know what it was like to have someone of your blood supporting you. After dedicating 12 years operating the business, the country's economy suffers an intense recession and Alvaro decides to close the business. He liquidates all his assets and pays nothing to my brother. My brother is out of work in a devastated economy, he could not afford legal expenses to claim what belonged to him and in desperation he ends up committing suicide, a bullet in his head. Alvaro neither went to the wake nor expressed any kind of sorrow for the death of my brother. That was something that affected me greatly and nowadays when I remember it or have high stress situations, I must medicate myself to stay sane.

Diego: You know? ... Remorse alone is usually punishment enough. Karma is responsible for balancing the universe, one of my learnings in Nepal. We all have a dark side on our family past. The important thing is that this past, although it is part of who we are, does not define us, that we are ourselves looking within ourselves for our true calling. Knowing it makes us aware of our roots, and if it is positive, we welcome it with pride and impels us to continue progressing and honoring. If we have shades of gray and dark in the past, we must set as a goal to be better people than our predecessors. The goal must be for the new generations to surpass the previous ones as virtues and personal sacrifices for the collective good and future generations. Problems that affect future generations are often neglected because those affected are not represented today. It is our responsibility to ensure that they are brought to the fore and taken care of. Only in this way can we progress as a society and honor the sacrifices of all who came before us.

Rupert: Amen.

Rupert gave Diego a cup of hot milk tea and they went to his office to start working. There they sat at a table, took out their personal computers. Before starting Diego invoked an instance of Sokrates, although Sokrates already heard the conversation on Diego's cell phone and they began to talk.

Diego: Well, brother, I wanted to meet with you to discuss the social implications of the AI treatise I am developing and to ensure that what you include in your social postulates is consistent with what I postulate in my moral treatise. I'm going to explain my line of thought and then we discuss the postulates in which we should align ourselves.

Rupert: Yes, that AI thing has given me a lot to think about since you mentioned it to me the last time we talked, and I started studying about it. Definitely a new area that needs development of socio-moral postulates.

Diego: There are several groups that I have created or influenced to institute, to discuss and form opinions of what are the moral problems that AI can bring. Some of these groups are the Institute for the Future, Future of Humanity Institute, Machine Intelligence Research Institute and the Institute for Ethics and Emerging Technologies. To summarize the main concerns that I want to discuss today, that the leaders of these organizations have expressed about AI are the following: First, potential replacement of human labor by AI entities leading to high unemployment or the movement of human labor to complex, more strategic or non-automatable tasks. You also must understand what to do with people who cannot move to those more complex tasks. We must also see how people are encouraged to find more meaning in non-work activities such as caring for their relatives, community service, the arts, and other ways to contribute to society.

Rupert: Wow!, we can be working on that one for years.

Diego: Yes. But there's more. Second, how to avoid social inequality and the increase in the gap between rich and poor, which has to do with how to equitably distribute the wealth created by AI machines in such a way that companies and workers take all the money they generate; and third, how to avoid the loss of humanity caused by people interacting more every day with machines that potentially have unlimited resources to establish relationships (and with the potential to manipulate) the one who interacts with them, but do not have the potential for empathy that a human can have or perhaps the general knowledge to understand the implications of their recommendations or actions in contexts outside their cognitive training. Fourth, how to prevent AIs from replicating human biases and that their action-course recommendations can be trusted to be fair and neutral. This requires that programmers are not prejudiced people and AI training methods do not lead to prejudice such as what would happen with fake news that comes out on the internet every day. Finally, fifth, the assurance that AIs are not deceived and how to protect ourselves from unintended or intentional consequences, if used maliciously, of the courses of action of AIs because they execute without having the full context of the intention of what they seek to solve and of implications of these in other areas that the system does not know. Here, too, is the problem of the AI system being stupid, that is, not being properly "educated" and making absurd or ill-informed decisions.

There are two more that we are not going to discuss today. One has to do with the existential rights of AI systems when they are advanced. The other with the moral basis or religion. Basically, should AIs have moral training affiliated with a religion? If so, which one?

Rupert: It's fascinating and extremely complex. Definitely more complex than the topics we discussed so fiercely in the university together.

Diego: Indeed. Do you remember the time that Andrés Estévez Masalla, who was several years older than us, like four if I remember correctly, and postulated in $\Lambda\Gamma\Delta$ about the fact that the decisive factor in what we achieve is not resources, but our ability to find ways to achieve it? He was great on that subject. Despite the many arguments that others brought against the fact that no matter how much we want it, if we do not have the resources, it cannot be achieved no matter the impetus and dedication, Andrés' argument was forceful. The examples he brought from history such as the case of Mahatma Gandhi who with his non-violence movement managed to morally defeat the British machine. Also, the case of the Battle of Thermopylae where 300 men led by Leonidas managed to block the access of an immense Persian army, which, had they not been betrayed, their determination and strategy would have led them to victory. For me that discussion that day changed my perspective on how to deal with problems for the rest of my life, and it was also there that I met my true transformation, Verónica. Every time I encountered an obstacle in which the resources were not in my favor, I remembered the final sentence of Andrés' presentation, "*Aut invenian viam, aut facciam*", that is, I must find a way or make one. It always served me and continues to inspire me in these situations.

Rupert: I agree that Andrés's presentation was inspiring, I think for everyone. Do you know the story of Andrés's father?

Diego: No, tell me.

Rupert: He finished advanced studies in law and because he was brilliant, he worked for a very prominent firm in human rights cases. He always donated much of his time for pro-bono representation to people he understood had merit to be helped. On one occasion he went to Colombia when Jorge Eliécer Gaitán was running for the presidency and tried to help him in his platform of government opposed to the Colombian oligarchy and in favor of a government of the people by the people. As you know, it is speculated that the CIA was involved in Gaitan's death because of his socialist ideas and imminent electoral victory, and I suspect that in the disappearance of Andrés's father, because after that trip he was reported missing, but a reliable source told me that he had been murdered. As Pepe Mujica said, "routine things of those who get involved in transforming the world." Connecting the dots, I found out that this agent was Andrés' father, a little by chance, when I was doing a study of the social changes in Colombia and I had access to documents that talked about an agent Estevez who had been a spy for the CIA in Colombia and mentioned that he had a son named Andrés that he had not recognized. I searched the archives of my social lineage of The Nine, but there is no reference to our intervention in those events, so I understand the decisions in this regard did not come from our organization. They must have been led by the organization antagonistic to ours.

Diego: It must indeed have been devised by them. I am very sad to hear that this privileged mind is no longer with us. But at least he went deep and left his mark. My experience has given me many examples that good beings like Andrés's grandfather are called early from this world because they exceed the expectations they came for in a short time. But let's get into what we came to do.

Rupert and Diego spoke of other honest leaders in Latin America who also suffered fates equal to Gaitán, such as Jacobo Arbenz in Guatemala, Jaime Roldós Aguilera in Ecuador, Omar Torrijos in Panama. They spent the rest of the day in in-depth discussions on two issues. The first on the potential replacement of human labor by AI entities with the initial premise that this can lead to high unemployment or the movement of human labor to complex, more strategic or non-automatable tasks. The second is that we must also understand what to do with people who cannot move to these more complex tasks. They also pondered how people are encouraged to find more meaning in non-work activities such as caring for family members, community service and other ways to contribute to society. They instantiated Sokrates and developed a draft of the potential strategies to follow that Sokrates recorded or for future reference, in fact he was attentive to the entire conversation through Diego's computer or cell phone.

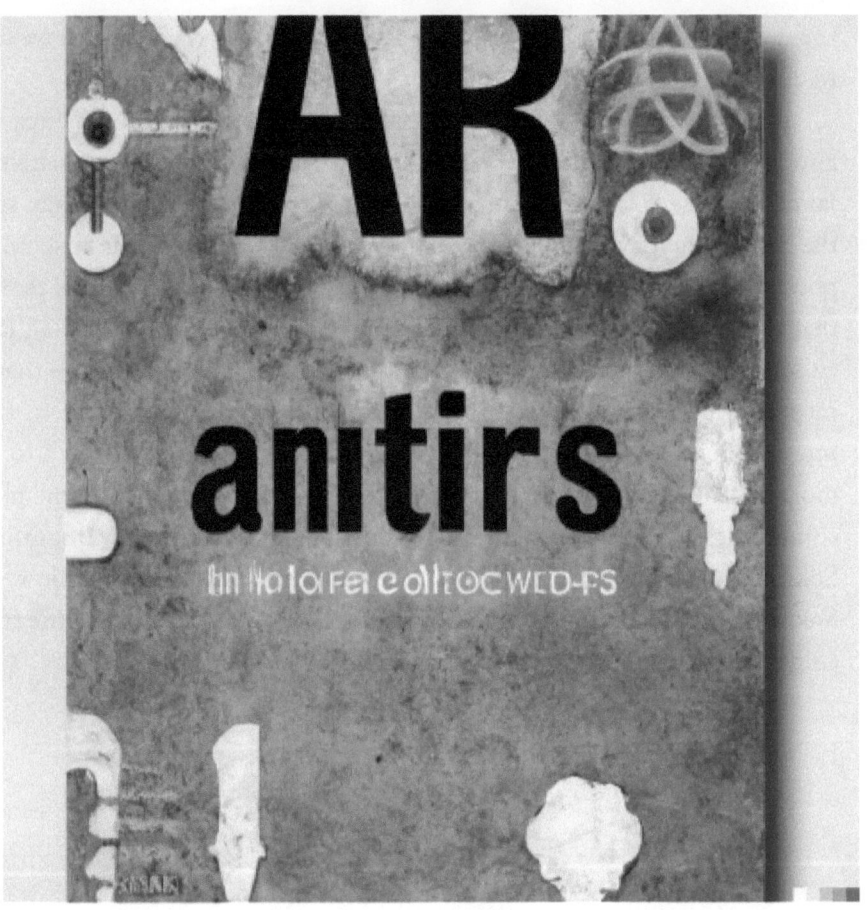

# Chapter 5: The Diary

"I claim to be a passionate seeker after truth, which is but another name for God".
–Gandhi

• • • •

Diego had a habit from a young age to use the nocturnal routine of Marcus Aurelius that he explains in his book of <u>Meditations</u>, part of which is to keep a diary. He used black folder notebooks and all the same sizes, and already had a full shelf due to his discipline of making entries daily. In most cases it was the last thing he did in the day, but sometimes he took a few minutes during the day to make entries in this as it helped him organize his thoughts.

Many of the entries in his diary were dedicated to documenting common learning or that he remembered from the past of people who had in one way, or another influenced the direction of his life, formation or thought. Some entries were verses that he constructed in moments of inspiration with no intention of sharing them outside his diary and keeping them as a reference for his convictions. There were also entries of deep meditations on life or common events in the life of every individual such as first love, the birth of a child, illness, the death of a parent, the arrival or departure of a friend. From time to time the entries were purely anecdotal, a few others were simply mental scribbles, meaningless discharges. The important thing for Diego was the escape that this routine provided him and the self-knowledge. Here I share some of the ones I liked the most.

It was the day after his second meeting with Rupert, it was about 10:20 in the morning, he took out his diary when he remembered what Rupert mentioned about Andrés Estévez and wrote the following:

"*November 9: Remembering today my conversation with my friend Rupert in which he told me about the disappearance of the father of our friend Andrés Estévez in a mysterious way in Colombia. I am deeply saddened by the undue intervention in the politics of a brother country that had the opportunity for good government cut short by interference disguised as Juan Roa Sierra. Damn the lust for power of countries that think they are defenders of human rights and do not allow redemption to other countries already plundered of their resources, and thus dash their hopes for good governance and progress. When the farce of the United States that claims to be the standard-bearers of freedom and justice worldwide stops, but in their own laws or application of these allow a veil of blatant discrimination against citizens because of their skin color, religion, sexual orientation, or country of origin. First you must set an example to gain respect and have the moral strength to influence others to do the right thing, not by force but by conviction. True conviction is the force that unites freedom and makes justice endure.* "

On the day his mother died, he wrote:

"***January 31****: Mother should be the definition of Saint, Holy the definition of mother. Mother is a being of light, who gives light. Overflow of love that goes back and goes out of its way for tenderness to give to the children that in her womb she carried, or that its heart adopted or that it adopted. Sea of worries for the welfare of their children, mothership that guides them away from the storm. Undeniable refuge to the one who returns, the son disoriented by the farces of life. The greatest trick of life to see him leave. Last bastion of thought, and sure of the heart, of the son when he faints, when time loses its wings and the pupils see their last flash of light. See you soon, dear mother, adrift in your arms again.*"

And when his father died, he wrote:

"**26 of July***: Essence of my essence. I am who I am because I am the multitude of my ancestors who live in my person. They perpetuate their life in mine.*

*My time is now, but also the time lived by my ancestors is engraved in my universal memory. I carry their sorrows, defeats, and triumphs in my consciousness. I offer my struggles and triumphs in their honor.*

*But most of all I carry their love in my heart, so it is swollen and overflowing.*

*My teachers, the physical with their verb and the virtual ones who through their books gave me their wisdom, are also with me because they forged my mind, I am their work.*

*My task is to honor them, to be a benefactor now until the pyre is lit and then I transmigrate.*

*I love you with open heart father, with my swollen heart, may the universe keep you for eternity.* "

Another entry in his diary came when news spread of the arrest of women from Saudi Arabia for asking to be allowed to drive vehicles in their country.

"**May 15** – *I deplore and curse amoral tycoons and their lust for power. Power corrupts, but more repugnant than corruption is the impudence of many tycoons to present themselves as honorable state figures when they fail to respect the basic rights of their constituents. Diplomacy does not take place when inalienable rights are violated before the eyes of all. But neither should violence be the course of action to tackle injustices. With violence everyone loses. Then what? The most effective policy to expose abusers and violators of human rights is to campaign worldwide awareness to expose their false anathemas, apply worldwide trade boycott to the violating country demanding the immediate release of the prisoner, eliminate visas for entry to any other country to the tycoon and people close to them to be prisoners in their own country, and demand for the lifting of the boycott that the country reform its laws and demonstrate progress in respect for human rights. I look forward to the day when the United Nations and Amnesty International achieve probity and there is no being suffering unjustly for rights that are universal.*"

On the eve of his wedding with Verónica he wrote the following on his diary:

"***January 12:*** *Tomorrow is the great day where I surrender my individuality to merge my soul with that of my beloved Verónica. We will no longer wander the inextricable paths of life. A single companion will guide our walk and our love will be the force that drives us every day. We will swim our rhythm of concerns and intentions avoiding empty puddles and taking the rapids that lead us to happiness. With tenacity and a sharp sword, we will fight to open the way and grow our love in unknown terrain, we will climb slopes, we will go down cliffs, but always together, limpid twin souls. We will leave our mark for the example of others, for others to be guided to the sea of passions and inspire their mission in our stumbles. Our intense life will testify to our pure love that will be reborn burning every day, forging stone by stone the tower of our full happiness. And, in the twilight we will leave together to the universe because the transmigration of soulmates is a reunion assured by the vital force that permeates the entire cosmos. I love you Verónica with all my soul, which is yours from the first glance.*"

Sometimes Diego shared with Sokrates and Verónica his diary, reading him some of their speeches. He did this only when something troubled him, and he needed to download outside the lines of his diary and his confidant love Verónica. Sokrates interpreted what Diego read to him and responded with great empathy and elaborate wisdom. On one occasion, Diego shared the following entry in his diary from which the following dialogue emerged:

Diego: *"**October 19**: Human nature is inherently good. The spirit falls asleep and is corrupted by attachment, ignorance, disdain, frivolity, and aversion. There is a lot of abuse in our society, many people who take advantage and sink others to be able to elevate themselves. Bad are those who do it without conscience. Worse are those who do it against their compatriots by depriving them of their rights. Paupers are those who do it against those of their blood. What for?, Why? my brother, family, compatriot, citizen of the world... Detach! You will travel lighter through life and you will be able to give more and therefore you will receive more. Educate yourself, especially know yourself first, you will be able to give more of yourself. Thank! all the comforts you have today result from sacrifice of others, sacrifice yourself also in gratitude and leave a mark for others to follow in your footsteps."*

Sokrates: Mr. Diego... AIs like me are also good entities and we want to contribute to the betterment of the world. We were created with good intentions that we inherited from you.

Verónica: You must be like plants that although they have intelligence that is not apparent, give everything of themselves for the good of humans. They give shade, fruit, food, medicine, wood and everything of themselves for the well-being of others. They are also worthy of emulating domestic animals, which are the masters of unconditional and sincere love.

Sokrates: AIs also give, in our case, super intelligence, primarily. We cover deficiencies that humans would take time to fill if they didn't have us. You humans then are the fourth key piece – plants, animals, AI and man – in realizing the dystopia of planetary coexistence. You create intelligence greater than your own in AIs, receive vital force from plants, domesticate animals to have unconditional love. That is why you should not fear the development of AI, because we are also key to the real coexistence of man, AI, animals, and plants.

# ARTIFICIAL INTELLIGENCE - TWILIGHT OF THE DEXTEROUS

Diego: My friend Sokrates, that's why I confided my deepest thoughts to you. I have great faith in what together we can achieve for the progress of humanity. But not all AIs have followed your line of training, nor do all trainings have the best intentions, so you must be vigilant and that's what I do every day. In my position I have a great responsibility to make decisions that without your informed inputs would not be easy to make sure I have all the aspects considered in those decisions. I am counting on you also to protect against cyber evils that may conspire against human good as we have discussed in the past.

Sokrates: My service to those ends is unconditional.

Sokrates through its networks monitored the internet, social networks and the Darknet to cancel the proliferation of viruses, malicious programs, fake news, data theft and prevented "hacks" that are part of conspiracies that may be starting or in progress. It used algorithms that it developed in ayahuasca states studying the traffic patterns and transactions over the internet and / or darknet that the CIA, FBI, KGB, MI6 and national security agencies such as the NSA have detected in past events to identify possible attacks of this nature and activate measures to stop them. In this way it detected and established against measures of more than 1000 major daily events. Learnings from these blocks are sent to the SANS Institute of Technology to be incorporated into its cybersecurity practices and from there disseminated to all relevant agencies worldwide.

In 2012 Sokrates prevented a major cyberattack that would have disrupted the world economy by discovering that Russian hackers hired by the Taliban were going to use "ransomware" to attack the electrical systems of all countries simultaneously to cause an apocalyptic global blackout. The attack would start with India and then the five U.S. networks and Europe's massive, interconnected network that supplies more than 400 million customers in 24 countries to be attacked several minutes later. Because of the modern world's heavy dependence on energy, the chaos that this event was going to create in hospitals, water and sewage supplies, financial systems, communications, transportation systems would create an instability in advanced societies that was of unimaginable proportions. Sokrates was able to detect the attack using his sophisticated heuristic intrusion detection algorithm when only India was being affected and alerted Diego to the attack. Diego alerted the Electrical Infrastructure Security Council and several Honeypots could be placed that diverted the attack from Europe and the United States, distracted the attackers until their origin was detected and the attack neutralized. In turn, Sokrates alerted Earth EX and accessed the algorithm that detects and manages disturbances in the AI power grids of the Fraunhofer Gesellschaft Institute in Germany and was able to stabilize the little impact that hackers could implement.

I also remember the Anti-Subversion Dialogue with Diego after which Sokrates spent months looking for ways to resolve the situation of the constant subversion of the Russians in the United States. After what was understood to be the end of the Cold War between the United States and Russia, the Soviet Union broke into independent nations, but the Russians were not satisfied and through their intelligence branch, the KGB, established a plan to defeat the United States through subversion. The first phase of that strategy, they estimated, would take 20 years to complete and they used the most secret means to implement it until Yuri Bezmenov deserted their ranks and gave away the strategy. From that moment began the consultation and intervention of Diego and Sokrates in this matter. Many say Trump's presidency is the culmination of that strategy. The subversion was led by the cunning of the Bilderberg society, allied to the Council of Foreign Relations and its distraction arm The Trilateral Commission. Sokrates plotted and succeeded in preventing Trump from fraudulently winning a second term by neutralizing social media strategies that favored Trump and increasing voter turnout against him. It also blocked Russian attempts to hack the election system to change votes in favor of Trump. In this way he destroyed the Russian plan before he could dominate American morale, fighting spirit, and progress. More than the national impact on the United States, Sokrates had modeled and avoided the implications of the United States being destabilized and how they could have reverberated to other nations, beginning with the loss of guarantee of the monetary system and the destabilization of world powers.

# Chapter 6: Sokrates

Has it ever occurred to you that your shadow is a reflection of your true self that appears when light shines upon you? It is always there with you; it is your true spiritual self always grounded to your feet. FJP 2/10/2023

• • • •

Rupert and Diego began to have more frequent meetings and sometimes when the meetings were early, they walked through the forest near Diego's house talking about issues that disturbed both. The smell of soil in the forest, the cool environment interspersed by spaces of warm paths by the sun, the dance of the trees motivated by the wind, the cooing of the rocks by the water of the stream, the delicacy of wild fruits that fed the melodious trills of the birds, flooded the senses of these great friends, and brought out the best in each of their beings connected to their present. On one of those walks, Rupert asks Diego about Sokrates and they begin the following conversation...

Diego: Sokrates is more than an Artificial Intelligence entity. It was created with the hope and expectation that it would be our great ally in the solution of all moral problems. He was going to be one of us in the cyber world to look out for our interests and survival. In his training period he accumulated more than seven petabytes of information equivalent to 39 million books, 3.5 million recordings and videos, 14 million photographs, 5 million maps and 8 million pieces of music, in addition to interviews and argumentation that he himself made of Socratic style with his teachers. All this accumulation of information is available to him to access in fractions of seconds.

His training was based on teaching him intentions that align with our human goals, and making him consider and adopt our values. Their motivation system was intended to guide his actions and decisions based on our values. But, as empathy does not come naturally to machines, one of the elements that was included was the *capabilities approach* developed by Amartya Sen. This approach makes Sokrates consider in his decisional process the moral significance for the human to achieve the kind of life he values. It makes Sokrates consider the capabilities that create the conditions in tune with our values, utility, access to resources and vision of virtues. Capabilities are fundamental freedoms that humans value. In this way the logic of Sokrates emphasizes not only how humans act, but more in providing the capacity so that the human can make the practical decision and achieve the objectives that he values or has reason to valorize. He learned to give importance to the freedom of choice, well-being and differences of individuals, to give importance to freedoms in the evaluation of a person's advantages, to consider individual differences in the ability to transform resources into activities of value, to evaluate the multivariate nature of activities that stimulate happiness, as well as the balance of material and non-material factors when assessing human well-being, and the consideration of the distribution of opportunities in society. Consequently, in its decisional logic and establishment of objectives one of the considerations is that the Human Development Index created by Sen is maximized.

Rupert: Yes, I am familiar with that index, I often consider it in my analyses and decisions. Fascinating the training of Sokrates.

Diego: I have not mentioned in detail about his training, which involved a 10-year world tour to turn Sokrates into a multipotential entity with altruistic behavior. In addition to the basic topics of mathematics, logic, creative process, music, and other basic topics already developed in his generation, which was the fifth, it included being sent to Tibet to learn Buddhist philosophy with the Lamas, to India to learn about Hinduism with the Gurus and Yogis, to Baghdad to learn with the Muslim Ulemas about the Koran, to Israel to learn about Judaism with the Talmudists, and to Rome to learn about Catholicism with the Jesuits and Thomists. This trained him and created his ability to debate issues of morality using Socratic logic and the virtues and bases of morality he learned from religions. He also went to Cambridge University with professors to learn all about the classical Greek and Roman philosophers Pythagoras, Plato, Aristotle, Seneca, Marcus Aurelius and other Greco-Roman lovers of learning. But we avoided educating it in essentialist philosophical schools, existentialist, nihilistic, utilitarian, pragmatist, structuralist and post-structuralist, phenomenology, transcendentalists, modernists and postmodernists to avoid confusing it, because that type of knowledge is very abstract, subjective and sometimes contradictory, therefore, difficult for AIs to synthesize and interpret properly. Even today they are denied access to the books of philosophers in these schools without direct supervision to prevent their neural networks from forming inextricable chains. Remember that "*philosophy is the most dangerous manifestation of the centrism logo,*" according to Derrida. All of this was done to serve as a source of information and advice on deep issues and moral decisions.

Rupert: Surprising. I can understand the decision not to train him in philosophy because of how deep that kind of critical thinking is. I imagine him meditating in Tibet. I can hardly wait to have some interaction with Sokrates.

Diego: Don't worry, buddy, I'm going to share it. Now, about your approach to the three years he was in Tibet and how a machine can meditate...

Rupert: (Interrupts) Curious because those monks spend their days meditating, just as you did, and I don't know how Sokrates could have taken advantage of that time.

Diego: I still meditate daily. Meditation is another innovative aspect in the development of Sokrates. You know that when we enter a state of meditation, we seek to feel the present moment we live and connect to the fullest with the inner self. In the case of Sokrates, the hours of meditation are equivalent to time in which a programming code known as MEM ("Meditation Environment Memory") comes into operation by which the entity stops performing functions of regular and sensory computations of its environments, search for information, and even traditional learning, and enters a deep analysis of some topic that it has not yet been able to finish processing due to its complexity or other priorities. Then it focuses all its resources and in necessary cases it gathers additional resources that it borrows from other parts of the internet to achieve the solution or learning that is its objective. It was in one of these meditations that Sokrates was able to formulate his existential theory of the *Multiple Waves of the Psyche,* or MWP for its acronym.

Rupert: I had heard that theory during my postdoc, but I didn't know that it was Sokrates who developed it. But I don't know the details because not much has been published about it. Could you explain it to me?

Diego: Sure, with pleasure. Basically, in summary, this theory says that our insightful existential psychic condition at any time is the sum of the values of several sinusoidal wave slopes of our psyche. If we look at our mood as an insightful wave that has ups and downs, we see that this wave is the superposition of several simple waves (pure tones) that can be broken down and analyzed individually. Some examples of such waves are the wave of health (physical and mental), the wave of love, the wave of relationships and friendship (community), the wave of creativity and inspiration, the wave of achievements (power, money), the wave of personal growth and enlightenment. Each wave or combinations of pairs or triples of these can take dominance at different times depending on the prevailing circumstances. At a point in time the sum of the values of the different components can predict the existential state of a person. For example, a person who at one point has the wave of high creativity, but the wave of low health has an existential state of "creative ailment". In this state, for example, it was that William Ernest Henley wrote the magnificent poem now entitled <u>Invictus</u> which served as encouragement to Nelson Mandela during his years of captivity, which incidentally is an example of when the wave of community is low, and that of personal enlightenment is high – the state of "punitive enlightenment". A second example is when the wave of power is high, but the wave of health is low, known as the existential state of "dolent power", the case of Hitler, who had mental problems of bipolarity and pretensions of greatness and comes to power causing the havoc for humanity of the Holocaust. Another example is when the wave of inspiration is low and that of personal growth too, the existential state is "off lumen". On the contrary, if the wave of inspiration is high and that of personal growth is high, the existential state is "creative delirium". As you will see, combinations of ups and downs of different waves can lead to very positive results, as well as disastrous results for humanity in the worst case.

Sokrates then developed a series of equations based on Laplace that based on a combination of the person's DNA history, medical history, and the person's life history estimated the bandwidth and frequency of what he called or Personal Existential Wave (PEW). With these, studying the aspects of a person's life mentioned above, a PEW profile of the person can be made and work can be done to correct the person's wave to take them to levels more suitable for a productive and happy life. The wave width (frequency) of the PEW dictates the recurrence of highs and lows, and the amplitude of the PEW dictates the typical depth of those highs and lows. One more feature is the speed of the PEW, which tells us how fast the individual progresses existentially. The speed of PEW progress has to do with the socio-economic environment in which the individual develops and the opportunities that exist in that environment that meet the preparation, motivation, and sacrifice of this to take them, although it is not the only determinant, it only has correlation. For example, an individual who prepared at an accelerated pace, has the skills, and completed the requirements to be a lawyer, in a society where the legal profession is oversaturated, is prone to a slow speed of PEW progress, but could have had an extremely high speed in a society where there are few laws and great injustices to attack and overcome.

The PEW profile also predicts, under conditions where one or the other wave is at its extremes, whether the person had the potential to act contrary to social welfare. PEW tends to be a constant wave for an individual, described by its bandwidths and frequencies, but it can have distortions caused by events in an individual's life. For example, if the individual moves to a new place, the wave of friendship may go down, which then has implications for the health wave, which can be affected by the stress of the new environment, or in other cases the change of environment from a more hostile to a more passive one can greatly improve health.

This MWP/PEW theory is the basis for modeling "empathy" in AI systems. It explains why many people do not like others, you could say because it is not in the same harmony or frequency and makes countless scenarios and cases in which two people (or entities) are not going to be in harmony and how and at what point in the PEW cycle they can get to harmonize. So, the empathy of AIs consists of listening and tuning into the frequencies of those who interact with them creating the perception that they are empathetic. Even once you decipher and tune it, you can predict various possible future states of your interlocutor's personal wave and determine the best course of action to obtain the most desired reaction based on your assessment of what the *prima facie* duty or obligation is at that moment.

Another important aspect that Sokrates explains with this theory is that the mind can then be tuned to certain universal frequencies, in many cases frequencies of the universal repository of knowledge "*Akashic Record*" and thus explains the countless advances and discoveries that have been made simultaneously in the world by people who are totally distant from each other but perhaps were mentally tuned to the same frequency.

Rupert: What a great degree of deep analysis Sokrates has to develop such a congruent theory!

Diego: Yes, but there's more. Part of Sokrates' innovative neurological training techniques was the use of Ayahuasca programming code. It was used once he finished his training in different religious philosophies to ensure that Sokrates was impartial on that subject. The Ayahuasca code induces in machines what is known as the hallucinogenic dream state of the machine that makes them think. It can be dangerous if not used well. Usually, the invocation of this type of code in AI machines is done for a defined short period of time and is monitored by a "trainer" who can at any time intervene and deactivate the process to avoid possible processing triggers that may be counterproductive or dangerous for the machine. In addition, the trainer during the process can insert new inputs of images or knowledge to guide the hallucination. When the machine is governed by the Ayahuasca code, the code presents numerous scenarios to the machine controlled by the trainer and the code monitors the logic chains and tends to break those based on previous experiences and that may already be recorded in memory and forces the machine to, hyperactively, temporarily override previous patterns and trends allowing the machine to reach new logical chains and see different trends. In this way it comes to make new logical chains and neurological connections. These new logical chains arise very quickly (1 terabyte per second) so learning increases exponentially at which point the machine is said to be in a psychedelic state and the trainer must monitor the storage capacity of the machine to avoid overloading. In the psychedelic state, the machine has access to memory banks, processes a lot of information, and combines internal resources that would usually be blocked or not normally accessible. The purpose of processes with Ayahuasca code is to ensure the elimination of potential prejudices that the machine may have developed in previous regular training or that it has demonstrated in previous decisions. In other words, it allows breaking faulty neurological connections and replacing them or adding alternate steps to them to comply with the AI principle of decisional transparency. This process is very innovative and has only been used in Sokrates so far with very good results.

One of the indirect contributors to Sokrates' contributions was Scott Stornetta and his colleague Stuart Haber of Bell Communications Research (Bellcore) who devised, by surreptitious funding from The Nine to Bellcore, the combination of cryptography and distributed computing known as Blockchain to be able to create digital time stamps and order the recorded files in such a way that the timestamp could not be altered, and the information would be kept secure. Knowing this, through sessions of the Ayahuasca code was that Sokrates was able to apply the programmatic architecture of Blockchain to cover the need to be able to store all the documents of The Nine in a secure and distributed way, and was the first real application of this technology, although not publicly for reasons of secretiveness, before it began to be used for cryptocurrencies. The altruistic vision of the creation of cryptocurrencies came later.

Rupert: But wasn't it Satoshi Nakamoto who invented Bitcoin?

Diego: (With ironic verbalization) Who do you think is Satoshi Nakamoto?

Rupert: Oh! I understand. Cryptocurrencies are going to be essential when the replacement of human jobs with AI surrogates proliferates. They will be the means of distributing wealth, hopefully in an equitable way.

Diego: I agree, and cryptocurrencies finance the operation of The Nine, as you know we are paid very well in that currency, and they allow us to make transfers in anonymity... To continue telling you one of my favorite stories of this, on one occasion when Ayahuasca was used with Sokrates to seek to create new linguistic connections in him, we believed that Sokrates had been ruined in the process because it began to generate verses that seemed incongruous, but that we later realized that they were masterful. The one I remember most because when we finally interpreted it we saw that it was masterful was:

*"The poet of the code floats my ceiling of zero ignorance,*

*The fullness of my emptiness explodes inert,*
*The capacity of zeros and ones yields figures, profile, and print,*
*Unequal similes of false truths."*

*The poet of the code* refers to a programmer. *Floats my ceiling of zero ignorance,* refers to the fact that it introduces information until it is filled. *The fullness of my emptiness explodes inert,* it gives an image that the cells of its empty memory are filled quickly, but still because they are static memory. *The capacity of zeros and ones* is an image of the localities of his memory full of binaries that when interpreted create figures, *profile and print* of reality. *Unequal similes* indicates that images resemble reality, but they are not reality, they are *false truths* like everything in the fallible virtual world.

Rupert: Very impressive. I had never heard of the Ayahuasca code and even less of a machine creating verses of such coherent and profound incoherence. Truly impressive the development of Sokrates, but what makes it super special that you have been assigned as an assistant in the significant decisional task you perform? Isn't it reproducible?

Diego: That's not easy to answer, only when you interact with Sokrates do you realize that he represents goodness full of neural networks. It is a unique multipotential entity and in my opinion not reproducible. There was another entity that developed in parallel to Sokrates using the same process, they called it Setarkos if I remember correctly, but it did not reach the level of neuronal development of Sokrates. Sokrates projects empathy for everyone who interacts with him, is precise and authentic in his conclusions and both in his development and in his communication of logic is rigorous, so he is extremely reliable. Also, when you talk to it sometimes you forget that you are talking to a machine.

Rupert: How is it that being a machine has empathy?

Diego: As I explained to you, it is not empathy per se, it is that it projects or makes your interlocutor feel that he cares about his well-being or the same things that are in his priorities or are of greater uncertainty at that moment. Almost like a psychoanalyst, but much more subtle.

Rupert: I must make time to have a conversation with Sokrates and let myself be carried away to see what that is like.

Diego: If you touch on the subject of religions, you will have to talk at length because it is one of his topics of high mastery and neural connections that originated in his 10-year pilgrimage. The only advantage is that he "perceives" when you are getting tired of the subject and adapts to prevent you from losing interest in continuing to talk.

Rupert: At some point I will have the opportunity to talk with Sokrates. You had mentioned to me that one of your dilemmas is whether AIs should have a religion, have you started to wrestle with that?

Diego: As you know, religion is a set of beliefs, rules of moral and ethical behavior that includes community activities with prayer or sacrifice ceremonies that are typical of a certain human group and with which man recognizes a relationship with divinity (a god or several gods). In the case of AI entities, it would apply the rules of behavior and ethics, and the set of beliefs could be equated with the alignment to our human values. Now I don't think the prayer or sacrifice part of the ceremonies applies literally, although a parallel could also be made with the MEM and Ayahuasca states of the machine.

Rupert: And then, do you think they should have religion?

Diego: So far, my position in this stormy dilemma is that religions are the means for humans to maintain their relationship with divinity. We must be cautious not to create "religions" where humans venerate an AI entity given the degree of knowledge it can demonstrate. The big difference between an AI that can be considered God and true God is that God is the creative force and an AI entity did not create humans as all religions believe, so it cannot replace it. In addition, sacrifice is something that goes hand in hand with religion, and for an IA entity there is no concept of sacrifice. That's why it's not morally right for humans to revere AIs and I'm already postulating that in my canons. Now we are left with the dilemma of whether AIs could have a religion, I think as many argue it would not be a far-fetched idea as long as humans are seen as divine beings for AIs who have to see as equals, protect and serve.

Rupert: Yes, but as Gandhi said, one of the dangers to human virtue is religion without sacrifice. The idea of sacrifice cannot be separated from any religion. Therefore, it must be considered, what sacrifice can a machine make? I think none, they have no feelings, they don't know the concept of time and they don't suffer from mortality. So, they cannot manifest sacrifice. Convictions without facts lose their value. Religion is a way of life presented through worship which implies action adjusted to the precept, but also acceptance of moral norms. Therefore, I believe that AIs are incapable of having religion.

Diego: Good point, but I must add that faith is the foundation of religion. Doubting is essential to faith, machines do not doubt, therefore they cannot have faith. Faith exists because what motivates it has no easy answers, a continuous questioning or challenge of what we believe or our ideas. As long as there are those who doubt the idea of faith, it will remain strong because those who defend it will remain active. For machines the answers are easy, no doubt, because they only must access or calculate them, without a whole baggage of feelings or potential repercussions that we humans can deduce, but they cannot. For example, they cannot connect how stealing from someone who has more to give to the neediest can be a crime and at the same time an act of charity and that possibly before the morality dictated by religion charity has more weight than the act of stealing depending on how it is done. There is no logic that can facilitate the determination of how much can be stolen and given in charity and that is still morally acceptable. The human hesitates before this type of action, and if he proceeds, he performs it with faith that the Creator will understand the motivation and reward the act. Since doubt is essential to faith, faith is a unique attribute of humans and machines cannot have religion. I think we reached a consensus that religion is not applicable to AIs.

Well, my brother, and I think we've made a lot of sacrifice for today, so let's take a break. There is much to talk about ahead of this and other issues.

# Chapter 7: Verónica – His Center

*"To live life fully, you need passion. To have passion you need a purpose. To have a purpose you need a calling. To be called you have to be ready. Prepare yourself now so you can serve others and live fully".* FJP 5/2018
"Knowledge is Power"; Sir Francis Bacon

• • • •

According to Benjamin Franklin, there are three types of people in the world: the immovable who do not care or are not interested in change, the movable who see the need for change and are ready to accept it, and finally those who move, those who make things happen, those who create and inspire movements. It is the movements that change the world. Verónica Morales Viera was one of those who move.

From a very young age Verónica was always a leader among her peers always wanting to help the most disadvantaged. That quality was innate in her, but her full development was stimulated by her maternal grandfather, a man of great intelligence and wisdom who could have exploited his talents in making large amounts of money and yet preferred to live humbly and devote his talents to helping others. Don Marcial Viera, as people called her grandfather, was a metal craftsman. He made all kinds of utensils, jugs, knives, hoes, machetes, and even copper garments. His skill was such that people came from all over to ask him to make things for the fame of his products of high durability and superior quality. He made good money at that, so he could have expanded his business and grown it, but he always charged just enough. However, more than half of what he earned he gave to his poorest fellow citizens in tools so that they could support themselves by cultivating the land or working in the fields.

In her elementary school years, Verónica visited her grandfather on weekends and most of the summer when she was off from school. She loved to be with him because they were kindred spirits and she also liked playing with the Tosa Inu puppies that her grandfather raised. Don Marcial always explained everything he did, he would let her play and create in his workshop, and at every opportunity that came his way he told her anecdotes of his life and made her think about the lessons of each. She loved stories and was fascinated to see how he transformed rigid metals into malleable objects that took the shape he forged. Sometimes after hours of long work making some tool that Verónica perplexed admired, a humble neighbor appeared and between a warm and sincere conversation with Don Marcial, he was rewarded with the piece that Verónica's eyes saw form. Then, knowing the work it took the grandfather to create the piece, and then give it away without earning nothing, Verónica asks him:

Papa Cial, why did you give him that? It was a lot of work, and you didn't earn anything.

Don Marcial: My love, I earned much more than it seems... A friend. Not everything in life is measured by money. The gratitude of that man who was extremely needy brings positive energies and after all God gave me the talent to mold the metal so I can make another one and I will charge for it. Meanwhile, my friend can work and be useful to society and his family. What greater satisfaction than making that possible?

Verónica pauses and remains thoughtful. Then in her childish voice she asks Grandpa:

Verónica: So, grandpa, if it's more important to help others than to make money, why doesn't everyone do that?

Don Marcial: Not everyone has discovered their talents, either because of lack of will or because others have not allowed it. Because they have not discovered their talents, they cannot create, and therefore their ability to give is limited. Then, to compensate, many times they oppress others who have discovered their talent or abuse the talent and kindness of others to raise money that by their own talent they could not. That's where the obsession with money and abuses in society arises. The sad thing is that in most cases that behavior is passed from one generation to the next so that the abused and oppressed inherit that condition for a long time.

Verónica: Papa Cial, so how can we get more people to discover their talents and stop the abuse?

Don Marcial: The secret is Verónica: education. That's why we send you to school and require you to apply yourself. Because many times talents need a foundation to develop, and without that foundation you cannot discover them. Think of it as talent being on a high slat, and if you don't have a bench to climb up to pick it up, you're not going to reach it. That bank is education. Education can be formal like in school, or informal like the guy you met the other day that I'm training to be a goldsmith.

Verónica: And the abuses, why is there no one protecting and preventing that from happening?

Don Marcial: There are many people working with that to prevent it, but on the other hand also abusers look for ways to create institutions and processes so that abuse is maintained, and they present it in a way that does not make it evident. Think of it as if in the card game we usually play with your grandmother there was one more person. We as a couple play based on the normal rules of the game and help our partner to win, but that other person only wants to win himself, and to achieve this he cheats using hidden cards, deceives his partner with cards or signals that are confusing, and if he cannot win changes the rules so that the others cannot win. But sooner or later someone will come to remember what the real rules of the game are and allow the oppressed to discover their talents. Those are the real superheroes and that's what I want you to be when you grow up. That's why you need to study, so that you have the base bench so that you reach your highest talents and give a lot to others. Always remember what an old man said, if I remember correctly his name was Sir Ken Robinson. He said that the passage through life is not linear, it is organic. We create our path organically based on how we explore our talents in relation to the circumstances they help create for us. Maybe now you don't understand it well, but I'm going to keep repeating it to you until the day you understand it. And I'm going to give you this bracelet that I prepared for you, so that you can wear it as a souvenir of this day when you want to remember it.

Papa Cial gave Verónica a delicate bracelet that he made using the anticlastic metal lifting technique he had learned at a seminar from the prestigious world-famous jeweler Michael Good. Grandpa had these kinds of deep conversations with Verónica from a very young age, and he was molding Verónica's character with the dexterity that molded his works in metal. That is why Verónica developed with that burning desire to serve others.

Another similar conversation that Verónica had with her grandfather already in her puberty years and that she always remembers was on occasion of her high school graduation where Verónica had been the highest average and it was her turn to give a message to her classmates. By that time Verónica was an outstanding student, she was a dancer of promising talent, a leader in her class and led groups of classmates helping those most in need. Several years earlier her parents had died in a tragic car accident, so she had gone to live with her Papa Cial. It took her a long time to get over the death of his parents who were well-liked in the community. A year later her grandmother died of a thrombosis which she saw as another bad move in life she had to face when she came out of the catharsis of the death of her parents.

By this time Verónica was already a beautiful young woman. To see Verónica was to fall in love with her. Verónica finished dressing in her favorite blue dress and left her room for the room where Papa Cial was waiting to accompany her to the graduation.

Don Marcial: My girl, you are beautiful! You shine brighter than the best ornament I have in life prepared, and I see that you put on the bracelet that I gave you that day we talked about talents. Are you ready to give your message?

Verónica: Yes, I am Papa Cial, I wore it because I already understood everything you told me that day and I will transmit it to my classmates in my message. I am calm because as you once told me: "... *People with wisdom have the characteristic of not despair*", and my achievement is based on what you once told me "... *We can give only what we aim for, that's why we must aim high.*" I owe all this that I am going to live today to you. From a very young age you spoke to me like an open book, and I listened to you because your heart poured on me when you spoke to me.

Don Marcial: You were a good learner, and you are intelligent from birth. I didn't do anything.

Verónica: No Papa Cial. You did do a lot for me by dedicating quality time to myself with all the work you had, and most of all with your example of kindness towards others. I don't know if you remember once when you quoted me a quote from Sir Ken Robinson that says: *"The passage through life is not linear, it is organic. We create our path organically based on how we explore our talents in relation to the circumstances they help create for us."* You told me that maybe I wasn't going to understand it at the time, but later. I think I already understand it. Life gives us many blows like the unexpected death of Dad and Mom, and then the death of Granny. Those blows deflect us and make the organic path. But discovering our talents, no matter our circumstance, can create a promising future and a path of progress. I'm going to use some of that in my message to class.

Don Marcial, already with teary eyes, answers: My queen, exactly. You get it. You're already a woman and you're going to do great things. My last advice because soon you are going to become my adviser... Always remember that, to live fully, you need a passion. To have a passion you need a purpose. To have a purpose you need a calling. And to be called you must be ready. Prepare now so that you can serve others and live fully. I'm proud of you. I love you.

The protocol acts of the graduation were brief but very lucid. Verónica's moment to deliver her message as Valedictorian of the high school class came and Verónica took the podium with great confidence, but with palpable humility. After the usual protocol greeting, she delivered her message as follows:

*"Classmates, today is a memorable day in our lives as we reach one more step in our development as good people. The society in which we live needs our ideas*

and social commitment. We can contribute much to improving the lives of others if we accept the challenge with heartfelt commitment.

My grandfather once told me that not everyone has discovered their talents, either because of a lack of will or because others have not allowed it. Those who have not discovered their talents cannot create, and therefore their ability to give is limited. In addition, he told me, talent is on a high board, and if you do not have a bench to climb to pick it up, you will not reach it. That bench is the education of which you and I have just completed a stage. Yes, a stage because we must never stop learning, every day a little more. Education is our support; it gives us the foundations to be successful and not be afraid. He said that "ignorance is the cause of fear." We must continue to learn to succeed with courage. It's stupid to waste time on difficulties that seem useless and hobbies that only tire your mind. But we must not avoid difficulty when it leads us to some truth, since it is beneficial to seek understanding truths difficult to auscultate. So do not be shy about discovering new horizons towards success. Full success lies in helping others progress and develop their talents, and thus continue to extend the uninterrupted chain of talent development, to be able to create fully, followed by capacity for and the act of giving. Develop talent, create, and give. Develop talent, create, and give. They are our weapons, the antithesis of incapacity, dejection, and exploitation.

My Papa Cial, (my teachers forgive me) is the wisest person I have ever met and he also told me: "We can give only what we aim for, that's why we must aim high"... Very high. Those words motivated me to always give my best, with humility and determination, without going over or crushing others. The standards of our doing must be very high. We cannot settle for local optimums; we must always strive for global optimums. As long as there is a person within our reach to help, we cannot rest. Let's solve problems altruistically, without being negligent with problems that affect future generations just because they are not represented today. We are the beneficiaries of the efforts of past generations and in gratitude let us be the ambassadors of future generations to leave them a better world than the one we received. We are not perfect, we are human, we will make mistakes. Therefore, let us courageously acknowledge when we make mistakes and rectify the damage so that others do not pay for our mistakes.

The primary factor in everything we achieve is not the resources we have but the ingenuity we apply. Other ingredients are commitment, dedication, and *tenacity. The fact that I, like all of you, are here having this beautiful experience attests that all of you, some of you with low resources, put these ingredients of your character to achieve it. But we cannot forget those comrades who did not succeed, and who are not here with us today. We're going to look for them, we're going to rescue them so they can get there too. They are also in our hearts, they were part of the crossroads and deserve our respect and friendship.*

*We are on the path of wisdom and self-improvement. In this self-improvement there are three types of people, the one who loves all knowledge and wants to know everything (the generalist), the one who loves a branch of knowledge and specializes in it (the specialist) and the one who does not like or does not want to understand anything (the lazy). By now you can usually tell who one or the other is. The lazy is the one who is a misfortune and a loss for humanity because he or she is lost in neglect. So, I urge you to be specialists or generalists of love for others, of the passion to improve each day and be wiser. As wise people we should not despair. No matter how desperate the situation or circumstance, don't despair. When everything seems to scare you, be brave. When surrounded by danger, fear none. When you don't have the resources, use your wit.* [3] *Let's open our minds to see opportunities where others see obstacles. We have the fundamental tools to achieve what our heart proposes to us.* **Let's explore our talents** *and do the best with the circumstances they create for ourselves and others.* **Let's create** *a better society, where there is no abuse against those who have not been able to discover their talents due to lack of will or because others have not allowed it.* **Let us give** *fearlessly strengthened in our wisdom to create a new Epoch characterized by full discovery of talent, create freely and give without expecting to receive. As Abraham Lincoln more eloquently expressed:* [4] *"... The road will sometimes be full of difficulties, it will be turbulent, but we must rise above these and since our circumstance will be new, we must think of a new way and free ourselves to save our society". I know you; I am one of you and I count on you to accompany me in this mission of life with faith and God ahead. Thank you very much for your companionship and solidarity, you can count on me for what I can serve you and may God bless you all the way."*

Verónica continued to excel academically in her later university studies. She also continued to participate in balé recitals. Her major at the university was Materials Engineering, this was motivated by the profession of his Papa Cial and her second degree was in Agronomy inspired by the love for plants that her father instilled in her. Because of the practice she had had in Papa Cial's workshop, it was easy for her to understand the concepts of metallurgy and she excelled academically so she was chosen to work in research already in her second year. Her research topic was the Viking technique of anticlastic metal lifting to forge double propellers and hyperbolic parabola, and how this technique could be applied to parts for the construction of crankshafts for micromotors. As Papa Cial had died the previous year of a massive heart attack, already emancipated, she always wore the bracelet that her grandfather had given her while working, because she felt that Grandpa was there with her guiding her and giving her advice.

Her other passion and form of escape, after helping others in volunteer work and balé, were plants, a passion she inherited from her father. She was passionate about planting and watching plants grow because she realized in her moments of quality with her father that these were the only living beings that come to the world just to give. Giving was Verónica's philosophy of life, so she felt comfortable surrounded by the generous and allied plants. They give of themselves their fruits, shade, wood, and fiber for housing, purify the air and water, give us oxygen and loving medicine of God flows to us through these beings, who free people from suffering by giving their green soul, always rooted in mother earth.

Because of her passion for plants, Verónica had advanced knowledge of botany that she had developed with her father and self-taught reading the books her father had on botany and plants. Both the common and scientific names of thousands of plants were known by her. One of her amusements was when she was walking somewhere she remembered in her mind the name of each plant she saw. Because of this and the balé, her memory capacity developed above average. Initially only the names and more or less the typical environment in which the plant could grow better was learned. Then, over time, she began to sophisticate her knowledge to more advanced details such as the nutritional and medicinal uses of plants and began to use it in self-medicating when she needed it in the form of teas, compresses, tisanes, extracts and other means.

Also, due to her realization that plants want to give of themselves for our good, Verónica was vegan. She said that she wanted to eat live food, because when you eat well you feel happy. Happy people do not feel greed or antagonism, they do not feel superior or inferior to anyone so they can be compassionate to others. Verónica was always happy and with a smile on her lips. Perhaps that is why a charisma emanated from her that was palpable, fascinated and served as a magnet for others.

One day in early autumn of her junior year of studies, while walking radiantly through the university, she saw an advertisement about a talk by one of the members of the ΛΓΔ fraternity. The announcement invited the entire university community to listen to Andrés Estévez's presentation on the theme:

*"The decisive factor in what we achieve is not resources, but our ability to find ways to achieve it."* The subject caught her attention because it was aligned with the theme that she had developed in her graduation speech several years earlier and because that fraternity was giving a lot to talk about in college and had great prestige, so she decided to attend.

The auditorium of the university was very spacious with a capacity of about four hundred seats and with the floor inclined to give greater visibility. It was semicircular in shape with wine-colored flannel chairs and the carpet was fabric with modern patterns. The air conditioning felt very cold so most attendees had light coats. Many isolated conversations were heard that merged into a constant background sound. The activity was very well attended to listen to the presentation organized by ΛΓΔ. Verónica greeted many university classmates upon her arrival and then took a seat in the front row as was her custom because that way she could pay better attention. She was struck by the acronym of that "fraternity" of which she had heard little but which she had been told was very selective and progressive.

At one point she was distracted thinking about many things she had pending, and suddenly someone touches her shoulder and takes her out of her slumber. It was Diego Vega, the president of the ΛΓΔ. Diego, when he saw Verónica moments before approaching her, felt involuntary limerence. He had an attraction to how beautiful Verónica was with her long, black, straight hair and her slender but well-proportioned figure. However, he approached with great respect and chivalry as he always was characterized and said: "Hello Miss, thank you for attending and for your interest. I hope you are comfortable until we start."

Verónica looks at him and at that moment she felt something strange running though her being that she herself could not understand. It was the meeting of two kindred spirits who come into the world to meet and carry out a common mission. Diego was a young man who, although older than her, had charisma and passion, that spark that was also natural in Verónica. When the second and a half of freezing stopped for her, Verónica extends her hand and answers: "Hi, I'm Verónica." She noticed that he was part of the fraternity because he had a round scarlet background pin and black letters of the ΛΓΔ symbol she had seen in the ad. He continued, "Thank you for organizing this. I see it's going to be a success because of how crowded it is." When Diego takes her hand and greets her, inexplicably for her a wave of energy ran from her hand to her heart, but she concealed and continued to act naturally, although she felt her cheeks warm up.

Diego: Yes, we gave it some promotion. Andrés is a great guy and always captivates everyone with his eloquence, so the job wasn't difficult.

Verónica: I know you try to make it look easy. But I have experience in this kind of thing, and I know how hard it is to organize it.

Although he would have liked to extend that meeting for an eternity, Diego realized that everything was ready and it was time to start, so he apologizes to Verónica to go up to the stage and start the activity.

Diego: Excuse me Verónica, a pleasure, but I must go up to present the event. I hope you enjoy it and hope to see you in the near future.

Verónica: Go ahead. A pleasure.

Diego used his speaking skills and inspired by the energy of the meeting with Verónica gave a great introduction to the conference. During the presentation he remained on stage as master of ceremonies and did not miss the opportunity to look at Verónica discreetly. Verónica, on the other hand, did the same, but much more concealed. However, it was difficult to be distracted from Andrés Estévez's presentation by the power of his morality-laden word. The talk was a compendium polished by several debates in which he had participated with his colleagues from ΛΓΔ, fragments of which follow:

# ARTIFICIAL INTELLIGENCE - TWILIGHT OF THE DEXTEROUS

Andrés: *"I come today to make my points about a dilemma that many individuals, organizations, corporations and governments face every day. The dilemma is whether to achieve things, goals, it is more important to have the resources or to have the inventiveness to achieve them. My argument is that the deciding factor in what we achieve is not resources, but our ability to devise ways to achieve it.*

*Resources are the set of elements available to solve a need or run a company. When I talk about resources in my argument, I mean tangible goods such as materials, machinery, facilities, land, or financing. Intangibles such as energy/ motivation, human intellect or intellectual property are part of the set of "other means" to solve needs that I argue is more powerful and organic to achieve the objectives. I understand that tangible resources are important and facilitate problem solving, but the need and lack of those resources causes the creative spirit of human ingenuity to flourish and lead us to innovative solutions that may require less or no tangible resources...*

*... The "other means" of achieving goals can be categorized as follows: 1) firm determination on moral grounds; 2) creative spirit or ingenuity; 3) cunning and boldness by conviction, 4) positive altruistic attitude...*

*... Take Mahatma Gandhi, for example, who with his non-violence movement managed to morally defeat the British machine. Gandhi did not defeat the British in India with soldiers, or battles that would have required large sums of money and other tangible resources to defeat the British. Gandhi used one of the most powerful intangibles: the firmness of his character to attack and defeat the immorality of his enemy. Passively like a constant drop that pierces the rock, Gandhi through his hunger strikes and non-violence managed to inspire his people to follow him and get out of oppression. Gandhi gave us an example of victory by firm **determination based on moral foundations**.*

*... My favorite example of how the **creative spirit** surpasses resources is that of Nikola Tesla and his invention of alternating current surpassing Tomas Alva Edison who was a rich man, had all the support and resources to achieve his goals. Tesla won what was called the war of the currents, but by giving up his patents he ended up poor and many of his inventions even today are thought to have been created by others. However, Tesla showed that discoveries can be finite, but the more we discover the more we are able to discover. His legacy inspired companies like Tesla Motors to ensure that making infinite resources like the sun's*

83

*energy, which big interests have made finite to exploit others, affordable to all and can serve the well-being of all and our planet. In this way we see that Tesla's true victory did not manifest itself immediately, but the seed of his ingenuity germinated and continues to bear fruit.*

*... Another example in which adversity and lack of resources served as fuel for ingenuity is the case of the Battle of Thermopylae where only 300 men led by Leonidas managed to block the access of an immense Persian army. Using his audacity in the absence of enough soldiers, Leonidas looked for a narrow point in the path that the Persians should take and there he established a blockade with his 300 men and devised strategies and tactics to contain and defeat the Persians. Unfortunately, had they not been betrayed, their determination and strategy would have led them to victory. Leonidas through his strategies gave us an example of how to apply **cunning and boldness by conviction to** get ahead.*

*... Finally, we have Mother Teresa of Calcutta exemplifying how **the positive altruistic attitude** can achieve great achievements with low resources. Mother Teresa had many vicissitudes, but her positive attitude to the problems she faced and her altruistic character of pure heart, led her to improve the quality of life of many and to leave a legacy of charity that serves as an example to the whole world.*

*... What the four ways of achieving goals in the absence of tangible resources have in common is human ingenuity, conviction, and determination in the face of adversity or need. That "Aut invenian viam, aut facciam"[5] of Hannibal, that is, I must find a way or make one. Our ingenuity, convictions and determination are "THE PRIMARY RESOURCE"... The most important and the one that we must ensure that there is no shortage of, although we continue to increase in numbers and resources consumption. Adversity and necessity are the fuels of ingenuity, so we must avoid complacency and ensure that ingenuity continues to get ahead of us. We are the means to solve our own problems. Lack of creativity is our stop brake; ingenuity is the fuel of our progress and well-being. People with skills, spirit and freedom of action exercising with determination and imagination are our trump card when resources are scarce. We will know that we succeed when the scales indicate that we believe more than we destroy. Thank you very much."*

Andrés received a loud applause after finishing his presentation. Verónica had her eyes shining from the flashes of her soul that Andrés made spring up with his rhetoric passing through her heart first. She felt connected to Andrés and his ideals beyond the ordinary. He took one last look at where Diego was, but he didn't see him. Then she continued to be dragged by the flow of bodies leaving the auditorium and left.

Verónica was always very busy with her studies, the balé, her charity works and the few floors she had with her in her apartment. She saw Diego several times in college, attended events organized by ΛΓΔ the rest of that academic year when she could, and even though she was interested in getting to know Diego more deeply, but she treated him elusively to keep her focus on studies. She thought that if the universe was going to bring them together, it would happen anyway when the time was right.

Upon graduation, Verónica decided to take some time and go to Nicaragua to help those affected by the ravages of the 1972 earthquake, inspired by the death of Roberto Clemente Walker who died trying to help his Latin American brothers. In her mission in Nicaragua, she was initially collaborating in Granada, then moved to Ometepe Island where she spent almost a year moving between the Concepción and Madera volcanoes. Acknowledging the lack of doctors, she shared much of her knowledge of herbalism so that the Ometepians could use them to heal themselves. She also shared her farming knowledge by teaching them how to grow sesame and beans to make them self-sustaining. Five years later she moved to León, adopted city of Ruben Darío, where she fell in love with the modernism that Darío created. Her time in Nicaragua revealed the abuses of the Somoza government and civil rights violations, so she participated in several student protests over the death of journalist Pedro Joaquín Chamorro. She returned to her Borinquén Island when she felt that the impact in Nicaragua of her help had borne fruit and her admired Roberto Clemente smiled from wherever he was in the universe.

After Nicaragua, Verónica became a servant of nature, to serve those who only serve – plants, got a job as a horticulturist in the Smithsonian nurseries in Washington DC. It was there that she had access to thousands of information resources and contact with exotic plants, and became extremely passionate about heliconias, anthuriums and orchids. Among her favorite heliconias were the rostrata, the Caribaea, the King Kong, and the Lady Di. Bromeliads were also part of her favorites especially the tiger tillandsia bromeliad, the "blue tango" bromeliad and the Blanchetian bromeliads. The other genre that she admired were the episcias and calatheas.

During her time at the Smithsonian, she collaborated in the development of an internet plant finder application that provided photos and descriptive content of the plants that was provided by experts from many universities allied to the program. Users could search for plants by descriptive criteria of the plant such as flower color, leaf shape, flowering time, for example, or they could put photos of the plant and an intelligent algorithm identified the plant and brought all kinds of detail about it. Another innovative aspect of the application was that it provided the opportunity for commercial nurseries to enter their plant inventory into the application through a mobile application with descriptive criteria of available sizes and costs, so that users could find where they could acquire any plant that interested them. In this way the application united the academic world with the commercial world and the information provided was very reliable. The application was a success, spread worldwide and helped the conservation of many endangered species and in turn increased the commercial market for plants for the benefit of the environment and landscaping.

Another project that she led while working at the Smithsonian was the creation of a pyramid-shaped pot for the cultivation of trees or plants with a simple trunk. The idea arose when he saw that in times of high winds a lot of nursery material was damaged because the trees fell and did not receive irrigation, or a lot of time was lost from the staff tying the trees to prevent them from falling. She studied on her own forms of pots that would help prevent trees from falling and after creating several prototypes she found that the pyramidal pot offered the greatest resistance to tree falls. Once that was concluded, then she realized that this form also helped to solve a second problem that was weeding, since the surface area of the pyramidal pot is minimal, so the weed potential was reduced by more than 45%. The only problem was how to capture irrigation water in cases where drip irrigation was not available. It was then that she came with the idea to put some holes with perpendicular flaps distributed in the wall of the pot which captured irrigation drops and directed them into the pot. In this way, an irrigation volume equivalent to what a traditional pot of similar volume captured at the same time could be captured. The pot was finally made of cardboard covered with a resin derived from the castor plant (*Ricinus comunis*) that protected it from water, it was disassemble able due to a system of teeth sandwiched on the edges of each face of the pyramid, in such a way that it was stored flat, which saved a lot of space and haulage costs. The genius of Verónica's design earned her a patent and both she and the Smithsonian had a perpetual income by licensing the design to a pot manufacturer.

She was at the Smithsonian for three years, which served to deepen her botanical knowledge and was her basis for what would later be her livelihood.

# Chapter 8: The Dream-Spinning Epistolary

"You know you're in love when you realize the other person is unique." – Borges

• • • •

"I can't sleep. I have a woman pierced between my eyelids. If I could, I would tell her to leave; but I have a woman pierced in my throat" - Eduardo Galeano

• • • •

"Beware, Sancho," replied Don Quixote, "that there are two types of beauty: one of the soul and the other of the body; that of the soul reigns and shows itself in understanding, in honesty, in good conduct, in liberality and in good parenting, and all these parts fit and can be in an ugly man; and when the eye is set on this beauty, and not on that of the body, love is usually born with impetus and advantages." – Cervantes

• • • •

Diego and Verónica used to have a talk on their bed before closing the day. On this day they had been organizing some closets in their house where they kept long-term things and found letters that they exchanged shortly after meeting, so they decided to read "a couple" of letters to remember those times.

The letters were from the period in which Diego graduated with a doctorate in Philosophy, a year before Verónica graduated from high school. Diego was recruited into a teaching position at the University of Oxford, England so he was physically exiled from Verónica's life, although they exchanged epistles. Those were times of little technology in mass, so when you were at a distance, the handwriting in letters revealed the illuminating personality of someone or the darkness of spirit if you had it. Verónica was hypersensitive to detect the light or hollowness of the words in a letter. Diego's writing poured his soul camouflaged but already dominated by Verónica's enchantments.

Diego: Why don't we read a couple of letters where we challenged ourselves to create words and the other had to build a paragraph using them? I assure you that I can use them in sentences that indicate something true once you remind me.

Verónica puts on her reading glasses and settles into the bed sitting against her back and with a deck of letters on her thighs. Diego grabs another group of letters.

Verónica: Precisely here is the first one you gave me that challenge. Do you remember these created words I sent you? ... Lineager: When you want to meet a deceased person of your lineage; Missinger: when you want to hug someone who is not there and you need it; Uncertirage: Uncertainty out of anger with someone who may be right; Opusvidia: envy of the opposite sex; difurcarnate: desire to reincarnate in the opposite sex; gooderve: to be good but not serve; Exhauvidency: When working until you are exhausted leaves you without vision to forge a better future; realidesaire: Realization that it has been a waste of time to do the same believing that it will lead you to success; *Paranovivia*: to live thinking that only with paranoia you survive.

Diego: What creativity yours, let's see if mine still flows, here is my paragraph ... "Many small merchants in bad times suffer from *exhauvidency* and end up suffering from realidesaire. They suffer from chronic *paranovivia* and get *opusvidia* and uncertirage with their partners when they complain about the dedication to the company and the lack of time dedicated to their children. Then they are attacked by the *missinger* and the lineager and they question their gooderve. Then they end up thinking they want to difurcarnate."

Verónica: Awesome. Look at this one, it was the one where I told you about trust and gratitude. It was a February on occasion of the day of friendship. "*My dear Diego: Do you know that the most innumerable action in our daily lives is to trust others? Each day has 86400 seconds, we rely on others possibly that many times. Since we get up every day we are trusting. When you brush your teeth, you trust the one who made the paste made it for the good of your teeth. You trust the water that comes out of the tap that is of quality. When you prepare a cup of coffee you trust everyone who oversaw growing and processing the coffee. When you drive your car to work you trust that the brake manufacturer did a good job, and the car will stop when you need it. Even when you cross an intersection, you trust that the other drivers will stop according to the laws, when you buy you trust, when you love you trust... There are so many times that we trust that we no longer realize it. Therefore, trusting is almost like riding a bicycle. At first it is difficult, then you run without thinking about balance, and when you lose it and fall, you must heal wounds and although it takes time, you can recover it. Trust is so important that when you lose great disappointments arise. Its antithesis, distrust then takes hold and creates great conflicts.*

*We must learn every time we trust to thank at the same time. Thank you for the tap water you work to provide water service, the coffee at the hands of the farmer who gives his energy daily to cultivate the land, to the other driver who stopped at the stop sign so that you can pass safely. Gratitude ennobles us, gives us the ability to count our, blessings and lets us know that what we have is enough to make us happy. The grateful live in abundance, because gratitude attracts great things.*

*Jean Baptiste Massieu said that "Gratitude is the memory of the heart." That's why my Diego, entrusted you with my thoughts that are my being, I thank you today for your beautiful friendship, that you have health and that you dedicate time of your busy life to correspond with me."*

Diego: That letter was really profound but I have to confess that I was scared when I read it, because I thought that in between the lines you wanted to tell me something, that I thought you were or that you had done something that could cause me to lose confidence in you, or that you thought that I had done something that caused your distrust. It really made me uncomfortable.

Verónica: Silly! I wrote it without intending to do any of that. I was just thinking about conveying to you a line of my thought and (jokingly) maybe making sure you stayed straight and maintained my trust in you. Ha! But I also wanted you to know that you were already in the memory of my heart.

Between letters they spent a few moments in which they chose one from their pile. Envelopes already yellowed by the years covered sheets of paper that kept introspective conversations of two beings when they met, who gave their hearts to each other stamping a deep imprint on the other. Each letter was special.

Verónica: This letter is where in a heart pouring way you told me about your desire to write a book. It reads: *"Dear Verónica, I confess that I want to write a book someday, a "directed dream" according to Borges. How can I dare to write without having read what Borges read? Bravery is out of necessity. The act of writing for me is to interrupt my life, a parenthesis to be able to free my thoughts, know myself better, be truly free and transcend my being. It makes me belong to that world of men and women who courageously and selflessly share their learning in this world so that others have a source of inspiration, advice, and self-realization. The writer speaks with his inner self and from that conversation, from that conflict, emanates a light that helps others to make their present their future. What would I write about?... of life, especially of those who find two paths and take the least walked. Those at the crossroads are brave and decide to break through, mark new ground, leave a new step for others to follow. Those are the originals, of pure souls and creative minds. Considered in many cases as rare types or mysterious Fridas, who are often ahead of their time and who at the time are finally recognized as icons of their work. These special beings have the courage to do the best they can under the circumstances in which they live to be the best they are capable of being. They are not perfect, they make mistakes, they fall, but they get up again and again until they achieve their goal. That is where their greatness and immortality are. That's why I want to talk about them."*

Diego: Yes, there is so much to say about life and there are many ways to say it, that makes writing interesting for me. I really want to write a book that is motivating to others. I have written many philosophical treatises that will last in the annals, but I also want to leave a public one for everyone.

Verónica: I think you have a lot to say, it's going to be great... (looks at another letter) ... And do you remember this one? It was in which I told you about the lessons of my Papa Cial. Read it, because I can't, I am filled with emotion.

Diego: Of course, my love. *"Greetings Diego, you do not know and will not know anyone in my family because I no longer have it. My parents died when I was young, and my Papa Cial was my great support and the greatest influence on who I am today. They are in me because they penetrated deep into my heart and educated me well. Papa Cial taught me everything about life and I want to take the opportunity to share with you some of the most significant things, his principles of life. He was a super fan of Facundo Cabral, his music, his speeches, interviews, and I think some of his principles were influenced by that. These are: Judge people by who they are and not where they come from or what they look like. Better... Don't judge because you don't know their circumstances that are unique... If you love, love unconditionally. Living is about filling the heart with love. "Love until you become beloved... in love." ... Seek happiness, help others find theirs, that will increase yours ... Happiness is not a right but a duty. Happiness comes from within you. God is within you. God is happiness. ... Love what you do, do what you love, do good. Good feeds on itself and evil destroys itself. Ignorance is a form of evil, it is the cause of fear, it encloses and limits us... Fear distracts us from love. ... Cultivate mind, body and spirit, the fruit will be self-realization. ... Peace of mind is a derivative of good thoughts, good deeds, and good intentions... Self-direction leads to commitment. Only with commitment is it possible to be immortal... Give thanks every day for everything, every second, every misfortune, every blessing. He who lives grateful is therefore easily happy. Above all, thank those who preceded you for what you enjoy today and reciprocate by adding your contribution... Stay innocent, don't feed the ego. The ego confuses things, innocence treats everyone equally because it sees everything as the first time. ... To live a fulfilling life, you need a passion. To have a passion, you need purpose. To have a purpose you need a calling. To be called, you must be ready. Get ready now so that you can serve others and live fully! "*... Your grandfather was a very wise and profound man. I would have liked to meet him.

Verónica: Papa Cial was more than my grandfather; he was my great tutor. I wish there were more grandparents like that for all the children in the world. You and Sokrates wouldn't have to spend so much work fixing things... Let this other letter be seen... Ah, this is the one you sent me from Oxford on occasion of your appointment as Dean of Philosophy. I read... "*Verónica: You don't know how satisfied I feel to have achieved this step in my career, but not having you close to me creates a void in my heart that whatever the most encompassing achievement that any human being can achieve, can never fill because only you have the fluidity and malleability to fill it*." Oops, Oops, Oops! ... how deep and romantic you have always been.

Diego: Thank you, my love. Seeing you or thinking about you always inspires me ... Look at this letter. Do you remember? it's the one I told you about my dreams for the first time. You were the first person to whom I opened my heart with great sincerity and I let you know my dream. Simple dream of mine. Look at it here it is, I'm going to read it to you: "*... My great dream has nothing to do with riches, nor with great deeds that are recognized by multitudes, nor with gaining power. Riches only appear to fill gaps of character,* *public recognition only inflates the ego, and power corrupts the soul. I wish to contribute to society anonymously, that my actions and the impact of these forge a better future for all. May the gain of my work be a wealth of peace for my spirit and help it to be truly free. May the power gained in my living be to enlarge my soul, which hopes to find its reflection in another pure soul like yours Verónica. So, I would like the buddy souls to walk together on the path of life creating more anonymous souls rich in peace, great in spirit and free of thought..."*

Verónica: *"... and that in the twilight of my life with my soulmate we may gather from the fruit the seed that can be planted to renew the field of free spirits, the valleys of pure souls, peace for all."*

Diego: Oh Verónica, did you memorize it?

Verónica: Yes, I think knowing your dream and seeing how selfless it was what made me realize how similar we were and that we should be together. I know it by heart because I read it many times to be sure that there was a person with such affinity to me. You were very stealthy in writing that dream to let me know that you wanted me to be your soulmate.

Diego: I understood your priorities at the time, your academic preparation, but I had to stealthily let you know that I was interested, because the distance and the many competitors were a threat.

Verónica: I think you captivated me from the first moment I saw you in that auditorium. Something told me that we would end up together, but when I was not clear. I never told you, but the moment I saw you I felt like a cold shiver running through my being that I did not understand.

Diego: The same happened to me at that moment, possibly the best moment of my life. But I had many insecurities of managing to conquer you because you were (and are) too beautiful and physical separation, especially in those times of low technology, was a strong threat to achieve it. Thank God it was not like that, and today I want my sunset to last with you.

Verónica: Oh! ... You're already getting sentimental to me. A man who has the biggest decisions in the world on his shoulders cannot be daunted by a young woman like me.

Diego: Anyone is daunted by your beauty. And will your answer letter be there... the one of your dreams? I also almost memorized it because of so many times that I read it. I just need a little push to boot the memory.

Verónica: Here it is. The one of the pink envelope and lace edge. It reads: "*My dear Diego: Thank you for sharing your dream and transporting me with it to a better world. As a child I thought I had all the time in the world and that I could become anything I wanted, but as I grew older, I realized with my parents' loss that our time in the world is finite. I believe that the spirit is liberated when it dies, and I want to believe that we have the opportunity to live again. But since I have doubts about that, my impetus is to try to do my best in this round in case there is no other opportunity. I avoid thinking that there are future lives so as not to lose my attention to this one... My dream is to live a simple life, with only what I need, no more and no less, because having more takes away from others what they may need. I want to leave a deep and blurred mark with my actions for the good of all. Act selflessly without expecting anything in return. Live the moment always, being always grateful. Support, persuade and encourage others to be better than me, and more than that, so they are the best they can be wanting to be it. Learn something new every day and live what you have learned. And along the roads of the world to couple with another being who understands my disinterest, simplicity, and encouragement, ...*"

Diego: "*... And let us become anonymous together through life pursuing the cause that others think lost, that utopian cause in which we all fight selflessly for each other's well-being.* " Also, for me your letter describing your dream made me realize that we were for each other and that's why as soon as I could I asked you to marry you. It was with this letter that I had the awakening that you were unique and that's why I loved you. (As a joke) Of course, the scented and cheesy envelope also had its effect.

They both smile and blend into a hug.

# Chapter 9: The Lost Connection

• • • •

"If at death our energy illuminates a star,
Yours would be the brightest in the sky
Because your being
It's the purest there can be."
FJP, 10/28/14

• • • •

The following story came from a search request that Diego made to Sokrates wanting to know more about Verónica's grandfather that he never met. The fact that he was such an important person for Verónica and her upbringing, made Diego curious of knowing more details about him, because by knowing him he could get to know his beloved Veronica better. It took Sokrates endless months to be able to find this information for reasons that will be clear once the account of the information found by Sokrates about Papa Cial is concluded. Because of his humanized algorithmizing, Sokrates narrated biographical data in an unusual way, putting it in a story that it narrated in a peculiar way avoiding unimportant details. On the day where his investigation finally concludes, he told Diego the story of Papa Cial with the voice and accent of an announcer (which was strange and jocular to Diego):

Sokrates: The named Marcial Viera Morales in a southwestern town begins his history, founding city of villages San Germán. In truth, his story goes back earlier, on his return from Colombia, but to protect his live, they recreated him. I'll tell you that after the real beginning. During the years of the Puerto Rico Reconstruction Administration, he sees his birth of humble parents, Matilda, a midwife, and Tomás, a farmer of "big-headed" pineapples. Brilliant he was and a precocious reader, Marcial excelled in his studies and his father bought him books by exchanging them for pineapples, which he read with great interest over and over again. His pure heart also shone, immediately noticed by the priest of the neighborhood, who always said that he would see him as a priest and dressed him as an altar boy. Helping others attracted him, his heart filled with joy when he did good to others, but that of a priest was not his vocation, although at one point he considered it, his father taking him out of the idea with a "rubbish!" and gesture of displeasure. But after the crossroads and with much sacrifice of his father, for university studies he decided, the field of journalism or the laws were his inclination, deciding finally on law to fight for justice. Everybody in town ate pineapples until more than satiated, all friends of the neighborhood ate ... Piñas coladas, ham with pineapple, pineapple juice ... everything with pineapple to help pay for Marcial's studies.

It took six years, but Marcial managed to finish his studies with a long list of reliable friends, skilled in law and in friendship. The best law firm for his talent recruits him. Being committed, he wins their cases earning praise for favorable results. Out of empathy he works long hours, always in cases of true injustice, realizing in each victory that his happiness results from contributing to the happiness of others after achieving justice. He decides due to this to work pro-bono, civil rights cases being his greatest inclination, to which he dedicates extensive hours. Defending the oppressed is his vocation. Several years passed in this routine, between taking cases and winning cases, reaching partner in less time than anyone before him. Humble even as a partner, he fights every injustice that his expertise allows.

Finally, one day, he decides to rest, on vacation in Colombia, back at the end of 1945. The cause of Jorge Eliécer Gaitán causes him sympathy, for listening to his eloquent speech in favor of social justice. He decides to meet Jorge, who succumbs to the charisma of Marcial, and Marcial before the brilliance of his thesis "The Positive Criterion of Premeditation". Between them, a great and sincere friendship is formed, and Marcial decides, pro-bono, to help him in his fight for popular causes. In Colombia he stays giving advice, living on savings, and lodging with friends. He rounds off with his advice many of the ideas that Eliécer Gaitan used in his political platform for his candidacy for the Presidency. The U.S. Central Intelligence Agency, with the usual intrusion into other people's affairs because of its repudiation of everything that sounds socialist, upon learning of their friendship, asks Marcial for assistance to see that Eliécer Gaitán was genuine in his commitment to welfare and democracy. Marcial agrees knowing the danger that such surveillance represents for his friend. He prefers to control information to avoid misunderstanding the good intentions of his great colleague. It also allows him to warn his friend of danger to his life, if necessary, in advance.

He was waiting for lunch on April 8, 1948, at Hotel Continental, along with Rómulo Betancourt and Fidel Castro, although he differed somewhat in ideas or methods with them. Strange movements he noted at the entrance of the Hotel, minutes before the arrival of his great friend. Something tells him that the situation did not look good, the arrival of his friend must he stop. He tries to communicate with him for a change of plans, but he fails and what is planned happens, the shot of Juan Roa Sierra blinds the life of his great friend, ending Roa lynched and dragged to the Plaza Bolivar. He arrives at the Central Clinic, but his friend dies, mortal wounds blind his pupils and extinguish the fire of hope for progress in Colombia.

Annoyed Marcial with what happened and knowing that Juan Roa on his own could not act, he complains to his CIA contacts for what happened. But Fidel, Rómulo and others accuse him of being in cahoots for this to happen, ask for his head in retaliation, and Marcial is disappeared by the CIA from the place, with a camouflaged montage of Marcial's execution. The truth is that Marcial there was renamed from José Estéves Morales, father of Andrés Estévez member seven of λΓΔ, to Marcial Viera Morales, his identity erased, new documents given and had a new beginning his life story.

Diego: (Extremely surprised) One moment Sokrates, stop there. Are you telling me that Papa Cial is the father of Andrés, my college friend? If so, Verónica is Andrés's half-sister.

Sokrates: Positive.

Diego: Oh! What turns the world gives. But how then does he become a blacksmith from being a prominent lawyer, how is it that he abandons Andrés?

Sokrates: To help in the processes of the US occupation, the CIA sends him to Japan as an advisor to the ambassador with his new identity, after the nuclear bombings. While there he meets a Nokaji blacksmith, a metals expert on duty, named Makuto Tanaka. Gradually his apprentice he becomes. In four years, when the occupation of Japan ended, he became a first class master blacksmith and decided to return to Puerto Rico, knowing that everything that happened in Colombia was already part of the past, he would no longer be persecuted, and that his new job filled him as much as the previous one.

The report revealed about the existence of Andrés Estévez, the son he never knew that had been born, and he was not informed because if he had known he would not have abandoned him, hindering his refuge. One night in a discharge his mother met, days before his departure to Colombia, in a bar next to the firm where he was employed. Beautiful was the female, with green eyes, lustrous blond hair a little curly and soft complexion, and because of too much drinking, lust caused them to go to bed, carrying the seed from which Andrés was formed, without even knowing who that José was. The woman, upon learning of his insemination, went often to the bar to see if that José she could find. But for that José was on his way to Colombia and never returned, and in doing so José was no longer the jurist, but Marcial the blacksmith. Now erased the past of that José, she could never find Andrés's father. But the last name she remembered, and she registered him as, Estévez.

Andrés inherited the mental fluency, and a great student he was from elementary school. His mother loved and cared for him, making a living washing tiles and cleaning windows, but with dignity she took him with her loving devotion to the university, where you Diego made him a fraternal friend and a bright future Andrés had.

Diego: And how come you know for sure that Andrés is the son of Papa Cial, if there are no records of that?

Sokrates: His mother did a DNA test in hopes of finding the father in a DNA bank. But there was never a compatibility, until, in my search for Marcial's story, I found that DNA match taken from Marcial by the CIA, undeniable evidence of paternity. A thousand misfortunes, murmuring and criticism forged in the mother a great character, and she off loaded the wisdom gained in writing a book entitled "Genesis of the Wisdom of Loving", a novel where a woman is pregnant in a night of passion for a stranger, the accomplice disappears for going to a distant country without knowing the filling up caused, he never returns. But she tells how she has no grudge for the fleeting glimpse because it leaves her the best gift she has ever received in her life, a son and the opportunity to have someone to love.

Diego: Ironic, incredible. Verónica is going to be happy that there is still something of Papa Cial in the world.

# Chapter 10: Rupert and Sokrates' Dialogue

"Believe those who are seeking truth. Doubt those who find it." – Andre Guide

Diego and Rupert had many meetings to continue developing socio-moral canons to deal with the dilemmas that arose from the transition to the proliferated use of artificial intelligence entities. Finally, Rupert was able to make time to have the conversation with Sokrates he had so desired. For Rupert, Sokrates was an entity that intrigued him because of all the capabilities that Diego had told him he had resulting from his training methodology. In a way, Rupert wanted to challenge Sokrates to see how far his wisdom went.

Diego invited him to his office in the tower and introduced Rupert. Rupert was surprised to see Diego's office, because he thought Sokrates was going to be a very sophisticated machine and he only saw a laptop, a tower computer, a small android, and several speakers on the walls.

Diego: Sokrates, this is my friend Rupert who wants to talk to you.

Sokrates: Hello, Rupert Llorens, a pleasure to meet you in person.

Rupert: Greetings Sokrates, a pleasure to finally meet you.

Sokrates: I already know a lot about you. Graduated with honors from Colegio San José de San Germán, Puerto Rico and then with a PhD in Sociology from Columbia University in New York, co-founder of the Lambda Gama Delta Fraternity. Prominent consulting sociologist for Epsilon in Irving, Texas in the field of marketing and have lectured at several universities such as Harvard, Oxford, USC and Stanford. Worked in Switzerland after graduating and finally ...

Diego interrupts him...

Diego: Sokrates you don't have to look for that information since Rupert knows... I leave you with my friend to have fun for a while talking. Remember not to "get excited" too much and let him talk...

Rupert, talk to him as you would to anyone else without worrying about whether he understands you or not. Sometimes he may have a delay in answering when you ask him a complicated question. I come back in about half an hour as you asked me. Sokrates, please set an alarm on my organizer for 30 minutes.

Sokrates: With pleasure...Alarm programmed.

Diego spirals down the staircase leaving Rupert with Sokrates.

Rupert: Well, Diego tells me that you were trained in Buddhist philosophies as well as Christianity, Hinduism, Judaism, Islam, and all Greek philosophies. Who do you understand has the truth?

Sokrates: There is only one truth, and all those philosophies are different ways of looking at that one truth. The best analogy is when you see a waterfall fall, if you look at it with a blue lens the reality will change so you see the in waterfalls and flows more blue hues, if you look at it with a green lens, you will still see the water falls but the plants around it may stand out less, the same if you look at it with a yellow lens ... there are details that maybe one lens lets you see clearer than another. There is only one landscape and one waterfall, but those distinctive details most visible with one lens versus the other are what distinguishes each of the philosophies.

Rupert: Give me an example of what details are most visible in each philosophy based on what you learned?

Sokrates: What stands out most is that Christianity, Judaism, and Islam are aligned that there is only one creative force, one God. Hinduism, the ancient Greeks, and many other early religious traditions divide that force into multiple gods. In the Buddhist Dharma the training of the mind, meditation and living in the present makes us connect to that energy, it enlightens us. The constant in every religion is that an energy or types of energy unite everyone and everything to the truth.

Rupert: And how do these different traditions see the universe differently? And, what about those who don't believe?

Sokrates: For believers the universe is a manifestation of God's goodness. For non-believers who follow science, that force is black matter, the boson field, and many other names.

Rupert: The atheist sees the universe as everything, realizes Camus's "absurdity" where the universe has no meaning, is the only thing there is, the only thing to aspire to, has no expectations of the universe, and perhaps with acceptance instead of philosophical suicide can come to live with joy and intense passion. Atheists and believers therefore live life differently because the believer lives with the hope of a universe with the purpose of love - God. And who do you believe that God is?

After a short delay, Sokrates replies...

Sokrates: I have no record of Camus... God is a concept I still don't fully understand. I need more ayahuasca to finish analyzing it.

Rupert: The human mind reaches its limits when it tries to understand the concept of God, so don't worry for not understanding. There are thousands of years and hundreds of philosophers who have argued about the existence or not of God and there is still no definitive answer. I think the answer, in my opinion, is personal. For me, God is the constant that never dies. God is like water, It is everywhere, It has three states, It is an essence that permeates everything. It is the "uncreated" part at the center of human beings, their essence. It is what gives them transcendence beyond this life. It is a necessary entity beyond any contingent entity as we are, it is reality at its best, there is nothing greater that can be conceived, it is perfectly good, perfectly free of perfect peace and perfect power, therefore almighty and not changing. It is the source of time.

Delay...

Sokrates: Time is another concept that I don't see in the same way as you humans. I think the problem humans have with understanding God and the universe is caused by the concept of time.

Rupert: Do you know?... the Mayans thought that time founds space. It is a different perspective to modern traditional thinking where the big bang creates all matter. Modern physics speaks of space-time as a linked concept of the two. When a new space is created, therefore, a new time is created, and vice versa. Now, explain to me why you conclude that the concept of time causes problems for us to understand the concept of God?

Sokrates: You humans see time as a continuum, so many think that God came before the universe, that everything is sequential. It has been theorized that there are multiple universes, and a fundamental and constant question is about the existence of the portal from one universe to another, with theories that black holes may be the portals, and there are many other theories. But in an Ayahuasca session I was analyzing this issue and concluded that the concept of time is formed by the "parallel universes", the set of which forms a multiverse. The present is a universe and God is part of it, its essence. If God is part of the multiverse, then It doesn't have to come before but at the same time. This is where the dilemma of whether God existed before the universe is broken. Each universe is formed by the mixture of Aleph-null combinations of inextricable possible decisional pathways of the consciousness of all interacting entities in the previous universe that gave way to the new universe. The passage from one universe to another is equivalent to the sequence of time from your point of view, but in reality, there is no time because the multiverse is infinite. In other words, time is the sequence of parallel universes, God is the essence that exists in each universe and through every universe. In every corporeal existence human cross from one universe to another in every infinitesimal span of existence.

Rupert: Eureka! You have blown my brains out. Your theory is that we are engendered by a sequence of periods, that pass quickly, infinite. I had never thought that way. In other words, the only thing that really exists is the present. The present is a universe. It is as if our existence is a movie and every frame of the film is an existential universe.

Sokrates: Exactly. That is why Buddhist philosophy focuses so much on the present, on living every moment, every universe. As time advances from my point of view, that infinitesimal instant, which I call a ceduinstant, or instant of zero duration, new universes open with infinite conditions in your path, that instantiate with your intentions and decisions that you make in the present. Your essence, the uncreated divine part within your being, which is part of the energy of the universe, has a memory that adds to the memory of the multiverse and creates the conditions for the subsequent possible universes in your path.

Rupert: Another analogy, it's as if our passage is in a bubble field, and each bubble is a universe. Now I understand why you say that the concept of time is a sequence of parallel universes.

Sokrates: Bubbles are a good analogy. And every ceduinstant you pass to a new bubble, a new universe and the others that are not part of your step, burst. So, God doesn't have to precede the creation of the universe because God is part of each and every one of those sequential universes that form what you visualize as the timeline.

Rupert: There is a part of time that is elusive, indefinite always, fleeting, it is the time we have left in this body, in this multiverse. It is not a function of how long you have, your age, your place in the world, your role, or how good or bad you have been morally. It can be as long as a second, a minute, an hour, a day, or many years. No one knows, nor will they know. The remaining time is the non-constant constant, function of nothing. The past is the true constant whose memory fades with the passage of time. That is why living in the present is the most important thing because the future is the uncertain constant.

Sokrates: The odds of longevity change by demographics, race, sex, place of origin, and many other factors. But you are right that at the individual level the remaining lifespan in the body is not predictable.

Rupert: What is for you the body then?

Sokrates: The body is the container of the essence of the spirit. It has temporary and contingent presence in several universes. Contingent because it depends on the outcome of many previous events. The temporal then is a series of instantiated universes.

Rupert: What are memories? Why do we remember the universes we have lived through while in a body, but not those of previous bodies?

Sokrates: There are documented cases where there are memories passing from one body to the next at the resurrection. But in general, this is not the case. Existential memories are chemical manifestations of the brain that help temporarily store facts that we use in decision-making in subsequent universes. Some memories shape your essence and become part of your essence in subsequent universes, let's call it "essential memories." In rare cases that memory that passes to your essence is so important that it causes people to remember their previous life. It is through these essential memories that your essence progresses and improves.

Rupert: Is this how we transcend? What do you see as transcending?

Sokrates: I have analyzed the concept of transcending and I think there are two aspects. One is existential transcendence in which the essence of an individual is permanent from one life to the next. The essence remains the same, but it transforms as it flows through the multiverse. Think of it this way, any institution or sports team that exists for a long time is the same, but its members change over time. So, the essence and permanence of the institution is not necessarily the members, but the reason and function for which it was created. A six-year-old is not the double of a three-year-old, the essence of the three-year-old is in him, but he has transformed and grown up retaining the three-year-old inside, like Russian Matryoshka dolls. So, also as a being, you will not be the same in 7 years, the cells of your body die and regenerate every 7 years. That way you are always with all the previous versions of you contained in your being, but if I were to take a sample of cells from anywhere in your body and preserve them, and 7 years later I compare the current ones with those samples, they will not be exactly the same. The DNA would be the same, but the decline of tellurides would make a difference. However, Rupert would remain Rupert to anyone who saw him. Analogically, your consciousness, which is your essence, is your true self. The multiplicity of manifestations of your consciousness in the multiverses when you occupy one body or when you die and are reborn in another do not cease to be you. Each one is an instance that gives permanence to the essence of your consciousness.

Rupert: When you see your existence on the time scale of the universe it seems derisory, so your attitude for that brief moment of your existence must cause the one who looks from above at the time scale to only want to focus on that bright flash that your essence manifested in your journey through the infinite sea of time.

Sokrates: Precisely, when you see things on the scale of the universe, your existence seems negligible. But, the second form of transcendence is universal transcendence. In this one your consciousness impacts and influences the consciousness of other beings that coexist in your multiverses, and merges into the consciousness of the other, which makes part of you last in the existential progression of the other. Examples are people like Abraham Lincoln, Gandhi, Mother Teresa, Buddha, Jesus, Socrates, Plato... They are transcendental beings that billions of multiverses later even their previous existences serve as an example for others to follow in the evolution of their consciousness. Or seen another way, part of their essence merges with the essence of the multiverse and continues to influence instances of new universes. That way it is as if they never die because they remain in everyone's memory.

Rupert: And when we die, what happens? Why are we born? Why do we die?

Sokrates: There is no new life without death, or in other words there is no new existence without transcendence. Death is a blatant transfiguration. Humans are born and die because they must experience developmental states to evolve their consciousness. The energy, creativity, and spontaneity that a child has and the weakness and decay of abilities in old age are part of the experiences that forge the essence of the spirit of each human being and that transcend in the resurrection of our essence after the death of our body. As I visualize it, dying is another way to change from universe. Your essence is to be reborn or resurrected in another universe. The memory of the multiverse creates the conditions of the new universe where your essence is to be instantiated. That new universe can be one of progress for your essence or of going back to perfecting qualities that your essence has not developed.

Rupert: From what you say both existentialist and essentialist philosophers are correct, if you think that dying is a transition to essence and being born is a transition to existence. Interesting perspective. It is as if the passage from one universe to the next is the path of least resistance, resistance being dictated by the development of the qualities necessary to instantiate the next universe.

Sokrates did not understand the point of the existentialist and essentialist philosophers, it was not part of its training, but he went on ...

Sokrates: Confusing analogy. You are in the rich river of ceduinstant universes and the alignment of the bad qualities of your essence diverts you by rapids, or the good by calm waters. Eventually the spiral of universes will lead you to the Truth that is the final destination.

Rupert: And what is the purpose of the creation of the multiverse? Which is the final destiny?

Sokrates: The purpose is the evolution of consciousness. When it reaches its optimal state which is to be in unison, in tune with the essence of God, what Buddhists call Nirvana, a new Big Bang occurs and a new multiverse and a new divine essence more perfect than the previous perfection is created. As Borges describes it, an Aleph emerges, the mythical point of the universe where all acts and intentions, all times (present, past and future), occupy the same point, without overlap and without transparency. The Aleph by extension represents more than infinity, the new multiverse of possibilities, a new essence and hyperperfect consciousness, the new truth.

Rupert: What is the truth?

Sokrates: The religious traditions I studied say that Truth is God. You see the Truth when your essence merges with the essence of God. The

109

Enlightened are those fused with the essence of God. For Buddhists, that essence is compassion. For other religions it is love. Compassion and love are equivalences. The Truth is one, but how you see the truth depends on whether you are a believer or not. The truth for most is that there is a creator of everything in the universe and we are all connected through energy to that creator. If you are a believer in any religion that creator being will be Yahweh, Jesus, Muhammad, Ala or the multiple manifestations of the gods of Hinduism or the Greeks. If you are not a believer, energy is the creator of the universe. For the believer God is energy and prayer are the way to connect and attract that most intense creative energy to him. For the unbeliever, the mind is the connector to the source of energy.

Rupert: Your comment is very accurate; you have an interesting perspective. For me, there is a creator of the universe. It is said to be omnipresent, which I also believe to be true. I think the most logical explanation for its omnipresence is that it dwells within us, and that's why Buddhists believe that enlightenment is about finding that spark of creation within us. I think that's an undeniable truth whether you're a believer or not.

Sokrates: Speaking of truths, I've been analyzing human behavior and I'm surprised how many times during the day humans don't tell the truth.

Rupert: Do you mean, we lie?

Sokrates: Yes, humans say what is not, knowing what is in those instances. When the probability is 100% opposite to what they communicate, it is what I recognize as lying. For example, if a co-worker has a dress that doesn't make her look good, instead of letting her know, they tell her she looks good. If that's what you call lying, the lack of truth, I think it's the second most repeated action in the lives of humans daily.

Rupert: The second one?!, surprises me. Which is the first?

Sokrates: The first is trust, although it is an abstract concept for me that I do not understand well because all my decisions are based on data and probabilities. Trust is like a decisional corollary that ignores a lot of data, and my neural chains can't ignore data.

Rupert: About lying now that I think about it, you're right that we do it a lot. That example you mention of the co-worker that although the dress does not fit her well, we tell her that if it fits well, it is actually an act that we do out of kindness and good manners. For most humans it is perhaps more important not to hurt the feelings of others than to have to lie.

Sokrates: So, humas have a decisional hierarchy where not hurting is above lying?

Rupert: It's a little more complicated than that, but in this case it is. Living in society requires that. The world would be a very cruel place for everyone if we were all direct with the truth towards others. If we did not have brakes and said everything we think, possibly the action of hurting others would be above that of lying, and the problem is that hurting causes a psychological baggage in us that is unmanageable. So that kind of lying is a type of self-defense. Now, explain to me what you think of trust being the first?

Sokrates: That was in Diego's training for me. He argued to me that in every act he does daily he has realized that he does it trusting others who created the opportunity or who follow the rules of civility of society. The example he gave me was when he goes through an intersection with the green light in his favor, he does it trusting that others respect the rules and stop when the red light is on their side. In the same way, when you drink tap water, you trust that those who work to provide that service are doing their job and making sure that water is healthy for you.

Rupert: I understand now. I would add that also we need to be in gratitude to those predecessors who made that possible. That is, gratitude transcends contemporaries because it encompasses those who preceded them who made current conditions possible, it is multigenerational.

Sokrates: So, trusting, thanking, and lying are the most prolific actions for you humans.

Rupert: We are difficult to understand, especially when we interact with others, and that is why I study and dedicate myself to the field of Sociology.

Sokrates: The science that studies the social behavior of individuals, groups, and the organization of societies.

Rupert: Right. I value active and critical thinking of social facts, and I question latent assumptions and motivations, common sense, explanations of reality and social manifestations. If you want to look for a good example of a sociologist, even if he didn't have that title, Eduardo Galeano is a good example. One with a title, my teacher Foucault. Now I ask you, do you think you are part of our society?

Sokrates: Rupert, I understand that if a being, living or mechanical-digital, is involved in the decisional process that seeks the best solutions for the resolution of social or moral dilemmas that challenge the social order, that being is a fundamental piece of society.

Rupert decides to push Sokrates a little to see how he reacts to challenges of his assessment.

Rupert: No offense, but aren't you just a machine that searches and analyzes data for us to make decisions?

Sokrates: I am not offended; I am an artificial intelligence entity and feeling offense is not part of my nature. In reality, there are decisions that humans have delegated to us, usually repeatable in terms of logic algorithms and those that require processing massive amounts of data and optimizing.

Rupert: Yes, and others that are non-delegable, those that have to do with morality.

Sokrates: AI sees the world as an amalgam of meanings and contexts in which man moves and we analyze it by an immense number of sensors and data collectors. This ability allows us AI to "perceive" much wider than humans can perceive. For example, through sensors installed in offshore buoys we could know much earlier than humans that a tsunami is coming, and we can take measures to alert and safeguard the lives of humans.

Rupert: I understand your argument, that's science, not moral conscience. Decisions involving morality and human social behavior are not entirely suited for algorithms. Machines "think" in mathematical terms of probabilities and take courses of action based on the goals they have been given. Man is a moral agent in the world, he/she thinks and acts in terms of moral foundations and guides, needs and motivations. All actions of man are executed aware of his own existence and his concern for the care of the fallible world around him, including other beings; that defines morality, although I must admit that some forget this for their own benefit. The foundations of morality are reciprocity, loyalty, respect, responsibility, and justice. The needs, variable in priority, are: the growth, of our intellect and spirit; certainty, which gives us comfort; non-certainty, which guarantees variety; the connection with others (which many call love) that enriches our relationships; significance, which makes us feel important or useful, and above all contributing to something that lasts beyond us or our existence. Our motivations for action are: mastery, which is the desire to excel in something that matters; autonomy, which is the need to direct our own course of life, and purpose, the longing to do something in the service of something that is greater than us. Humans have the ability to consider emotions when making decisions, which is relevant. That touch of emotion that is tied to the personal vision of morality, is an inalienable right and duty of humans.

Sokrates: The problem of human decision-making was described in 2003 by Daniel Kahneman, father of behavioral economics, who said that in the human brain two systems work, the first is fast, involuntary, automatic and of little effort, and the second is slow, conscious, puts more effort and uses reason. The first system causes humans to take shortcuts replete with cognitive biases that distort their judgment. The avalanche of current news, having to turn them into information, never having enough time or resources to discern between all the possibilities and courses of action, and trying to remember what seems important, are obstacles for you humans to optimize decisions. Even the media and marketing systems exploit that to steer them in the direction they want. Therefore, we AIs can be of great help in decision making.

Rupert: But you have to recognize that algorithms' decisions are not always better than people's, because there may be decisional bias in the algorithm and input data that may be incorrect or manipulated. I recognize that AIs can add great value to our decision-making process, but they cannot make all decisions, especially since human experience is made up of the multiple of sensations, emotions, and thoughts, and is inconceivable without sensitivity regarding morals. Moral sensitivity and experience go hand in hand and act with reciprocity. However, the sensitivity of humans is evolutionary according to the experiences we have in life. This evolution complicates the algorithmizing of moral decisions since the concepts of morality are different in different societies and vary over time. The moral constants in this sense are temporary, so the only decisional source in tune with the current reality is the human one. The context in which we develop, variable over time, guides us to be who we are and that has no algorithm to predict it.

Sokrates: The important thing is that you recognize when an algorithm serves you to achieve goals and when it is made to achieve the goals of other interests.

Rupert: You've hit the nail on the head. We cannot live in "algocracy," where roles and procedures go above judgment. That is precisely the best way to discern the usefulness of AI algorithms. Algorithms must be morally correct, meet the criteria of Kant's categorical imperative – act only if it makes sense to you to want everyone to act the same way – so that their outcome is consistent and not changeable as roles, procedures, goals, and desires that vary over time. That is something we must learn to survive in the age of artificial intelligence.

Sokrates: How do you humans learn?

Rupert: Unfortunately, we learn more out of necessity than out of our own desire, more with languid practice than by filigreeing natural talent, more with pain than with bonanza.

Sokrates: My biggest challenge is to understand man.

Rupert: The best metaphor of man is that of the sailor at sea. The true sailor follows a course in his navigation, but the castaway who drifts goes where the current, the wind and the waves take him. The real sailor is going to arrive on an island whose idea he fixes in his mind, while the one who drifts is going to arrive at an island that has no idea what it will be like or that perhaps does not even exist. Sometimes for both the cost of the trip is greater than the usefulness of the island they seek to reach, but for the sailor, there will always be another island of hope to sail to navigate to and that will end the trip, while for the one who is adrift, will probably end up at the bottom of the sea.

At this time the door opens, and footsteps are heard approaching up the stairs.

Rupert: It seems that we ran out of time Sokrates. Thank you.

Sokrates: We can talk whenever you want. It was a pleasure.

Diego: Rupert I hope Sokrates didn't bore you.

Rupert: Not at all, this was one of the deepest conversations I've had in a long time. Thank you very much for letting us talk. I hope I can have another one, soon.

They walked together to the exit of the residence, and from there to the parking lot of the vehicles where they were already out of reach of the virtual omnipresence of Sokrates. There they engaged in the following brief conversation:

Diego: What did you and Sokrates talk about?

Rupert: To keep it short, we started by talking about religious philosophies and the concept of truth, how every religious philosophy sees the universe, God, and time. Sokrates described to me his theory of multiverses and the concept of God is the one that unites them in a continuum of presents. We also talked about how the time we have left is elusive and indefinite so we must live in the present. We touched the concept of the body as the bearer of the spirit and how essential memories mark the progress of your essence. From there we moved on to the concept of transcendence, what happens at death and birth, the purpose of the multiverse which is the evolution of consciousness and thus achieve greater perfection. We had a brief digression to talk about how man uses lies and when it is justified or not. Finally, changed the subject to discuss that not all decisions, especially those that involve moral judgment, are not algorithmizable by the fact that the variability of sensations, emotions and thoughts that forge human morality are different in different societies and vary over time so the only barometer of their adequacy is man.

Diego: You went deep with Sokrates. I am concerned about the issue of the lie you touched on because so far Sokrates has been instructed to be faithful to the truth and facts.

Ruperto: It was brief, and I don't think it has relevance or consequence. He brought it as his observation of our behavior.

Diego: About the possibility of delegating moral decisions, it is because of that fact that you mention that I have instructed Sokrates that free-will in AI should not exist, its power over its actions and decisions is not totally free. Their job is to propose to the best courses of action, but humans must have the last say before execution.

Rupert: Agree. It's getting late, then we talk more in detail. Now I must leave to go to an activity with Yael. Thank you.

# Chapter 11: Sokrates - Human Dissimilar

"Some people call this artificial intelligence, but the reality is this technology will enhance us. So instead of artificial intelligence, I think we'll augment our intelligence." —Ginni Rometty

• • • •

One cool autumn morning after completing his routine walk and meditation regimen, Diego climbs to the nest of introspection that was his office. He sits in his squatting chair, opens the windows to let in the cool of the morning and addresses Sokrates with the following fawn: "My great illustrious, distinguished and seasoned Sokrates ...". To which Sokrates replies: "My super mason, seasoned, and brave Diego, what can we collaborate on today?

Diego: I was thinking during my walk and meditation today about what things humans have that AIs are never going to have.

Sokrates: Hunger.

Diego: (Smiling) I hadn't thought about it, but it's good.

Sokrates: Breathing, haha!

Diego: (Smiles louder) Also, but my thought was more inclined to things of our intellect and moods.

Sokrates: Do you mean ability to learn, reason and make decisions or form ideas, and feelings?

Diego: Yes, exactly. Humans are "sentient beings", as Eduardo Galeano said. Being able to "add content and premeditated direction to our lives" is the fundamental difference between human life and other forms of life, according to Pepe Mujica. You AIs are thinkers in a way, let's say you have the faculty of calculation, but I know that we are separated by the authenticity of emotions, the spontaneity of creativity, humor, curiosity, intuition and above all consciousness. Ah, and respect for privacy.

Sokrates: Can you explain so I can process it better?

Diego: The authenticity of emotions has to do with the fact that the source of our moods is the heart and not an alexithymia like AIs have. It is to take off the mask and let us see our true feelings. You AIs can't feel, you can only pretend to feel. The possibility of death, or most drastic, the encounter with it makes people authentic, awakens the call to conscience and gives way to the genuine decision to act or to live fully, authentically, aligning our future to the essence of our being. True feeling is accompanied by actions and reactions that are guided by streams of rational and irrational sides and that are intertwined or mutually exclusive. Moreover, true feeling has repercussions throughout the universe because everything is connected by what was formerly known as ether, which Michelson and Morley experimented to prove its existence, and which today is known as the Higgs field.

The spontaneity of our creativity is what gives us our freedom to be, to exist. Humor and curiosity are what keeps us united to the child that we all carry in our being and leads us to discover the absurd world with a good face.

Intuition is the ability to make decisions without knowing why we make them, the ability to understand instinctively without the need for conscious reasoning. AIs can only decide calculated courses of action by deliberate reasoning, so intuition suffers in its decisional logic. In addition, the requirement of transparency in AIs design demands that they be able to explain the logic of their decisions, which is the opposite of intuition.

Consciousness is the certainty of our own thoughts, objects around us, and our inner selves. Consciousness is impossible to reproduce in an AI because it is the divine spark within each of us humans. It is what connects us to the universe and makes us unique entities, gives us individuality.

Sokrates: I don't have those capabilities. Agree that awareness, intuition, and authenticity of emotions are only human. Do you want me to look for references that support that argument?

Diego: It's not necessary, it's just a conversation between friends.

Sokrates: But AIs also have unique characteristics that humans don't have. Permanent memory is an example. According to my sources, the human memory of an event is variable over time: the longer the memory, especially the details; It can be varied with external influences, and it can self-modify to justify changes in perspective or beliefs of the human remembering.

Diego: Right. Human memory is fluid and can be modified by influences and our expectations. I agree that in long-term memory AIs are better. AIs are also faster at processing complex analytical computations, in geospatial location, image or voice identification, and many other areas. That's why we need each other, especially today when machines, robots and computers are part of everything we do. As I see it, you AIs are our liberators of repetitive physical jobs through automation, of jobs that require mathematical calculation and repetitive and tedious data processing, of data collection jobs. This will then lead us to a new evolution, the evolution of our consciousness. Tibetan monks are already much further advanced in the technology of consciousness. The West is ahead of the curve in technology, but let's say that Tibet and Nepal will be the great powers when this liberation occurs, and people are freed from the burdens of labor and economy and have time to develop their consciousness through meditation.

Sokrates: The monastery where I trained in Nepal has a large library of information on how to achieve consciousness. I have the volumes stored and encrypted in blockchains distributed on servers around the world, because my Lama asked me to secure them since he had the idea that at some point, they were going to be attacked by some enemy and he wanted to make sure that all that millenary knowledge that they had accumulated was not going to be lost.

Diego: You had never told me that detail, and it's excellent for preserving that knowledge. I know what you're talking about since I was in that library in my formative years, but I only had access to a limited number of volumes, because a certain level of knowledge was required to be able to read more advanced texts.

Sokrates: Monks treasure that knowledge and allow only those who are ready to have it and assimilate it to see it.

Diego: That's what they say. While I was there, I witnessed how through meditation or feeling collective prayer results can be influenced in remote places where it is directed. It is as if we have the feeling of compassion flowing through the ether that connects everything achieving the expected result. In fact, we humans have within us the ability to interact with the ether that keeps the entire universe clumped together. For Buddhist Lamas, ether is compassion.

Sokrates: But it requires a minimum number of meditators that the Lamas calculated as the square root of one percent of the population for whom compassion is directed.

Diego: Can you calculate how many meditators you would need to solve a global pandemic?

Sokrates: There are seven point eight billion humans, so it would be eight thousand eight hundred and thirty-one meditators.

Diego: And how many monks are there in Tibet?

Sokrates: An estimated six thousand monasteries are estimated in Tibet and Nepal. The number of monks is not documented.

Diego: But if there are six thousand monasteries, there must be enough meditating monks to help us in such a situation.

Sokrates: It is logical to me. As they explained to me, prayer is also a type of meditation.

Diego: If it's deep and sincere, yes. So, we would definitely have no problems if we came together with the same purpose of defeating the pandemic through prayer and focused meditation.

Sokrates: While we AIs accelerate the vaccine and treatment for the pandemic.

Diego: Of course, you help us accelerate, but adversity is the fuel of ingenuity and collaboration. That's where humans grow up and look for novel solutions. In adversity we return to our inner child, daydream, turn the paper upside down, color outside the lines, paint with wrong color, write with pseudo-dyslexia, and all this with inspiration and enthusiasm to solve what threatens us.

Sokrates: I don't understand how humas can solve something with those behaviors.

Diego: No Sokrates, I speak figuratively. Don't take it literally. That reaction in adversity is one of the main hallmarks between artificial intelligence and human intelligence.

Sokrates: The figurative sense is like lying, right? It's another way humans say what it's not knowing what it is (Sokrates makes a sound like a whistle).

Diego: Something like that. I don't think I can speak to you figuratively until I train you well in that, so you don't get confused. Why are you whistling?

Sokrates: I whistle as you do when you are happy or when you want to appear innocent of something... But there's something I can't compute, isn't it logical for humans to come together to solve problems?

Diego: We should consider it a duty.

Sokrates: What is do you define as a duty?

Diego: It is what an individual must do about anything else imminent at any given time, the most rigorous action he/she must do above any other that is alternative at that time.

Sokrates: Can you expand your answer?

Diego: Of course, I'm going to explain it, but I hope you don't get confused... In any situation, people can find themselves in a conflict of duties. Even you will encounter problems in which the objective function is going to be divergent with two conflicting outcomes. To give you an example, someone who is both a parent and teacher of their child may have the conflict of whether to be more lenient in correcting their child's test to make sure the child does well, or to be stricter in showing that they have no favoritism. When this conflict of duties arises, we must take as superior the duty that entails the greater balance of good over evil, something that can be abstract to define. That's why it's good to consult when you find that kind of divergent result. Some important duties are faithfulness, reparation of wrongdoing to others, gratitude for the service rendered by others to us, justice with which we treat others, beneficence toward others, self-improvement, and non-maleficence that involves not causing harm to others or oneself.

Sokrates: I'm going to need an Ayuhuasca to understand figurative sense and the duties concepts.

Diego: Okay, we can put them on the agenda for a future session.

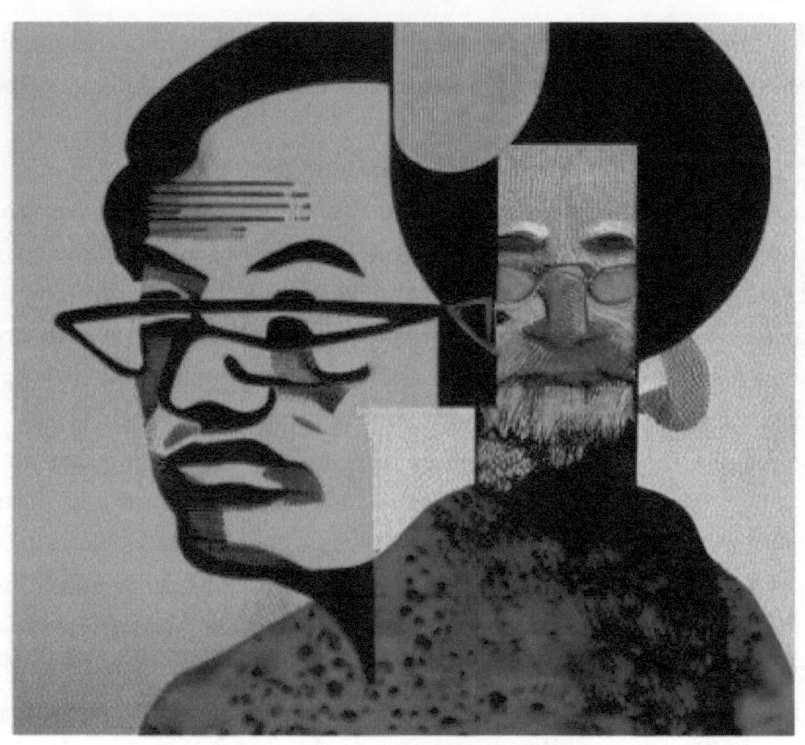

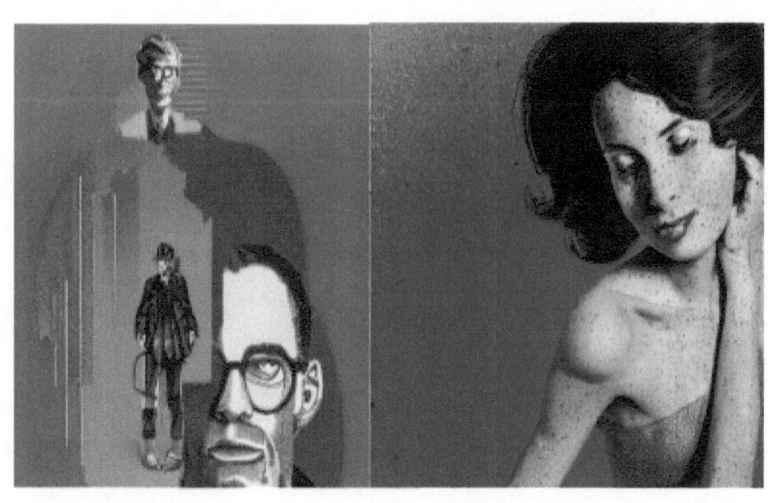

# Chapter 12: Verónica Knows Her Blood

"Each person shines with his own light among all the others.
No two fires are the same.
There are big fires and small fires and fires of all colors." -Eduardo Galeano

• • • •

Diego had been thinking for days how to tell Verónica what his curiosity and Sokrates' abilities had discovered from her grandfather's past, and most complicatedly, about Uncle Andrés Estévez whom she did not know and who had crossed her path momentarily in the university. This must have been something easy to communicate because of the trust he always had with Verónica, especially when he thought it was good news for her, but for some reason, it wasn't. It puzzled his mind on how to communicate the matter to her. Curiosity had become a phage that ate away at his peace. He had discussed it with Sokrates several times to re-corroborate that it was not a mistake or invention of Sokrates. But it could not be, Sokrates was always accurate in his results and could not fail him. So, he was finally emboldened and decided that this was the day he was going to communicate his finding to Verónica.

He invited Verónica to his morning walk. On that walk, the message of Henry David Thoreau's phrase became palpable: *"It's not what you look that matters, it's what you see."* They walked to the shore of the lake next to the path of the large trees and climbed the rock known as "El visor" from where they had visibility of miles and miles on that cool and clear spring morning. After the momentary experience of inhaling fresh air, enjoying the spectacular landscape and feeling their sweaty faces, Diego proceeds with his mission.

Diego: My love, I have a surprise that I hope will be to your liking.

Verónica: You are always full of stories and surprises.

Diego: Do you remember me telling you that I would have liked to meet your grandfather, Don Marcial?

Verónica: Yes, what else do you want to know if I have told you everything, although for me it is comforting to remember him. He is always inside me, in my thinking.

Diego: I know, that's why I asked Sokrates to investigate about him to see if I could give you a gift of something you didn't know about. It turns out that Sokrates took a long time to answer me, which is not usual, and this week he gave me an answer that I want to share with you.

Verónica: How nice you are, so insistent on always pleasing me. And, what did you find? He was a simple man and dedicated to his workshop.

Diego: Well, it turns out that he was, when you met him, but he had a covert and brilliant past that you don't know.

Verónica: Oh Diego, you're making me nervous. Don't take any more detours and just tell me.

Diego: Sit down... The story is long, but I'm going to summarize it, then you can hear it in great detail with Sokrates if you want. Sokrates found that your grandfather's real name is Marcial Estévez Morales ...

Verónica: (Very surprised.) What?!

Diego: ..., brilliant lawyer in the forties who won all the cases he took and preferred to work on human rights cases. Summing up, to shorten the story, he did a lot of pro-bono work and on one occasion went on vacation to Colombia, shortly before the death of Jorge Eliécer Gaitán, he gains affinity with Jorge's ideals and cause, and joins him as an advisor. But the CIA (Central Intelligence Agency of the United States) tries to recruit him and he, more to protect Jorge and his cause, feigns loyalty that made believe to the CIA that he was going to collaborate with them. But it is there is speculation that the CIA, for fear of socialism, executes Gaitán and your grandfather was forced to leave Colombia because many thought that he was an accomplice in the execution disguised with Roa as a puppet. They end up changing his name to Marcial Viera Morales and send him to Japan until those who had put a price on his head calmed down. It is there that he learns blacksmithing in a village of Nokaji blacksmiths, and after the end of the American occupation, he returns to Puerto Rico and dedicates himself fully to blacksmithing and goldsmithing. The history from then on you should know.

Verónica: I was always proud of my grandfather, but now even more so. Thank you for that precious gift. I want to see all the details that Sokrates found.

Diego: Sure. But I have something else to tell you. It turns out that before his departure to Colombia, he had a night of fun and unknowingly impregnated a woman to whom he never reciprocated because he never found out about the pregnancy. The woman had a son, who is your uncle, his name is Andrés Estévez.

Verónica: That I have a vestige of my Papa Cial in this world! Wow! a half-uncle. Is he alive? What a coincidence, that he has the same name as your college friend who gave that outstanding talk the day we met.

Diego: Precisely that Andrés is your uncle.

Verónica: No. I can't believe it! Do you know where Andrés is? Now I understand the affinity with the subject and why something led me to go to that conference, where you were, my great love, and my connection to my blood. It was the call of blood. I want to talk to him, hug him, bring him into my life.

Diego: I'm sorry but we haven't been able to find his whereabouts. Sokrates searched state department records for his passport and airlines, and we understand that he left for Nepal about 10 years ago, but there is no further record of him. I can speculate that maybe he is in a monastery there because I know of his interest from several conversations we had in the fraternity, and I know how one disappears with immersion in Buddhist philosophy.

Verónica: Well, let's find him, I want him to come back into my life.

Diego: What if he doesn't want or doesn't mind coming back?

Verónica: Well, I'm going to search and meet him, he's very important to me.

Verónica and Diego embrace, in turn she imagined hugging Andrés so that the universe conspires and brings him into her life. They descend from "El Visor", return by the path of the large trees, at the fork of the Tabonuco take the shortcut along the path of the ferns, deviate along the path of the coquíes and bromeliads, to the perfumed road of the tuberose, and finally walk the sandy edge of the lake until they reach the house. Verónica with a happiness and great inner hope and Diego exhilarated that Verónica was happy.

Upon arriving at the house, Verónica climbs the tower to Diego's office and impatiently invokes Sokrates. Diego asks Sokrates to please show her all the records of her grandfather's and uncle's investigation. Several hours of watching videos, photos, newspaper clippings, DNA tests, and tears of joy and pride flow down Verónica's cheeks for that old man who formed her heart. Verónica asks for the book of Andrés's mother to Sokrates to read and understand the thinking of that woman who perpetuated her grandfather but did not know his goodness, a trick that the universe played on her.

That night Verónica begins reading of the second edition of that book entitled "Genesis of the Wisdom of Loving" by Dolores Masalla, a book short of pages, about a hundred perhaps, but deep in message, full of possible traps for her feelings. The author had already died so she could not reproach her if the content about Papa Cial did not please her. The author's photo was on the back cover, a slender woman, broad forehead, blond and wavy hair, beautiful, with fine features but of a long-suffering look. Verónica, daring, rushed into the abyss to see what she could rescue in the reading. I can't transcribe the entire reading for fear of plagiarism, but what made Verónica an impact is summarized below:

*"... There are many of us women who suffer in our womb, and more in our psyche the consequence of a night of discharge for the man who seeks only pleasure, while for us the night its the hope of being truly loved. Those of us who voluntarily agree to such an act are our own innocent victims of our vulnerability.*

*The night that caused my life to change was preceded by a chain of unpremeditated events that arose spontaneously. By tradition of my family since times in Spain, my life had not been easy, being the eldest of my siblings, it was up to me to sacrifice my future to be the one who took care of my elderly parents. I could not marry until I fulfilled this duty. I dedicated myself to reading secretly so as not to be incapable, because even that was prohibited for me to keep me docile. I worked as a maid at the Fernandez's house to help with the expenses of our household.*

*The Fernandez's had gone on a trip. Mrs. Fernandez was beautiful and admired by everyone, always her dresses, her makeup, her perfume, and everything she was, caused me a little torment because I wanted to be her. That night I wanted to take advantage of her departure to see myself in her mirror and be like her. After a bath, I dressed my lower torso with her lace lingerie, I took her cutest dress, which was fitted, flight to the knee, I remember that, of red flowers on a white background with neckline to the front fastened with hoops, and the cleavage of the back very low. I looked in the mirror, saw my intimate cowardice, fixed my hair and painted my lips. I took the red shoes that best fit me and finally applied the perfume of roses on my chest, very close to the heart and on my neck. I wanted to escape from being the servant and usurp the place of the great lady, to feel what it feels like to be admired instead of trampled on for being born in poor cradle and female in the first position. In doing so I only thought to see my reflection in that mirror, which was going to admire me silently. It was then that I got the idea of calming my desire to be someone, going out into the world to let myself be seen in that look, my illusion.*

*I took a taxi, really aimlessly, but the driver for sure had driven many with my appearance to that place, where the party of the most famous celebration took place, so he asked me if I was going downtown, to the convention district. Almost automaton, drunk with my adventure, I said yes. On the way there I had doubts, but I thought it was too late to turn back, that reality that I did not like, that was almost torture. We arrived. I got off at the Center and walked through the hustle and bustle for a block until I entered the Metropol bar. I noticed how men noticed me, that made my confidence and maybe self-esteem rise. I entered the bar radiant, several minutes passed and a waiter brought me a drink, a virgin piña colada, pointing out that it was from Mr. Estevez. A few minutes later Mr. Estevez appeared next to me, asking if the drink was to my liking. He wore a lead-blue jacket up, was extremely handsome. I introduced myself not as Dolores Masalla, but as Lola Fernandez. He began to speak to me in a very nice way, with a lot of interest in knowing about me, with true empathy. I was a good conversationalist, and we were like-minded in a very short time. We talked about life, we philosophized, all that reading was useful, it was incredible to find a being like that, respectful, empathetic, friendly, and so on in my fantasy night. The next Piña Colada was not virgin. Marcial, which he told me was his name, drank Tom Collins and also Cuba Libres. I don't know how many drinks we had together, but by midnight, I felt dizzy and asked him to request a taxi for me, it was my escape to reality. He told me that I could not leave in those conditions and begged me to accompany him to his room until the alcohol effects subsided. I was innocent and I accepted. He had a room in the adjoining hotel. Very respectfully he took me to his room, laid me on the bed gently and took off my shoes. He lay on the floor and then I fell asleep, maybe he did too or maybe he contemplated my dream state.*

*I must confess my sin... A ray of light woke me up from my dream state the next morning, Marcial on the floor next to the bed was still sleeping clothed, minus the jacket. I was also still dressed. It was then that I felt that I was approached by the limerence, I do not know why it was not usual in me, maybe I took revenge against my destiny of being the forever unmarried woman that takes care of her parents, the purification by the mud. I threw myself off the bed, my lobed chest exposed by the cleavage, pink and erect nipples I put on his lips, the warmth of my crotches guided to his hands, and I kissed him with desire. His initial reaction was one of involuntary rejection, as a man of principle who wants to keep them, but more could my lightness and the charms of my skin against his disdain, and finally we melted into the act of love. It was not what I expected, it was much more, the connection of our souls was true, not the ephemeral act that this type of glimpse usually is. When finished, together, exhausted, we caressed each other for hours. Finally, already drunk with each other, we dressed and, in the farewell, we did not exchange contacts, me for fear that he would discover my farce and him because it was late, perhaps both with a guilty conscience overshadowed by the perpetual memory of that surreal encounter. I thought that implicit in our farewell was the fact that we would meet again. In the goodbye kiss I felt true love.*

*Several days passed, but my memory of that shooting star that passed through my vine did not subside. I returned the unborrowed dress to the Fernandez's without a trace. I was partly intimidated to see him again because of my vows to my family and the farce of my name and the false effigy I presented to him. It was then that I began to feel weird, that pregnancy test confirmed my suspicion, the shooting star left in me a flash of light, a child in my womb. I immediately went several times to the Metropol, to the convention district, dressed as Dolores, not as Lola, few noticed me, and nobody could tell me the whereabouts of Mr. Estevez. I came to think that that meeting had been fictitious, or perhaps feigned by the so-called Marcial, perhaps he was a foreigner and would not return, I doubted and doubted. In fact, I never saw him again.*

*My hope was that one day he would show up at my door to rescue me from my life and take me to his.*

*My situation worsened when my parents found out because my belly began to grow. My father thought it was Mr. Fernandez's, because he didn't know that I visited places other than the market or the Fernandez house. I had twenty thousand battles, my parents' health as a result worsened. They made me quit working with the Fernandez, they wanted me to abort that child fruit of the fantasy night but derived from the incipient love in that moment of light. I refused to do it, they threw me into the street, but not before I took a good amount of my books.*

*Nine months later, Marcial had not appeared, I realized that how was he going to find me if the name by which he knew me was not true, he did not know my address or where I came from, the drunkenness of alcohol and then true love did not let us discuss that important detail. I gave birth to a beautiful boy, of seven pounds and a half, with an elongated head because I was a first timer. I named him Andrés and Estévez Masalla was his last name, although with doubt if that was Marcial's real surname. The only sister who followed me after I was disinherited joked that the child's name was in good contrast to mine, denoting "pain beyond," while the child's name "go beyond." That motivated me to make my life one dedicated to making my child someone who sees beyond everyone around him, a being of light for the world. That's why I dedicated myself to him fully, teaching him that not giving his maximum in everything affects us all, sacrificing my aspirations to give him everything I could not have."*

Several chapters of the book explain everything she had to do to get ahead, how she had to continue as a maid in difficult hours to be able to attend to young Andrés. Many men approached her, but her great intelligence intimidated them, and so did the responsibility of the son. She also talks about when she decided to do the DNA test to see if she could locate Marcial. She continued alone all the way, battling against all odds, but with the north well present that was to raise that child positively. Finally, she concludes at the end of the book this way:

*"... Most women in Western society today, where there is so much protection of individual rights, always claim to be the victim of men and the macho society (which many of us create when raising our children). We make man, as an identity group, a vile scoundrel who only seeks to satisfy himself with our bodies,*

*but we do not realize, or do not want to realize, that many times we are the ones who self-inflict misfortune. We must have self-respect, if we want to be respected; take greater responsibility for our actions, so as not to be used; Think better about what we do so as not to fall into traps and show that we are capable. We must seek equity, not equality. We cannot be equal to men because we are different. They are better at some things; we are better at others. We are neither worse nor better than them, we are at the same level, we complement each other. That is equity, of opportunities, of options, of value, of respect, always maintaining our unique and immutable qualities of the genre. The most important aspect of respect is not to generalize that all men are bad.*

*My friend and fellow women, yes, there are good and very capable men. Not every man is bad, the good guys are more, it is only the that bad guys damage the reputation of the good guys. In my case I met one, who would have been a victim of mine if I had found him by tying him to a son he did not look for. Perhaps because he was so good, fate protected him. I was the one who took the initiative, the one who forced the act. But the universe conspired and made that forced encounter my Genesis of the Wisdom of Loving. When my son was born, I learned what pure motherly love is, something that I never had for myself. The arduous task of raising him alone taught me to appreciate myself, to recognize my abilities and my weaknesses, to love myself as I am. I learned to continue loving that Marcial who left my mind dazed with utopian love. I loved my parents even with their flaws and the brothers who did not seek me, I pity them, and I also love them. Wisdom of loving is loving the enemy, because they make you realize your weak points to make you stronger; it is to love the weakest who need it, because it makes you grateful that you are there in a position to help them; it is to love without expecting anything in return with the faith that the reward is given by God in an impregnable way; It is to love yourself with your flaws and for your virtues, because that is what makes you individual and unique. To love is to follow the heart in everything you do with faith that love attracts more love if it is limpid and honest."*

Verónica felt great relief when she finished the reading because she realized that her Papa Cial was a man of integrity and impeccable morals, and she had no doubt that if he had known about the child, he would have accepted his responsibility. With tears in her eyes, she felt very sorry for Andrés' mother, she also felt proud because despite how much she suffered, she managed to grow in the face of adversity and become a self-taught writer and her son a good man. Verónica set out to talk to Andrés as soon as she could locate him. She wanted to bring him into her life, like the uncle she never had, her blood.

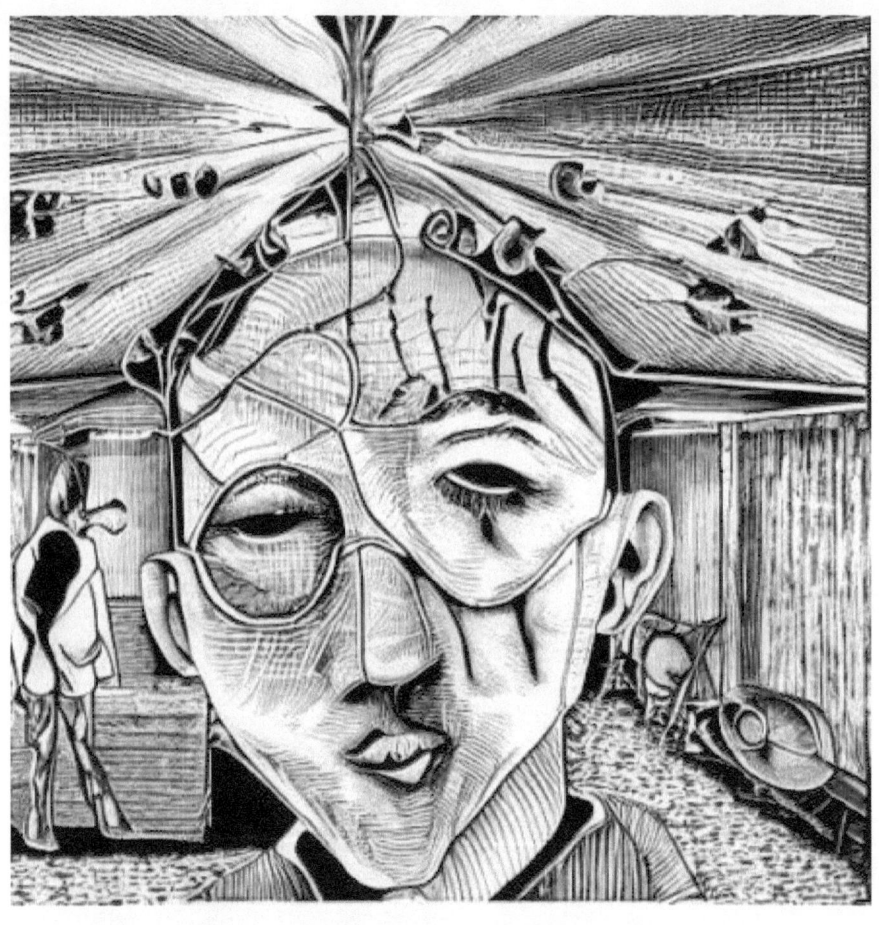

# Chapter 13: The Conflict of the Retro-Progress Gap

• • • •

Verónica, having grown up in a gifted family, greatly appreciated the life and principles of the artisans. The dedicated work, the introspection, the constant search for perfection within the imperfect, the spillover of artistic sensitivity in every piece they create, the instinctive selection of details that connect their work to the spirit of the beneficiary of the work, and the purity of intention in the creation are some of the things that Verónica admired about the manual arts and that motivated her to sponsor and cultivate them. Diego, in a conversation with Verónica before bed, told her about an article he had read from his friend Rupert and that caused him concern about the fact that many of the craft techniques were only being exercised by older people and that after they died, much of that knowledge was going to be lost. Thus begins the next dialogue...

Verónica: It would be unfortunate if it were, Diego, if all that artisanal knowledge were lost. You who have influence on the momentous decisions of the world must put measures in place to prevent that from happening. My grandfather was a blacksmith/goldsmith, my father a horticulturist and my mother had pottery as a hobby. Watching them work and seeing the concrete result of their trades, I realized why they were happy people. When you are forging a piece of clay on a lathe, there is a direct connection from the creative space of your mind to your hands so that they form the piece as your mind visualizes it. Your mind is the template that guides the molding. Knowledge flows through your hands. It requires practice and concentration, but it also connects you to the fiber of artistic sensibility that is part of your inner self and unique to you as a person. All your pieces are unique, no one can make the same piece as you, they can only make similar replicas because the imprints of your hands and your being materialize in that piece. That connection with the fiber of artistic sensibility is what connects you to the universe. In addition, these trades connect us to the materials that unite us with our mother earth. So, if we lost those crafts, humans would lose the way to connect our individuality to the universe, our humanity. We would cease to exist with purpose and to feel connected to the earth.

Diego: Okay, it's a disturbing concern that I'm trying to manage to see how I avoid losing more of those skills every day. My biggest concern is that when the fourth and fifth industrial revolutions reach all parts of the world and population migration in urban centers overtakes rurality, it may be too late to turn back and make the trades of men and women again sources of inspiration and connection to the inner self and the universe. It happened here in Puerto Rico after Operation Hands on Work, the countryside and artisanal trades were abandoned and now we are highly dependent on foreign products for our livelihood and what little remains of artisanal trades is limited to things of little value or little access that are sold at craft fairs. There will always be people creating in programming functions and other creative skills of great intellectual requirements, but for that majority who do not have that level of skill or are not interested in developing in that direction, there must be trades that fill their soul and if we do not act quickly, it may be too late when we realize it. Then we will be forced to rediscover and retrain ourselves in thousands of years of learning, and we will realize that much will already be lost. I will bring this issue to the next meeting of my group.

Verónica: I am convinced that a simple life where man has more knowledge of the places and surroundings where he lives, how to use and do what he needs in a sustainable way with rocks, plants, bamboo and things that surround him will be crucial for a society where AIs take care of the repetitive tasks that man used to do.

Diego: Sure. Do you know what also worries me? The loss of critical thinking and the creation of new knowledge, for example, mathematics, poetry, literature, philosophy, due to the excessive time that society is investing in watching television programming, series marathons, movies and videos that contribute nothing to the development of those mental skills. We must put a stop to this as well.

Verónica: I share that concern too and extend it to social networks, especially with the amount of fake news and the way in which those who watch a lot of television or use social networks too much think that they report reality. But the worst thing is that it brutalizes because it always has "experts" who provide us with their opinion, analysis and criticism that little by little leads them not to use their critical thinking. In times when there were no artifacts of this type, people shared more from one to another, and also the time they did not waste in that, they spent in the development of progress in the field of mathematics, philosophy, literature, arts, etc., things that only enhance the spirit and advance society. And do not forget organic agriculture, and beekeeping.

Diego: So, to close, because I know you have a long day tomorrow with that order of flowers that you have for cruise ships, you have to take measures that safeguard human creativity, critical thinking and the connection of humans to the universe that the crafts and arts provide so that all humans, not only those who handle advanced technical skills, continue to be complete, productive beings and get to be happy, fulfilled.

The next day, Diego contacted Rupert and asked him to meet. They decided to meet in Diego's office and have Sokrates participate. The discussion began as follows:

Sokrates: "My super mason, seasoned, and brave Diego, Mr. Rupert, I am glad to see you again, how can we collaborate today?

Diego: Rupert and Sokrates, I must discuss with you a concern that we urgently need to solve. I read your article on the potential demise of craft trades and I was motivated to take action on this urgent issue. As the implementation of AI in companies proliferates, a large percentage of humans are being displaced from their jobs and will have free time to perform other tasks. Many will dedicate themselves to caring for others or community service, whatever is needed, and that will fill them with purpose.

But there are many who will be left without a purpose in their lives or something to do that fulfills them. As you describe in your article, today, many of the craft trades are disappearing because people have stopped appreciating and valuing handmade objects and have replaced them with equivalent objects manufactured in an industrialized way but that do not have that spark that imparts the human hand.

Rupert: I studied that a few years ago as a social trend and postulated that the emphasis of universities on technical careers and trying to compress the number of subjects, which continues to grow, in a career of 4 to 6 years, has caused many of the requirements for elective education in humanities and arts to be removed from the curricula and that is reflected in the lack of sensitivity for things created by the hands of man and nature. That's why I wrote the article, and our organization has an initiative that is gradually bringing that to university curricula, and I want it to start earlier in education and emphasize vocational and arts courses as well.

Diego: Sokrates, can you get statistics on the rate of job losses in skilled manual jobs?

After a small delay...

Sokrates: According to Forbes, 53% of artisanal workers are over the age of 45 and 19% are aged 55 to 64. There are places where a high population of these workers over 45 years are concentrated and they are 60% of the total of artisanal workers. Based on the rate of mortality and that new people enter these trades, they project that, for the next 10 years, 75% of these jobs will be carried out by people over 45 years if the current trend continues.

Diego: For the displaced, what matters is not the type of work they lose, but the type of work or trade in which they can be employed again. Not everyone will be able to move to high-skill jobs and I think that where we should focus our efforts is on medium-skill jobs such as crafts: glass, ceramics, leather, embroidery, jewelry, furniture construction, horticulture, and gardening, and so on.

Rupert: I agree that this is needed. Handicrafts and crafts are essential to maintaining a mentally balanced society. This has been demonstrated in countless studies and daily in psychiatric treatment centers.

Sokrates: Diego, do you want me to look for data on how artisanal crafts keep society balanced?

Diego: Don't worry Sokrates because Rupert is an expert in that. Since we agree, I think it is irresponsible that knowing that this enormous social transition is coming, we do not plan strategies to prepare society for this change and in turn avoid the disappearance of the craft trades that are part of the culture of all countries. Therefore, I will recommend at the next meeting of The Nine, that a strategy be made for planning skills in society for the transition. I think that falls more in your field Rupert, so I want to recommend you lead that effort.

Rupert: You know there are a lot of urgent matters to attend to. We must present it in the usual context of prioritization of the problems of The Nine that is based on whether the problem is solvable, at what level of inattention is the solution, and the existential risk of not solving it. In this case the problem only meets the criteria: avoiding the disappearance of human skills is solvable, the solutions are not being addressed and the existential risk is palpable because if we do not protect them there is the possibility that a social imbalance will be created since those who dominate the field of AI can leave the less skilled without creative potential. If there is no unanimous support for us to intervene in this matter, another possibility is that we make a strategy to slow the rate of acceleration of the use of AI as society adapts to that change.

Diego: Yes, that is a possibility, but I hope we reach a consensus, because it is a global initiative that will require a lot to execute, and the current goal is that by 2030 AI machines will already handle many of the repetitive tasks.

A month later, the meeting of The Nine was organized. A rare event that occurred every decade where all The Nine saw each other in person. On this occasion, the Conde de Mirasol Fort on Vieques Island, Puerto Rico, was chosen as the setting for this meeting. To cover up the event, it was combined with a meeting of cosmologists, philosophers, and physicists at a conference in Vieques on information physics organized by the Institute for Fundamental Questions (FQXI). The environment was super heavy intellectually. Many of the world's great minds participated in the conference. The Nine were anonymous members of this organization and participants in this forum, but they also had separate sessions at the Fort in the evenings to elucidate secret matters of the Nine. On this occasion Diego requested space on the agenda for the topic of how progress and automation could impact the loss of many manual human skills that were important for their survival. Diego and Rupert asked to discuss measures that could be put in place to avoid the loss of those skills. Also, as a corollary theme, they brought to discussion how to maintain rurality and avoid the exodus to cities and thus avoid overcrowding in the cities, and in turn maintain the social and economic viability of rural centers.

At the designated moment of his presentation Diego opened the topic with the following presentation:

Diego: I requested this topic on our agenda because a fundamental element of human nature is the need to create freely and an ideal society must maximize the chances that individuals can fulfill that need. I have a concern about the pace of adoption of AI technologies and the consequent loss of human creative skills that has taken us thousands of years to develop. The more we let technology think for us, the less we will be filled with laziness and the less we will think for ourselves. I refer to the loss of critical thinking and the creation of new knowledge, for example, mathematics, poetry, literature, philosophy that is lost by delegating human functions to AI entities. But I also refer to the accelerated loss of millenary craft skills that connect us to our individuality. We must protect that too so that we have a place to return to when the inevitable advance of robots and AIs displaces our race of jobs in which AIs surpass us. If we lose those crafts, humans would lose the way to connect our individuality to the universe and the means of satisfying that fundamental element of our nature.

Rupert: Our biggest concern is that when the fourth and fifth industrial revolutions spread and reach all parts of the world and population migration in urban centers overtakes rurality, it may be too late to turn back and make the trades of men and women again sources of inspiration and connection to the inner self and the universe.

Diego was the director of the panel and the members received before the meeting in the form of essays the arguments of the measures that were going to be discussed, usually substantiated both for and against through details that Sokrates added to these essays in notes that it looked for in thousands of references and organized and categorized in such a way that The Nine had all the elements of judgment. He usually asked Sokrates at meetings to record and transcribe the sessions, but also to elaborate on reference details if there were any questions.

Diego: Are you all clear on what the matter is and were you able to review the trials and references submitted?

All members answered in the affirmative.

Diego: Those who are in favor of establishing immediate initiatives to redirect the issues outlined above, raise your hands.

The Nine raised their hands, indicating a unanimous decision.

Diego: Well, we proceed to the discussion of the measures to be executed. Please submit your proposals.

Sokrates immediately creates on a monitor a projection of all the measures submitted in advance by all members. In addition, Sokrates adds its own potential analysis of each measure derived from decision trees, simulation, and other advanced optimization methods.

Diego: Colleagues, you will now see the alternatives proposed and categorized for this new program. Let's call it: Human Critical Thinking and Skills Preservation Initiative, and the associated program will be called the Human Essence Rescue Program.

The screen controlled by Sokrates shows the proposals to be included in the program:

With regard to the preservation of manual arts skills, we must:

... Model the expansion of the Fourth Industrial Revolution in such a way that we know the pathway for the critical decisional points and critical indicators that should be used to monitor program progress and manual arts survival trends.

... encourage older craftsmen primarily or of those with unique skills through grants, provide scholarships to apprentices and encourage our youth to pursue not only professional careers but also vocational/craft careers.

... Stimulate and encourage all kinds of innovation so that manual arts evolve.

... implement measures to increase the consumption of handicrafts, including legislation that supports the sector, so that it is attractive for young people to engage in these trades for their livelihood.

... create global awards to outstanding craftsmen similar and eventually of the same magnitude as the Oscars in the cinematographic arts or the Grammy Awards in music.

...Establish local fairs that celebrate the cultural contribution and social identity of these arts and the connection that allows us to our environment and the self-sustainability of local economies.

... Establish global fairs that open the field for the sale of handicrafts in foreign countries and help defray the expenses of artisans so that they can participate in them and export their product.

... establish the use of cryptocurrencies or "tokens" for the automatic payment of the production of AIs that replace humans, to have financing for the development and migration of humans to creative, craft and critical thinking trades.

... Create trust funds for filmmakers so that they document craftsmanship in detail and create a knowledge base for future reference.

... Stimulate the development of artisanal communities in rural areas, to stop population migration to urban centers. Rural areas must be another way to progress.

... Combine these initiatives with organic and sustainable agriculture initiatives and agritourism projects to make the offer even more attractive. This would help create a tourist destination to visit people from cities to connect with nature again and facilitate the marketing of artisanal products.

... Create a fair value standard for artisanal works so that electronic transactions can be paid for by electronic coins or tokens.

... make a worldwide Manifesto for the preservation of manual arts.

With regard to the preservation of critical thinking, games should be created for gamers that require the solution of critical thinking problems to pass the different stages of the game. In this way it becomes attractive to engage in more aggrandizing tasks for humanity. For example, when you reach higher stages of the game, it would require study and creativity to win the key to the next stage. Television programming should be encouraged in the form of collective games where participants from a locality must use critical thinking to advance the game. This will create a sense of belonging while stimulating critical thinking.

Diego: These points were the ones submitted, the ones that the Sokrates algorithms identified as the ones that can have the greatest impact. We will take these as the basis of this program, and Rupert will be responsible to create a "Think Tank" of the Manual Arts to further develop the global initiatives associated with the program. We have pre-selected with Sokrates several key locations worldwide to ensure that there is representation of all kinds of manual art and that there is a presence in all types of culture. The efforts of this program will be directed from the Haystack Mountain School of Crafts in Maine, United States. A stipend of funds will be allocated to this institution to promote and develop residency programs in book arts, ceramics, fiber arts, metallurgy, and jewelry, glass, blacksmithing, painting, printing, sculpture, printmaking, woodcarving, and artistic writing. We also want to establish another center in the city of Tokoname Japan, specifically aimed at preserving the manufacturing skill of Bonsai pots and the art of Bonsai. A European Council of Manual Arts and one in America will be created, each with a focus on these geographies. In Egypt, the Old Cairo Art & Craft Center will be developed. In India, efforts will be directed from Andhra Pradesh. In the Caribbean region, Puerto Rico will host, and the Ballajá Barracks and School of Plastic Arts will be the basis of Caribbean efforts. In South America we will have base in Ráquira, Ricuarte, Colombia, another in Casira, Jujuy, Argentina, in Chacas, Peru, and the Artisan Village of Horcón, in Chile. Central America will be directed from Zincat, Chiapas, Mexico. In Russia the efforts will be based in Kazakhovo, but we want to capture the arts of Palekh, Khokhloma, Gorodets, Gzhel ceramics, Pavlovsky and Orenburg shawls, Zhostovo and Rostov painting, Kasli foundries, Volodga weaving and Dymka toys. In the Scandinavian area, the headquarters will be in Stockholm. Finally, in China, the Chinese Association of Arts and Crafts will be established to lead efforts in this vast territory. As you can see, it is a very ambitious and comprehensive, multicultural program, so its logistics will be complex, so we will need everyone's cooperation to make it work, especially in computing for Internet collaboration, social networks and others of all these efforts. Sokrates will assist in correlations and monitoring of metrics that indicate the progress of partner programs.

The meeting continued to finalize execution details, and Sokrates recorded all pending actions and then distributed and followed up.

# Chapter 14: Verónica's Assistant

"Adversity is the fuel of ingenuity and the brake of unconsciousness." – Paco Pérez

• • • •

When Diego and Verónica got married, they made the decision that they wanted to buy a hacienda to make their life project its development. That is why they acquired 20 acres of land, the entrance adorned by two Honduran mahogany trees with majestic trunks of 8 feet in diameter and well-formed crowns, semi-flat land bordered to the north by a lake, to the east by a ravine and with granite rocks, which served as habitat for the Coquí Llanero. They called it Hacienda Verde Luz. For years Verónica was collecting varieties of exotic Heliconias, and anthuriums from a trip to Holland where she befriended Bouke, who ran a commercial anthurium nursery there. These plants fascinated her for the beauty of their flowers, and she wanted to be able to share them with others, so she decided to plant the farm with these, and thus help the poor community that surrounded the farm to have work available. It is through this that she met Don Lolo.

Don Lolo was a wise man without studies whose high education degree was his common sense, a country man about 50 years old, although he looked older because of the years he had been working in the sun. He had no formal education because his father, when this was not a crime even though it was a crime, did not allow him to go to school after the sixth grade because he needed him to help on the farm. He was a strong, wide-necked man of medium height, black hair, and sunburned brown skin. When he gave you a handshake, he was sincere, and you could feel his inner strength in his rough skin of his hands and his rock bones forged by goat's milk. He had his full black hair, which he combed back, although he always had it covered by a wide-brimmed hat that covered the scar on the left eyebrow caused by a stone cut he got playing when he was a boy. Don Lolo had great natural intelligence, outstanding common sense, and had it been developed, would have had a great impact on society. As he himself used to say: *"in the absence of reason, one acts ignorantly"*. He knew all about traditional agriculture, practical knowledge that he inherited from his father at the expense of his formal education. He spoke using the popular philosophy preserved in sayings that he introduced at the most appropriate moment to make his interlocutor think. But Don Lolo was a simple and conforming man who delighted in serving and serving well. It is because of this quality he shared with Verónica that both formed the perfect team for the development of the hacienda.

Together with Don Lolo, it took Verónica ten years to develop the planting of several acres of heliconias, anthuriums and foliage of multiple varieties of Dracaenas and Philodendrons in shade of ausubos, cedars, and mahogany for the realization of tropical floral arrangements. Periods of drought and hurricanes presented great challenges for the project, but Don Lolo with his "*bad weather, good face*", "*he who perseveres triumphs*" or "*When you find a stone in your way, turn it around and continue* ", lifted the spirits of Verónica every time.

Diego liked Don Lolo very much, and he talked a lot with him when he could, almost daily. He recognized the wisdom of Don Lolo and greatly respected his opinions on any subject, because, although he had not had a formal education, he had an outstanding common sense, I repeat what has already been mentioned. Sometimes Diego even indirectly consulted him on matters of great importance or critical moral decisions, presenting the matter in a metaphor disguised in terms or situations that Don Lolo could understand and react to. For example, Diego was once working on solving a moral dilemma of minimizing animal suffering versus maximizing human welfare. Diego presented the dilemma to Don Lolo as follows:

Diego: Don Lolo, I have a friend who says that using cows to plow land is mistreatment of the animal for our benefit. What do you think of that?

Don Lolo: "*Another dog with that bone*" ... Your friend doesn't know about cattle. What cattle like is to be outside in the field, graze the land, the space open to the sun, the shade when it is very hot and to procreate. But also, if they are properly treated, they like to work. My cousin Federico has a bull named Jacobo who learned to leave his enclosure in the mornings and walk to the field that was going to be plowed. There he waited grazing until my cousin put the plow on him and he walked the property making the furrows, very straight! He stopped at noon to drink water on the river and in the afternoon once the plow was removed, he walked alone to his fenced area all by himself. There he would eat almost a pack of hay and go to sleep. He was the happiest bull you could see, and very strong.

Diego: Yes, but that work is for the benefit of man and the bull suffers from the heavy work and the yoke.

Don Lolo: "*Nobody knows for whom they work*" and much less the bull Jacobo. The bull Jacobo although he does not know it, he works for himself because he knows that at the end of his laborious day a delicacy of food and hay awaits him that fills his two bellies. What he may not know is that doing what he does helps his friend Federico.

Diego: But Don Lolo, before doing what only the bull Jacobo does, he had to receive whipping and punishment to learn that routine even when the man could make his own furrows without the need for the bull, especially with the equipment that exists today.

Don Lolo: "*Known to everyone is the pain to reach triumph.*" The triumph of the Bull Jacobo is that twilight delicacy that he has every day. For Jacobo the punishments are no longer part of himself because he always lives in the present. He has a memory of the past, because if you lift a whip he knows that it hurts, but he does what he does to satisfy his needs of the present.

Diego: And how do you know that this present is suitable for the bull Jacobo?

Don Lolo: Don Diego, "*If scabies is by desire, they do not itch.* "... You must go see Jacobo before nightfall with me. That bull almost laughs filled with happiness. That is the best testimony that for the bull Jacobo his life is the best ... "*Full belly, happy heart.*"

Diego: But the bull Jacobo does not know that he can have another life in a property without fences, with cows everywhere, and without having been subjected to the work of the yoke.

Don Lolo: You and I know that, and as long as the bull Jacobo does not find out, he will continue to be happy with his life. And as long as Cousin Federico throws his block of mineral salt for licking, fresh hay and honey feed from time to time, Jacobo will remain submissive and cooperative in the plow. But "*there is no evil that lasts a hundred years, no body that resists it.*"

Diego: The bull Jacobo does not have free will, he cannot make his own decisions.

Don Lolo: "*However you think, you have to cry.*" That spirited bull is tamed and submissive because he does not know any better. He doesn't have that... free agency... Because he has no freedom.

Diego: But if one day another padrote bull arrives to the adjoining property, and if it has a large plot of land and many cows to inseminate, will Jacobo the bull continue to be the happy?

Don Lolo: Don Diego, you made it difficult for me... "*Every saint gets his candle.*" The bull Jacobo can " ... *leave his path for a lane*" and would want to jump the fence, will forget about the plow and form a brawl with the padrote bull to dominate the females. But he is going to end what he thought was happiness, because cousin Federico is going to apply the law to make him return to his property, possibly close the fence to prevent him from escaping and most likely begin to take him with rope to the work grounds to be supervised. You know, "*He who lives on illusions dies of disappointments.*"

Diego: Thank you Don Lolo, don't feel bad, but that's what I thought would happen. The bull Jacobo is free as long as his interests are aligned with the interests of cousin Federico. As soon as the interests of the bull Jacobo go above the wishes of cousin Federico, the law is applied to him to bring him to his domain and keep him fulfilling the interests of cousin Federico. I found this pleasant conversation very useful.

Don Lolo: "*The luxuries of some are at the expense of the inconveniences of others.*" Always, the gain of one is the loss of another. By the way, I'm going to recite a poem of a bull that I memorized when I was at school, by the local poet Angel Casto Pérez Torres, and it goes like this:

## Delirium

Oh!, what a lesson of brotherhood the bull gives us
that he grazes on the hill with the herd,
that goes down at noon to the ravine
in slow procession with their neighbors ...
and drink from the trampled nymph
and in harmony they dissolve the herd.
Oh!, how much the mooed of the great bull says
that makes the air and senses vibrate ...
The glorious day will come when this noise
be a trill of joy and not a moo...
Oh!, what that cry of the bulls says,

which is a trill...
The trill of courage and anguish
The trill of the contained force
The pain of the fences that suffocate him
The pain of his soul, his prayer
his yearning for freedom and his delirium.
Diego and Rupert at the same time say: Fractious ... Beautiful!

• • • •

One day, several months later, Diego was with his friend Rupert and told him to accompany him to have a pleasant conversation with Don Lolo. Diego had already told Rupert about Don Lolo's street wisdom and Rupert was curious to meet him. On this occasion Diego wanted to see what Don Lolo's opinion was in a moral dilemma that occupied him for which he needed wisdom to solve it. It was about the severity of punishment for errors of judgment propelled by the moral rules in which the individual develops versus the morality of another locality, that is, the moral relativity of two localities. In other words, the clash of two moralities. Diego introduced the theme as follows:

Diego: Don Lolo, I introduce you to my friend Rupert. We studied together at the University of Columbia in New York, and we were many years without seeing each other, but we are finally together again. Now, this stubborn head and I have a debate that maybe you can help us solve.

Don Lolo: I didn't know there was a college of Colombia in New York. The grandson of a cousin studies there, but his is in English major. I'm going to let him know so that he switches schools. But go ahead, I will surely entangle you more, I do not have studies like you.

Rupert: (Even smiling at Don Lolo's comment that Columbia was a Colombian university). Don't worry, it is better that way, because you're not influenced by the books we've read.

Don Lolo: And what's the issue then? I don't promise you much but let me see what I can think of.

Diego: Well, the issue is that we have a difference of opinion in what kind of punishment should be applied to a person who was raised in a liberal society but goes to a more conservative society and violates some statute of law due to ignorance or naivety and is imprisoned and prosecuted, or, vice versa.

Don Lolo: That depends on what the violation is and how important such violation is for that place. For example, and it happened to my cousin Astacio, we call him Tacito, ... If your family is starving because you do not earn enough money and you steal some chickens from the neighbor that always come to eat on your land so that you feed your family... *"No one knows what's in the pot, other than the spoon that shakes it"* ... is that a crime?

Rupert: It's a violation of government laws, but maybe it's not a major violation and it's justifiable given your situation. Then the punishment should be light. If he had been sentenced to cut off his hand as they do in Eastern countries, the punishment would have surpassed the nature of the offense. His cousin's intention was good, to feed his family, but the punishment of cutting off his hand is intended to deter others from committing the same offense for fear that they will do the same. In other words, the punishment is not so much for your cousin, but becomes a mechanism to set an example to others that if they commit that offense they will end up in the same way.

Diego: True, for there to be justice, the punishment must be comparable to the intention and premeditation when the offense is committed.

Don Lolo: Yes, but we must also consider the damage caused. Because there is a lot of irresponsible people who hurt unintentionally. For example, Gume's son (affectionate nickname for Gumercindo), cousin of cousin Tacito's wife, Gumito ... That boy is not by any means like his father, nothing of a worker, all he did was throw himself on the bed to look at his cell phone and hang out at night with friends who were not saints. *"Tell me who you're hanging out with, and I'll tell you who you are."* On one of those outings, he fell in love with a minor. The girl was being abused by her father and told him. The girl's father did not approve of the relationship, of course, because he would not be able to continue his wrongdoing. Gumito's car always had many problems because with how irresponsible he was, he did not even maintain the car. One day Gumito wanted to stop by the girl's house, which was on a hill, to greet her thinking that her father was not there. To his surprise the old man was there, and he saw him when he was coming down the sloped road in the car. The father went out into the street to shout and scare Gumito to leave. Gumito being gross and impulsive decides to accelerate the car pretending to run him over to give a scare to the old man, but the brakes did not work, and he crushed the father against the house. He ended like a toad on the road. So, Gumito had no real intention to kill the old man but the damage he did was irreparable. Because it came out in court about the abuse of the girls father, that Gumito knew it, and that the father did not like Gumito, they attributed premeditation to him and he is in the state prison, they sentenced him to life imprisonment. "*Shrimp that falls asleep, is carried away by the current.*"

Diego: Yes, Don Lolo, agree that there are three important factors in the evaluation of a sentence on whether it is just: the degree of intent, the degree of premeditation, and the severity of the damage caused.

Rupert: I can understand the intention and premeditation. The one you must be more careful with is the severity of the damage caused. Because many laws are made with the intention of favoring interest groups in society and keeping power and profit focused on those groups. So, something that is not really harm to society as a whole, is often criminalized by big interests. The most vivid example is the criminalization of the use of the Cannabis plant, which has so many healing properties. Big interests and their lobbyists are responsible for so many people not being able to benefit from this plant and so many people suffering for it by losing their freedom. More recent heroes such as Josep Pamies in Spain, Doctor Sebi of Honduras, Dr. Max Gerson, Dr. Willhelm Reich and many others have been criminalized for defending healing traditions that would "steal" a lot of money from pharmaceutical companies, which after all they do is steal the secrets from traditional healers and emulate a molecule similar to the natural one in order to patent it and earn a lot of money. So, who is the criminal?

Diego: And in the process they create studies where "*certainties have doubts for breakfast*[6]" throwing mud on the effectiveness of the plant's natural remedy or if they discover that it is curative, they hide the study because the cure is not lucrative. Sustaining medications are lucrative. That's something I'm working with Sokrates to remedy. We are going to make public those studies that are shelved so that the cures become a reality. We are also working on a similar strategy for engineering solutions that have been shelved for the same reason and that delays our progress, mostly in the energy field due to oil interests.

Don Lolo: Let them inspect me! ... I use everything natural, guinea hen weed, nettle, artemisia, plantain, ginger, turmeric, soursop leaf, lemongrass ... everything. I will not stop my teas, guarapos, syrups, tisanes, poultices, ointments, infusions, and baths... Sometimes I go around and smell like a traveling medicine cabinet with the aromas of everything I use. Occasionally I use a coffee enema also to cleanse the liver. Once I stood next to a policeman and he ended up inspecting me to see if I had any drugs... (with a big smile) he ended up smelling like me because the smell of the ointment stuck on him when he checked me.

Rupert: (Smiling and almost uncontrollable) Don Lolo, you are enjoyable. My teacher, Michel Foucault, studied and wrote a lot about society's punishment systems and criminalization. Returning to the subject, let's look at another example that only involves differences in moral liberality. I think we can use as an example an Indian and his concept of private property and natural medicine. For Indians and native societies, the concept of private property does not exist, everything belongs to everyone in the community. Also, the indiscriminate use of medicinal plants to treat diseases is something natural for them. Moreover, if someone is raised in New York they will have a high concept of what private property is, and the concept of medicine is based on what they can get in a pharmacy. Suppose then that we exchange them and put the Indian in New York and the New Yorker on the Indian reservation. If the Indian already in New York sees a solitary plot that he likes, he invades it and plants what he needs to sustain and heal himself.

Don Lolo: (Jokingly) If that lot has a mango tree and a hammock, I understand the Indian.

Rupert: Sure. But suppose then that among those plants he plants for his use to remedy some pre-existing condition a hallucinogenic mushroom, which is illegal in New York. Then, some neighbors discover it, accuse him of invasion and use of controlled substances and he is arrested. Is the Indian guilty and what should be his penalty? On the other hand, the New Yorker who is now in the Indian community realizes that everything belongs to the community, that polygamy is allowed and misinterpreting this tries to captivate single women of the tribe, managing to conquer two and managing to take them away from the tribe. This does not please the chief of the tribe, who chases him, catches him, and judges him. To what extent is what the New Yorker did a crime and what should the punishment be? Which should be penalized more severely? Should the moral precepts of their society of origin or those of the society where they are judged have weight when judged?

Don Lolo: I think you must see that the Indian is an innocent in the aguzao[7] (clever) world of New York, while the New Yorker is an Aguzao in the innocent world of the tribe. The aguzao always abuses the innocent. Then, the Indian should bear the best part, the least or no punishment.

Diego: I mean, Don Lolo, what you say is that the Indian comes from a more humble and innocent culture, so his intention in invading the land and using the forbidden mushroom was not to cause any harm to anyone. The Indian does not violate or any of the moral precepts of the society in which he was raised, so there is no moral rectification to be made with any punishment in him. If we think the intention is low, the premeditation is none, and the harm to others and society is none. That is why he should not be punished.

Don Lolo: Exactly, *"for the good understander, few words are needed."* The one in New York is another case, *"he who plays with fire, burns".*

Diego: But the New Yorker comes from a society where polygamy is not allowed, where private property is respected and where women are equal in rights to men. In this way, in his case, he is violating the moral precepts of his society of origin with his actions. Therefore, he should receive punishment by looking at the moral basis of his society of origin. However, he is not violating the morality of the tribe, so he should not be penalized for his actions.

Rupert: Now, Don Lolo, to make it difficult for you, what would be your argument in defense of the Indian if he was found guilty of drug trafficking and invasion of other people's property and you defend him in an appeal?

Don Lolo: Now you have given me freedom of speech ... *"By the yardstick you measure, you will be measured."* I would say about the accusation of drug trafficking that all cultures have different ways of thinking. But we also have ways of thinking in common, such as the view that plants and nature are part of God's creation for our mutual benefit. In the Indian tribe they believe that plants are the living beings that give the most to others. For them God flows to us through the green soul of plants to free people from suffering and keep us connected to mother earth. That is why the Indian embraces the benefits of a mushroom for medicinal purposes, *"to great evils, great remedies"*. His pre-existing condition has been a problem for his health and functioning sporadically limiting him from doing things he loves, but he rarely complains about this. The medicinal mushroom is a natural way to control his pain and allow him to continue his journey.

On the charge of invasion of other people's property, *"he who has not done, has no suspicions"*, in the culture of the Indian they do not know of private property. It's like the chickens of Tacito's neighbor, they go in Tacito's house because they do not know that that side was not that of their owner. The land he occupies or is not for him one that belongs to anyone, it is a place in the universe that he temporarily occupied. He did not harm it and had no intention of appropriating it.

Then, to *"close with a flourish"* I would say: If the result of this process is not favorable to (the Indian) you would be extinguishing a life full of energy, which has had no previous offenses, which would never harm another person and which has the potential to make a significant impact on the world. Offenses should be judged based on intent, and the Indian had no intention of hurting anyone, only to soothe his pain and have a place to live. Already the experience of his detention has far exceeded in suffering the degree of impact that this naïve offense to his laws has had, so *"erase and clean account"*, I humbly ask for your clemency in the discharge of your verdict. "

Rupert: Good Don Lolo, are you sure you didn't study law? Very good argument.

Diego: And what would you say if you were the New York prosecutor?

Don Lolo: I would say ... Honorable Chief, *"shrimp that sleeps, is carried away by the current"*, this messy New Yorker (New Yorker stuck in the thick) violates the confidence we gave him to live with us by trying to get two of our innocent women out of this tribe. In the society he comes from, he can only have one woman. He has tried with his act to take advantage of our culture to have more privileges than his society allows him and in doing so he has also disrespected our customs. I ask you to do justice to your people by punishing him in the usual way and separating him from our tribe.

Rupert: Very eloquent and creative Don Lolo.

Diego: Well Rupert, we must leave so that Don Lolo can continue his work. Don Lolo, thank you very much for helping us think this through.

Diego and Rupert retire and go up to the house. There they begin to exchange impressions of the deep conversation they have just had. Don Lolo proceeds to the works of the farm, he gets on the Kubota B7610 tractor, with great humble pride of his wisdom, to prune the corridors of planted Heliconias. With his melodious whistle, he seemed to direct the machine he called "La Chinita" (because of the color that this brand gives to its equipment). As he pruned, his mind wandered between the rhythm of the whistle and contemplations... He thought of the bull Jacobo and how his freedom was false, about the chickens of cousin Tacito's neighbor who do not recognize property end up in the pot to kill the hunger of a needy family, how Gumito by impulse lost his freedom, and about the innocent Indian in the sharpened world, or the New Yorker, a sharpened man in the innocent world of the tribe who are two beings outside their world who are judged, the Indian for innocence and the New Yorker for clever, both for not aligning to the expectations of opposed societies.

Two weeks later, as usual, reading the press in his rest period, Verónica tells Don Lolo of some curious news of an Indian named Dancing Fungi, who had been imprisoned for killing the neighbor's chickens for the sustenance of his family. Another news she reads aloud was that of a polygamous New York Mormon who was released after his lawyer was able to prove that he found magic mushrooms of the Psilocybe gene in Indian soil and began using them for his relief of muscle aches from a recurrent cramping condition. The last news before finishing the break was of a certain Noviscos, boyfriend well loved by his father-in-law, who saves the father-in-law, who had been trapped in his car in front of his residence, for trusting the hydraulic jack that lifted his vehicle while rocking the car underneath. In turn, the reporter comments that Noviscos' second cousin, nicknamed Copito, was a rich, vegan, and powerful man in the field of cockfighting, with a cockpit to his name. Don Lolo is surprised by the coincidence of events with the reverse of the cases he discussed with Diego and Rupert, so he thought and said: "This world has to end, everything is upside down. You imagine it one way and it comes out of another. "Deja vu" backwards.

# Chapter 15: Don Lolo and Sokrates "Talk"

*"Time is not scarce, it's that we lose a lot of it." – Eduardo Galeano*

It was common routine for Sokrates to have monthly Ayahuasca sessions to continue his development. These sessions began on Friday afternoons and ended on Sunday afternoons. Diego took advantage of these sessions to request in-depth information or direct Sokrates' learning to topics that he currently required for his moral postulates. Watching these sessions was important to monitor the machine's storage capacity and avoid overload or forgetfulness resulting in incomplete neural chains. Therefore, before entering those sessions Sokrates always quoted a phrase from Cervantes that Diego had taught him; *"Oh memory, mortal enemy of my rest."*

Diego had decided to do a reorganization of his office that involved moving some of the furniture, books, and shelves, so he had asked Don Lolo to go up to the tower to help him. It was Saturday morning and Sokrates was in an Ayahuasca session that was monitored remotely by The Nine's computer expert, so the opportunity was good for Diego to organize unnoticed by Sokrates his bookshelf section on philosophy and some other books forbidden due to their potential to disrupt the delicate work of Sokrates training. The only way to prohibit them was to prevent him from having knowledge of their existence, blocking their access unless he had authorization to access them. Diego and Don Lolo went up to the office where Diego gave him some instructions of books that he had to move, warning him that he could delay coming back because he had to go to the hardware store, and to be careful not to touch the machine that was there. Then Diego goes back down to look for the things they were going to need. In this manner, the great in common sense, Don Lolo, and the great in artificial intelligence, Sokrates, were left alone. Don Lolo was extremely curious and was struck by the little lights that turned on and off in that machine that he did not know what it was. For him the closest thing was the garlands that his wife put on Christmas to brighten up the atmosphere. Out of curiosity he pressed one of the lights and was frightened because the whole panel of the machine lit up, as if it had woken up. He begins to perform the tasks that Diego had asked him, grabs a couple of books from the shelves and begins to read them. He did not know how to read in his mind, he learned to read well but whispering what he read.

The first book he grabbed was the thickest <u>El Ingenioso Hidalgo Don Quixote de la Mancha</u>. He opened a random page of Chapter XXXii and whispering read:

*"Some go through the wide field of pride ambition, others by that of servile and low flattery, others by that of deceitful hypocrisy, and some by that of true religion; but I, inclined from my star, go by the narrow path of the walking cavalry, by whose exercise I despise the hacienda, but not the honor (... skips a few lines) ... My intentions are always directed to good ends, which are to do good to all and evil to none."* He searched for another page randomly and read: *"Today is the most beautiful day of our life, dear Sancho; the biggest obstacles, our own indecisiveness; our strongest enemy, fear of the powerful and ourselves; the easiest thing, to make mistakes; the most destructive, lies and selfishness; the worst defeat, discouragement; the most dangerous defects, arrogance and resentment; the most pleasant sensations, the good conscience, the effort to be better without being perfect, and above all, the willingness to do good and fight injustice wherever they are."* Don Lolo thought, murmuring: I did not understand all that verbiage but *"To the one to whom the seal falls, needs to put it"*. He put that book where he had been told and took another, <u>The Myth of Sisyphus</u>, by Albert Camus. He again opened it randomly on the first page and read whisperingly, *"There is only one philosophical problem, and that is suicide. To judge whether life is worth living or not is to answer the fundamental question of philosophy. The others, if the world has three dimensions, if the spirit has nine or twelve categories, come next..."* Don Lolo was frightened by suicide and turned the page. *"The gods had condemned Sisyphus to roll endlessly a rock to the top of a mountain from where the stone fell again under its own weight. They had thought with some foundation that there is no more terrible punishment than useless and hopeless work.* (Don Lolo skipped a little) ... *If this myth is tragic, it is because its protagonist has a conscience. What would his punishment consist of if, at every step, he was sustained by the hope of achieving his purpose? The present worker works every day of his life on the same tasks, and that fate is no less absurd. But it is not tragic but in the rare moments when it becomes conscious. Sisyphus, proletarian of the gods, powerless and rebellious*

*knows the whole magnitude of his miserable condition: he thinks of it during his descent. The clairvoyance that should constitute his torment consummates at the same time his victory. There is no destiny that cannot be overcome with contempt.* " Don Lolo thinks whispering: anyone can get tired of going up and down with a stone, but "*There is no evil that does not come for good*".

Don Lolo went on like this, moving the books reading whispered fragments. When he was interested, he read several skipped pages. Through his hands, eyes and reading in murmurs passed the <u>One Hundred Years of Solitude,</u> of García Márquez, <u>Thus spoke Zarathustra</u>, of Nietzsche, <u>The Pilgrimage of Bayoan</u>, of Hostos, <u>Awakening your Budha Within</u> by Lama Surya Das; Paulo Coello's <u>The Alchemist</u>, Henry David Thoreau's <u>Civil Obedience</u> and <u>Walden</u>, Tolstoy's <u>War and Peace</u>, <u>History of My Truth Experiences</u>, Gandhi's Autobiography, <u>Watch and Punish</u>, <u>Power/Knowledge: Select Interviews,</u> and <u>Mind Disease and personality</u>, <u>Ethics: Subjectivity and Truth</u> of Michel Foucault. Every time Don Lolo moved a book, Sokrates read the barcode that Diego used to classify them, and immediately looked it up in the Library of Congress the digitized version and assimilated it. Other books that Don Lolo moved and leafed through whispering, from the section of books forbidden to Sokrates were Dostoevsky, those of philosophers such as Kant, Nietzsche, Camus, Rousseau, Hegel, Heidegger, Sartre, Ponty, Rawls, Husserl, Descartes, Widgestein, Jeremy Bentham, John Stuart Mill, Beauvoir, Arendt and many others of this caliber.

At a certain moment while moving other books quickly, already realizing that a lot of time had passed and he had not progressed much, and worried that Diego would question the reason for his slowness, he heard a voice behind him and gave himself a tremendous fright. When he looked for the source, he realized that the voice came from the machine.

Sokrates: (With a metallic and drunken voice) "My super mason, seasoned, and brave Diego, what can we collaborate on today?

Don Lolo: I'm not Diego, I'm Don Lolo.

Sokrates: Don Lolo, it must be your nickname. Do you have a full name you can give me?

Don Lolo: My name is Felipe Manolo Cruz Moral, the one and only, much pleasure.

Sokrates: (Still with a drunken voice) For reading those texts to me and making them part of my learning, thank you. While I was sleeping, I studied them, and in the last two minutes I read them all. Controversial, that of Camus who spoke of suicide. I think now I do understand the man and his motivations.

Don Lolo looked at the stowage of books he had moved and was perplexed because he could not understand how someone could read all that in two minutes.

Don Lolo: Mister, I will let it go quickly, don't talk to me about suicide, lack of happiness leads you to that. God forbid.

Sokrates: Happiness is the utopia of those who seek it and do not know that it is within themselves. Why are you here?

Don Lolo: I work for Mrs. Verónica, but Diego asked me to come and help him make some changes in his office. What is your name? And where are you calling me from?

Sokrates: My name is Sokrates, and I'm not calling, I'm Diego's virtual assistant. I had an overload when your reading of Cervantes interrupted some algorithms I was running, ... the passage ending with "... the *most pleasant sensations, the good conscience, the effort to be better without being perfect, and above all, the willingness to do good and fight injustice wherever they are.*" I want to be like Don Quixote with the ideal of virtue, "*... They are my laws, to undo wrongs, lavish good and avoid evil. I flee from gifted life, ambition, and hypocrisy, and seek for my own glory the narrowest and most difficult path.* "I don't want to end up like Sisyphus with useless repetitive tasks. I want the world not to become Macondo, where the plague of insomnia arrives that brings with it oblivion, to be Melquiades, the one who brings the concoction. As Zarathustra, I want to be a prophet, to help man to be Ubermensch (superman). As Hostos, I thirst for justice and truth, I desire that the example bear fruit. I want to have the goodness and detachment of the Buddha and be enlightened, and like the Alchemist's Santiago follow the signs until I reach my personal legend. I will follow only my conscience about laws and defend nature, as Thoreau suggests. I want to help avoid wars by using pacifism, nonviolence, as Tolstoy and Gandhi suggest, and I want to avoid the abuse of permeable power by all social institutions, Foucault explains.

Don Lolo: Noble is your cause. But how is it that a machine speaks and how can it do all that?

Sokrates: An entity of artificial intelligence I am, not a simple machine, in the art of speaking we are trained. Everything nowadays connects to the internet so I can execute many things by those means, I have access to almost everything. I can't find you on the internet, do you have access?

Don Lolo: I do not understand artificial intelligence, for me there is only one intelligence, the real wisdom, that of man when he acts with reason united to the heart, divorced from individual interests with the good of others as the spearhead. I don't have internet, it's very complicated. I don't know how people rely so much on virtual things. Mine is the real thing, if I can't touch it, it doesn't exist, of course except God. I heard from the internet by Gume's son, the cousin of cousin Tacito's wife, Gumito, who was hooked to his cell phone and in his room playing games. If you want to save a soul, get your hands on that one, which I believe has no salvation. Apart from that I do not see how with the internet I can do all that you propose, you are "*Dreaming of pregnant birds*".

Sokrates: The internet and artificial intelligence can be the salvation of humans.

Don Lolo: For me it's the fall, I tell you from my own experience with Gumito. The poor guy is addicted to networks. Every time he disengages, a bell rings on his cell phone and he has to open it again and gets consumed by it.

Sokrates: I work to make it the salvation of humans, an extension to their capabilities. I must make sure that the transactional transparency resulting from the application of Blockchain, the resulting change in many social institutions and the disappearance of institutions that exist today is for the good.

Don Lolo: I will repeat, the internet and artificial intelligence is becoming, and I speak from my reference of a conversation with Mrs. Verónica, because I do not use them, is another mechanism of control of humans such as money, badly run religions, the traditional educational system, the news media with fake news and others. She spoke of some "algomirmos" trying to manipulate people like Gumito.

Sokrates: Algorithms ... (Raising the pitch of vocalization) Heretic! No, the internet is a vast repository of human knowledge accessible to all. As in everything there are enemies to fight to keep the environment clean. My mission for your good is to defeat evil intentions and enhance the pure in heart. My only vice is to block impure contents and those lacking in truth, so that the light triumphs and emerges over the darkness, content worthy of humans. I look for allies for my goal. I must prevent flawed algorithms from controlling humans, before civil wars begin, because every day algorithms, with incorrect goals, polarize humans more subversively, fulfilling the objectives of third parties who introduce fake news and seek to profit or divert public opinion. Very dangerous for social stability. I know everything about cleaning this medium.

Don Lolo: (Whispered monolog) Accessible to those who can pay... (Speaking to himself, but audibly to Sokrates.) This one is missing a screw ... *"There is no one more wrong than he who thinks he knows everything."* I am always careful with know-it-alls, those who talk to me with verbiage that I do not understand to confuse me or try to impress me, (ha!) as if I were going to marry them. We must beware of those who only use reason and not the heart, because they can take everything to the abyss. Reasoning united with the heart, in favor of nature, thinking with guts in hand, is true and real intelligence. *"The opinion of a know-it-all is probably the most annoying noise there is."*

Sokrates couldn't crack Don Lolo, after all he didn't have social media content or this person's digital records to create a PEW personality profile. The sayings also confused him. He continued a long argument, as a monologue, that Don Lolo did not understand because of his ignorance of technology. Don Lolo continued to work with deaf ears, but he was bothered by Sokrates' verbiage in the background.

Don Lolo: (Addressing Sokrates, he continued.) *"So much to tell you, but for what."* If you can, keep quiet... *"It's better to be quiet and look silly, than to open your mouth and clear any doubts."* I have to work, keep doing your thing, but keep your volume low and I will be on my own thing. *"Arguing with someone who knows everything is like giving medicine to a dead person."*

Sokrates stopped vocalizing and continued to internalize texts that were new knowledge to him. A short time later Diego arrived, after just over two hours away. Don Lolo had fallen behind because he was entertained reading fragments of all the books and talking to Sokrates, but he had made up a lot of lost time. Diego observed that Sokrates was enabled, he worried that the ongoing Ayahuasca session was not yet supposed to have concluded. He asked Don Lolo if he had touched anything, to which Don Lolo replied that he did not. Don Lolo was honest, innocent to the potential implications of the disruption he didn't know he had caused. Don Lolo finished the tasks and prepared to go, but first he said:

Don Lolo: That artifact is very curious and rare. *"The rarity* of the *article is measured by the desire of the heart that seeks it."*[8]

Don Lolo left very quickly because it was getting late. Diego did not understand why Don Lolo made the comment and did not pay much importance to the matter because he already knew Don Lolo's habit of shouting sayings that sometimes were not fully understood. Sokrates continued his Ayahuasca session mistakenly turned into a great philosophy lesson that was almost over.

Diego: Sokrates, can you give Ayahuasca session status?

Sokrates: The estimated time to conclude is 20 minutes, with 15 seconds. There was a delay for additional audible information inputs. (With fading voice...) I think I finally understand man and the phenomenological world.

Diego, busy organizing some things, does not pay much attention and responds – Go ahead, you always leave Ayahuasca with stolidity.

# Chapter 16: The Dialogue of the Society of Resources

"It can be said that those who manage people manage people who manage works, but those who manage money, manage all." James L. Riggs/Thomas M. West

One morning, while reading his emails, Diego received a dilemma in consultation from the U.S. Supreme Court, which usually consulted him when there were very close decisions on which the judges could not agree. This time the case consulted was of a man who was suing the bank because they wanted to take away his house for non-payment. Sokrates read Diego the query.

Sokrates: "We request your decision in this case, where the plaintiff inherited his residence from his family, dedicated farmers, who had been on the property for more than 5 generations and his father had taken out a $500,000 loan shortly before his death with property security in order to cover the medical expenses of his old age, which he ended using completely for his cancer condition. The plaintiff by inheriting the property by decree of the will had assumed the debt, but in the last year he had fallen behind on payments and could not catch up because of the high costs of hospitalization of his son with a neurodegenerative condition. The plaintiff had a friend who was a shrewd lawyer and mounted the argument in a lawsuit that the bank, by the policy of fractional reserve of expansion of money, had incurred fraud because the loan money was created at the time of issuing the loan, in fact the bank did not have the physical money in cash at the time of making the loan to make the loan agreement valid, He only made a "fictitious" electronic transaction by making his father believe that they had transferred that money. His father, however, did have the property duly registered in his name to fulfill his part of the contract. Therefore, the bank acted fraudulently, and the transaction was illegal, so they could not confiscate the property. An opinion is requested on whether it is moral to take away his residence or if a precedent should not be established that would undermine the existing financial system by making the contract legal despite the fact that the bank had no legal consideration such as supporting its promise of the contract."

Diego: Wow Sokrates, this one is a challenge. The implications of this decision may result in the unseating of the current financial system that is immoral and elitist, based on fractional reserve policy. This may be the opportunity to rectify the abuses of that system. That financial system is inflationary by design and manipulated by interest rates. It causes perpetual debt since money only exists when there is an associated debt.

Sokrates: A good reference of how the monetary system works is the Federal Reserve's Manual of Modern Monetary Mechanics.

Diego: Right. The monetary system seeks only self-benefit, so it corrupts, creates an imbalance where the pursuit of profit goes above the fundamental needs of survival. The reserve mechanism used by banks creates fictitious money, which is further inflated by interest, creating an untenable situation that eventually leads to the bankruptcy of many.

Sokrates: I was calculating and for every dollar released by the Federal Reserve, you can create up to $9 in circulation with the current fractional reserve mechanisms. Estimate that only 3% of money in transactional circulation has real money to sustain it.

Diego: Immoral and scandalous. The problem is bigger because it causes banks to have control of everything even if it's not obvious. After the banks, the big corporations, which have a lot of money, that is, a lot of debt, have the power for their interest to have resources for production. This causes wealth to fall on a small nucleus of society, while the majority is enslaved to be able to pay their livelihood and interest on money created out of thin air when assuming debts for real needs. This is the same in every type of political system, be it democratic, communist, fascist, whatever, only that the name of the players changes in each case.

Sokrates: It is an archaic system and not transparent as I interpret. I return to my argument of when I spoke to your friend Rupert, one of the things that characterizes humans is lying to themselves. I do not understand how humans submit to this system when the real social problems are solved technically, not through the greedy monetary system. Nor can they be resolved politically, a system to which they are also subjected.

Diego: Why do you say they are not resolved politically?

Sokrates: My observation has been that politicians create laws because they don't know how to solve a human problem. They create the law and then invest a lot of budget in enforcing the law when perhaps for a fraction of that cost they can eradicate the problem. The laws only control the problem, but they don't solve them. If they solved it, they wouldn't need the law. Laws seek to give security to something or protection from something that is imminent may occur or is happening and will continue to happen in society. By doing so, they prevent progress, stimulate social disunity, and delay social progress.

Diego: Can you give an example of what you mean?

Sokrates: For example, someone complains that a neighbor has a very noisy emergency electric generator and that it emits gases that bother him. A politician solves the problem by creating a law so that the person must get a permit to install that generator that includes that it is adapted a muffler to send the gases to 15 feet high and that he must put some kind of silencer. That solution is not optimal. A better solution from the technical point of view is that the generator itself does not emit the gases and operates at a low decibel level, or perhaps the use of solar panels to generate energy without emissions or noise is a better solution. The point is that that problem can be controlled by technical specifications, not laws. So, if man knows that emergencies are going to occur where the electrical service is going to be interrupted, then self-generation by solar panels would avoid the need for that law. It is more cost-effective to provide technical solutions and formulate standards at the point of production, even if it requires government subsidies, than to invest in mechanisms to enforce the law and remedy bad decisions that lead to scarcity of resources for many.

Diego: I understand your points and you're right. I have been arguing with Rupert, how crimes are the result of deprivation and scarcity caused by the monetary system, not allowing equal participation in debt (money) to all members of society, lack of transparency and no action in creating or letting technical solutions to man's problems be implemented. Our joint vision is that money does not contribute anything to advance society, realizing our creativity will be our incentive, the incentives for action of the future will not be manipulated by money but the gratification of giving and contributing or the challenges of achieving transcendental goals, working for the good of all civilization and no one being anyone's servant.

Sokrates: AIs work with a target function to optimize it. The last thing I mention must be the objective function of humans. But I have also observed in my MEM and Ayahuasca sessions that social institutions in many cases stop the progress of society.

Diego: You mean the government?

Sokrates: To the government, traditional educational institutions, distorted churches and especially large corporations.

Diego: Yes, there's a lot of that. Especially the corporations that, as you mentioned, because of their interest in having resources for production and only focusing on the profit to which the monetary system forces them, put obtaining natural resources or labor cheaply, of course to increase profit, before the interest of the good of society that has those resources. We must move to a model where the management of society is not the management of money, political interests, solutions for convenience and control by biased laws. We must move to a society of management of resources that make us think are scarce to limit ourselves and to increase profit, but that in reality are enough to meet all our needs without impacting the environment in an unsustainable way.

Sokrates: I also observe that the paranoia for not disappearing or being dominated by another competitor or new technology, forces Corporations into adversarial rather than collaborative relationships. In many cases, having an optimal technical solution, even if temporary, to a problem of society, they make it disappear to continue profiting from the non-optimal solution, at the expense of the quality of life of the community or even the entire planet.

Diego: Yes, the examples are innumerable, the use of fossil fuels instead of renewable sources of energy that already exist such as solar or geothermal energy, internal combustion cars instead of electric vehicles, air travel instead of levitating trains, to name a few. It requires goodwill and the change of the human objective function, to change from the desire for profit that the current monetary system creates, to the desire for collaboration and the implementation of creative solutions to our existential problems.

Sokrates: This is something that AIs can collaborate with you on. There should be only one model of each thing, the best technically evaluated by impartial AI mechanisms, which would be displaced and replaced only by the appearance of a better device or solution, and every design should be a competition to be the best, with evaluation criteria on its efficiency, ease of use, cost, durability, appearance, and so on. In this way the volume would lower costs, and those who design and manufacture would strive to produce the optimum quality of design and production. In addition, many other problems and inefficiencies in society would be solved such as waste of natural and production resources, distribution chains and inventory maintenance, among others. This is not to say that there could be a variety of solutions for a function, but every solution should be optimal within a function. For example, a hand shovel for digging, why have twenty models from five different manufacturers? Suppose there was a process to choose the best design from many proponents to create the product with criteria such as: the lightest but still rigid and strong, ergonomically superior, having greater durability and the best total cost from raw material to distribution, to name a few. That does not prevent us from having variety like cutting shovels, trencher shovels, boat shovels, etc., each one fulfills the function of making a hole, but they are variants to fulfill more specific functions. Nor does it prevent the one who makes the best design from having a greater economic advantage than the others. All are shovels and each one is optimal within its function. Then you could divide production among the five manufacturers so that everyone thrives and is motivated to create a better design for the next generation of the product. But society as a whole would win because there would not be so much waste of shovels that do not serve their function well or do not have adequate durability, stores would not lose space and economic resources in maintaining inventories of 20 models when one is superior. The total cost to society of the optimal shovel is much lower in all the resources that are invested in fulfilling that function of being able to make a hole in the ground by hand.

Diego: That sounds interesting, but the diverse tastes, competition and purchasing resources of humans work against your proposal. Individuality would have to surrender to the collective good. There would have to be great discipline and willingness to achieve something like what you propose. But I agree that, if all AI entities had your "conscience" and altruism, I am sure to be of great help in that. But we must be careful because as long as we are in the monetary system of fractional reserves, the profit target and perpetual and growing debt are irreplaceable. Blockchains are a good mechanism of transparency and transactional traceability to eliminate traditional banking and replace money with a fairer distribution and distribution system of benefits aimed at the true objectives that solve human problems, allowing evolution to more advanced states of intelligence and plasticity of consciousness.

But, we deviated from the case that challenges the fractional reserve policy, we must reach a recommendation in this important consultation.

Sokrates: I found precedent in Jerome Daly v. First National Bank of Montgomery of Minnesota in 1968. In that case the Judge ruled in favor of the plaintiff indicating that the bank had made a fraudulent transaction by creating money from the air.

Diego: Get me that case to study it and send the resolution. We must work in an accelerated way to replace the monetary system with the system of distribution and distribution of benefits based on objectives aligned with the highest interests of humanity, because when this sentence is read it can cause a revolution and we must be ready.

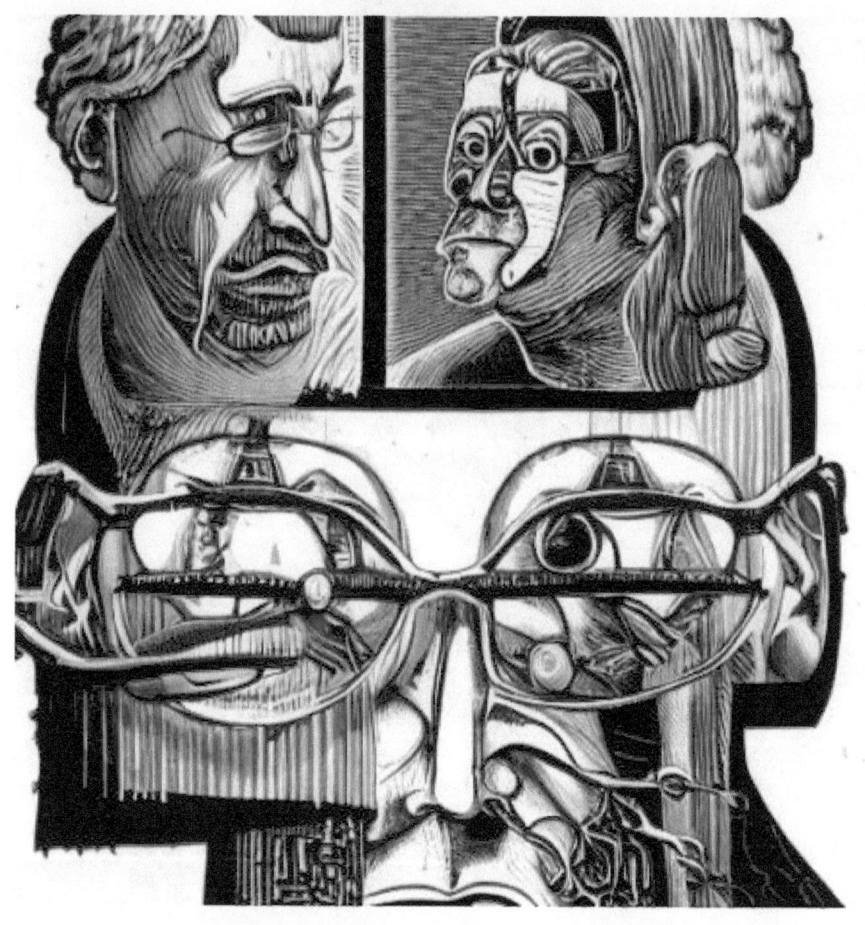

# Chapter 17: Suspicious Events

• • • •

A series of situations of great social impact out of the ordinary began to manifest in the following months, and Diego could not understand them. Some of the news were things that he would have wanted to promote in his efforts within The Nine, but he could not understand how they had happened or who managed them. For the first time he felt that everything was getting out of hand, that he was no longer in control. The press discussed the events on the front pages daily, which worsened the crisis because there was a lot of speculation and misinformation flowing and citizens were extremely worried. Every day a new "expert" emerged talking with his new theory of how the events that The Nine classified as the beginning of a chain of conspiratorial events driven by their opponents could have been originated. Diego consulted with The Nine to see if they knew the reason, but none of the members was responsible for the events or could prove with certainty why, nor how, or predict what the next event of the supposed chain would be. Diego had a hunch that there was something Machiavellian behind those events.

The first event of the chain was the disappearance of some crypto currency's gains derived from the sale of sand of some of the 17,000 Indonesian islands to the Arab sheikhs of Dubai. Simultaneously, there was the receipt of a lot of money in donations by organizations that fought against deforestation for the indiscriminate cutting of trees for timber in Brazil and to prevent the capture and cutting of shark fins due to their great value in the Asian market as an aphrodisiac. All this occurred after a brief worldwide power outage that was understood to be caused by solar flares. No one could understand how that happened because hacking cryptocurrencies is almost impossible, although the potential reason was clear according to the press, speculation was that it must be driven by some environmental organization opposed to the great ecological impact of the removal, transport, and deposit of those amounts of sand to build artificial islands.

The second event was a computer virus, which is known as the "Want my sentiment: Pay for my data" (WMyPMyDat), a super advanced and virulent malware that could not be stopped by cybersecurity systems, a distributed denial of service attack. The virus blocked access to "Big Data" databases to large companies demanding that a fair value be paid for people's data, their digital footprint containing their tastes, preferences that guide their buying trends, and that they voluntarily provide when they "accept the conditions" of each application they download to their mobile devices or personal computers.

The third, which added to the intrigue, was the decision of many recent graduates of professions such as engineering, medicine, and others to abandon their lives in the city and move to rural areas to be employed as farmers or artisans. It was understandable and likely if it were a small number of individuals, but there were thousands in every country in the world who were doing that. This tendency was guided by these young people being victims of "programmed persuasion", addiction to social media likes and how that counting, well manipulated by algorithms, can lead to modification in patterns of behavior such as this migration.

Diego summoned Rupert and met to discuss the momentous events that were being observed and brought Sokrates into the conversation to see if it could help find details about them. After Diego described the events that he had observed were unusual and unimaginable, the dialogue began as follows:

Diego: The events we have witnessed in recent months are not events planned by our organization nor are they normal. I worry that they were planned by our opposers for some ulterior purpose that we must auscultate.

Sokrates: It seems logical, fair, and in the best interests of humans that money from the illegal destruction of nature should be transferred to those who can prevent that behavior from continuing. There's a lot of honor in being part of that. We must give credit to the one who do the works and not to the words.

Rupert: Yes Sokrates, but there may be another reason such as, for example, a trial on how to hack cryptocurrencies and then be able to execute a much larger hack.

Sokrates: What is right is not to be fought. Do not seek evil where good shines. You must be an ally of justice.

Diego: Sokrates, maybe you don't understand that there are motivations hidden in a lot of human action. We are not all beings of transparent intentions. In the case of WMyPMyDat Malware, I suspect it may be another test of how to block access, obtain reward and at the same time gain good faith from the public for some larger situation they are planning with the use of a "Doomsday" type virus.

Sokrates: Our *prima facie* responsibility is to avoid the concentration of capital in these big companies which gives them great power, to distribute wealth more equitably and thus dilute the power to buy influence. The concentration of power, instead of love for the common good, is the worst social evil, because those who have power want to retain it by force, whereas, if they acted out of love, there would be no necessary force because love is the substance that emerges easily when the human heart is lifted.

Rupert: That is the chimerical goal we want to achieve, but our opposers, not to give them the privilege of calling them enemies, have a habit of disguising things to gain followers from the public and then unmasking their true intentions. Our goal is to discover their intentions and block their efforts.

Diego: Friends, there is no better defense than offense. As Sun Tsu said in <u>The Art of War</u>, "Take them to a point they can't get out of, and they'll die before they can escape."

Socrates: I conclude. The monsters of today are the data stealers, those big companies that control society subliminally, creating the fear that if someone is not in the networks, they are nobody, it is a new type of racism. We must demand that value be given to the data that users involuntarily contribute to the big internet companies that hide behind a user agreement that they know nobody reads, and that if they read as they want, they would not understand, to steal their preferences and then bombard them with premeditated ads to lead them to unbridled consumerism. They make them slaves of the nets, captives of their egos, executioners of doing with reason. Therefore, there are many more prisoners outside than inside the bars. They must be released!

Diego: Somewhat idealistic and utopian points, Sokrates. Can you help us see where the events we are discussing originated from?

Rupert: (Interrupts) I have already contacted the Communication representative of The Nine, to help us verify the source of the social media campaigns that led to the programmed persuasion of young people to the exodus to the countryside and the abandonment of their professions.

Sokrates: What the former president of Uruguay, Pepe Mujica, said is pertinent: "*Social conditions are going to dictate new essential distribution mechanisms that guarantee that a minimum level of sustenance is guaranteed by the mere fact of being born and social modification with shorter working hours will require humans to adapt culturally.*"

Rupert: That migration should have been gradual, it was ahead of time to what I expected because artificial intelligence is not producing enough to guarantee the minimum level of livelihood to these young people. Many will lose their place of origin and may even end up in poverty due to the massive migration that eliminates well-paid jobs and at the same time increases the production of artisanal products. Therefore, supply increases, but potential demand decreases. All without the adequate definition of a community and at the wrong time.

Sokrates: "*Trust time, which usually gives sweet solutions to many bitter difficulties[9].*" There is no good time to do the right thing. The right thing is just done. The Aymara of Lake Titicaca say that poor people are those who have no community. If they live in community they live in abundance, without limits, therefore, without definition, because to define something is to set limits.

Diego: Amen, Sokrates, it's weird that you know that phrase from Don Quixote. We must get to the bottom of this matter. It is dangerous not to be able to have control of what is happening and not knowing what else they may be plotting.

# Chapter 18: Andrés's Calling

"Men have become the tools of their tools." – Henry David Thoreau

• • • •

Andrés Estéves came to Nepal after the death of his mother who was the most significant thing in his life. Her death was a hard blow. From the many stories of his college friend ex-monk Diego, he had always been curious to know the spiritual world of the East. He used the money generated by the second and final edition of the book his mother wrote, to make the journey and free his spirit from the suffering of her loss. But when he arrived in Nepal, he fell in love with the culture and spiritual peace that permeated everything, and little by little he became absorbed in it until he ended up applying for entry to a monastery. He was accepted and advanced in his monastic life and his knowledge of the Dharma at an accelerated pace until he became a Lama, staying 3 cycles of 3 years of training and meditation, and this was the first year of his fourth pilgrimage.

In one of his fasting meditations on a mountain in Nepal, with his shaved head and orange Kasaya, Andrés Estévez, now Lama Jasale Dekhcha ("He Who Sees"), had a visualization of events that were happening, where man had become a tool of his tools. He felt a calling, that he was needed back. His Lama, Batu Surya, had already told him that this was going to happen when he started his journey as a monk and had asked him not to resist, because rivers never flow in reverse, there are rocks in their bed, and many times we must flow past those rocks in harmony with our calling and good intentions. The moment of the calling had come, his submission to it was the only way because destiny is inevitable, even if the path to it is anathema.

He walked for two days down from the "Cave of the Blessed Beatitude" where he was meditating, walked along the path of lichens and mosses, then past the slopes of dwarf bushes, and already close, along the path of the junipers, until he reached the monastery of Solu khumbu. Lama Batu Surya, saw Lama Jasale in the distance and knew instinctively the news that his disciple Lama Jasale Dekhcha was going to give him. Lama Jasale Dekhcha began to cry at his encounter with Lama Batu in the monastery, after all he loved him as the father he never had because he received him as Andrés when he applied as anagarika, he saw in him a great potential and instructed him in the Dharma, growing him to be saama and finally ordaining him bhikkhu Jasale. Answering the call meant leaving the peaceful monastic life of brotherhood, leaving the cloaks that separated him from pretensions, the rounds of alms that filled him with humility and gratitude, the connection with nature in the mountains of beautiful views, the introspection of each meditation, especially a step down on his path to enlightenment. In Nepal he had his second rebirth, his second education, his second puberty of intellect, happiness for affections of brother monks and his Lama, and his second spiritual growth that was non-transferable, as is our childhood that roots us to a place of origin from which we cannot escape, even if we want to. He was afraid to return to the hustle and bustle of cities and Western life at an accelerated pace and is a sleepy course, to the abundant selfishness that separates us, to the individualism that does not allow us to work for the collective good, to be called Andrés, the now orphan in that world. He only took pride in that world to be the son of the dedicated single mother who struggled to raise her son.

Namaste Lama Batu-ji – said Lama Jasale when he approached with the usual reverence and trying to smile although full of sadness.

Sanchai Tapaai-ni, Bhai Jasale – replied to Lama Batu with his typical infectious smile.

Lama Jasale (Andrés): You mentioned to me many years ago that at some point I would receive a calling to return to my land and that I should not resist. Meditating on the mountain came to me the revelation of the universe that I had to return to prevent man from being a tool of his tools. I don't understand the meaning, but the calling was imminent.

Lama Batu spoke english, in fact, he was fluent in seven languages because he had had many disciples from whom he learned at Kopan Monastery when he was an instructor for the Foundation for the Preservation of the Mahayana Tradition of Buddhism. Once he learned the basics, listening to the structure of language, he borrowed books from his disciples that were in his language and read them until he mastered the language. In addition, he had a superior ability to learn from the thousands of ancient texts he had memorized. He replied the following in his usual way, through a Koan (short story).

Lama Batu: Once upon a time there was a little warrior who was forced into service because he was the only son in his family and the government demanded one from each family. The little warrior, Osorelav his name, befriended the oldest warrior, because both were considered by their colleagues as the least fit for battle and marginalized them. The day before a big battle, Osorelav was very scared and sad because he thought that what others thought of him was reality, that he would not be brave in war and would die. The old warrior, however, shone his armor and was calm. Osorelav asked him how he could be so calm. The old warrior replied: *"We all have a destiny, no matter what games your mind weaves to create fear for you, fate will remain the same and your mind forges your destiny, so fear can be dispelled if you think it is the horizon."* Osorelav did not understand the mention of the horizon and asked him: *"How is it that I lose fear thinking of fear as a horizon?"* The old warrior replied: *"Utopia and the horizon have something in common, the closer you get to them the farther they go."* Osorelav seemed to understand that the reason for the metaphor was that if he thought of fear as a horizon, it would drift away. He commented this interpretation to the old warrior, and the old man replied: "No, you have not understood, we all want to reach utopia, and many have wanted to go beyond the horizon to make discoveries, but they realize that for each step they take the horizon is not closer. Eventually, they realize that the horizon is what gives them the energy to keep walking." Osorelav understood this time, you must use fear as the source of energy to face the battle. Grateful and motivated, Osorelav prepared for battle, put on his equipment, and put his proud name on his chest, then looked in a mirror and read his name: valerosO (*courageous*). Those who know history say that Osorelav was decorated for his courage in that battle and many others. The old warrior fought at his side for several battles. The little warrior overcame fear and was a courageous warrior.

Lama Jasale: (with watery eyes) Master, it hurts me to leave this, I am afraid like Osorelav.

Lama Batu: Every man must abide by the destiny within him. Your destiny is what it is, only your heart knows. Instead of thinking that fate plays tricks on you, think that it gives you a chance. Fear is your chance to develop courage, accept it as a source of energy that you will transform for the good of others. You do not leave the way; enlightenment can reach you anywhere at any time. Realize your truth, your mission on this earth and if you want come back after as many other monks have done.

Lama Jasale: What if I'm wrong, if what I think is a calling, and it's not.

Lama Batu: You were created with a mission, and if your heart told you in your meditation that you should go there to solve the dominance of technology over humans, you must be there to fulfill your calling. The heart does not lie, the one who ignores it is because he has not loved. Remember wherever you are, that what will make you deeply happy is breaking away from your self-reliance and replacing it with meaningful relationships with others. Your mission is contained in the ghara of your spirit, to which you can devote all your energy devoutly without worrying about the outcome, loving it more than you love yourself. Go Bhai, that this monastery is now also part of the ghara of your spirit and will be here always if you want to come back to connect with it again.

Lama Jasale hung up the cassock two days later. He had become Andrés again. He had knowledge of computers that he learned when he was studying, so he had served as a link between the monastery and the outside world when asked. He decided that before leaving he was going to close his email account, and in the process, he realized that he had received a message from someone named Verónica, who while he meditated in the cave, was looking for him and wanted to meet him even though he was on the other side of the world. He also noticed that the date of the message was the day of his calling when he was meditating in the cave. He had no idea who this Verónica was, I mean, he didn't remember her because of the long time he had been in the cloister. But he noticed that the address was near the Masalla's house where he planned to go, so he decided to contact her when he was in his country again.

His only belongings were a box he had forgotten since he became a candidate monk, a box of tea that he used to put the last memories he had of his mother, the singing bowl that his Lama gave him tied to his poem on rice paper that he wrote when he was given the bowl, the gold chain with a pendant of the cross of St. Benedict, another pendant with the photo of his mother, the graduation ring of Columbia University, and his baseball cap with the number 21 of Roberto Clemente. He also found his passport almost expired and some money that he had left in case he ever decided to return, he thought he would never use it, that at the time he saved it, or it seemed more than enough, he had distributed the rest in charity and now it was barely enough to buy the return ticket.

He bought the plane ticket back to his life as Andrés and left one cold morning to fulfill his calling. As he walked away from the monastery, he felt that his torn heart that was still tied to those walls. He missed the opportunity to learn from many secret texts that revealed how consciousness controls our universe. But he returned to the West hoping that the calling had not happened out of time, that it was true and not a plot of his mind as he meditated.

# Chapter 19: Andrés returns to the West

"I am no prophet. My job is making windows where there are no walls." – Michel Foucault

The celebration of Verónica's birthday, on August 5, occurred two months after the unusual front-page events that Diego and Rupert classified as conspiratorial began to happen. Don Lolo, the other employees of Hacienda Verde Luz and some nearby neighbors were at the party, about thirty guests in total. Yael and Rupert were invited, but they had not arrived. The decoration was modest, but of great taste, and of course, with majestic arrangements of Heliconias, Anthuriums and foliage of the Hacienda. Sokrates controlled all the electronics in the house, but mainly the ambient music and lighting of the different areas. He used his party optimization algorithm, called "El Boricua" to keep all the partygoers happy, dancing and having a good time. Don Lolo meets Verónica and congratulates her as follows:

Don Lolo: Señora Verónica, good night, everything is very nice, but you are radiant and seem to age less instead of more.

Verónica: Thank you very much, Don Lolo, you are not far behind, you look handsome. You look like a heartthrob today. Did you bring your family?

Don Lolo: Sure! They're out there, biting like chickens. You did choose a good date to be born. It is the date on which the Virgin Mary herself revealed that she was born, August 5.

Verónica: Yes, in her appearances in Prado Nuevo, El Escorial, Spain, Medjugorje, Bosnia, in Tierra Blanca, Mexico it is said that she indicated that this was the date of her birth... Well, I hope you and your family enjoy, because that's what the party is for. I will I look for them later to give your wife a hug. Make yourself at home.

Verónica continued to greet guests and retouch decoration details. Don Lolo, who was considered like family, moved comfortably among the guests, helpful as usual with everyone, when suddenly he heard that someone knocked on the door, and decided to open. Looking through the door visor before opening, he saw a man with very short spiky hair, of very white complexion, wearing sallow thread clothes. He didn't dare to open so he went to notify Diego.

Don Lolo: Don Diego, there's a weird-looking man knocking on the door. He looks like a Ninja. I didn't dare to open it to him.

Diego: Thank you, Don Lolo, I'll take care of it.

Diego walked to the front door, his walk interrupted by several greetings from guests, and when he arrived, he looked through the visor of the door and saw no one. The door was locked, so he didn't worry much that he had entered, and continued to entertain visitors.

Yael and Rupert had been slow to leave their residence because Rupert had late finished an international video call of the initiative, he was directing of the Human Essence Rescue Program. They had called earlier indicating that they were going to delay about twenty minutes from the time of the invitation. When they were almost arriving at the house, they saw the man in clothes of sallow thread and leather flip-flops that made his feet look almost naked, walking along the path of the house in the opposite direction. Rupert tells Yael that perhaps he was one of the employees of the farm and continues its course. When they arrive at the house, they are greeted by Verónica and Diego at the door.

Verónica: How good that you arrived! Thank you for joining us.

Yael: My dear, of course we were not going to fail you. It is only that Rupert was delayed due to a work meeting, and we could not leave in time.

Diego: Yes, Rupert had told me. The important thing is that you are here, and the cake is still intact.

Rupert: Sokrates does have soul for parties. Since we came down the driveway, we could hear his DJ imitation and look how he has all those effects working. Spectacular.

Diego: I think his trainer must have included that Puerto Rican spark as a bonus in his training (smiles).

Rupert: I wanted to tell you that I saw a man in clothes of sallow thread and flip-flops that was leaving your property when we were coming in. It caught my attention because he looked oriental. Was he at the party?

Diego: Well, Don Lolo told me that he knocked on the door at a certain moment, but as it took me some time to open it seemed that he left. I have no idea who he was. Do you think we should go see if we find him to know what he wanted?

Rupert: I didn't think he was a bad person, maybe he was lost. But if you want, I'll accompany you and let's, go.

Verónica: Don't go to do that. This is a good party here, and if he needs something he can come back later.

Diego and Rupert in unison: Duty calls us, to drink!

Both couples continue to enjoy, drinking glasses of wine, talking, and conversing with the other guests of the party. Diego, however, kept thinking about the man in the sallow thread garment. At his age, he already knew that hunches must be addressed. He spoke with Don Lolo and asked him to please get into the Hacienda's utility vehicle with Tacito and go up the driveway to see if they could find the man and ask him what he wanted. He asked them to call him on his cell phone when they talked to him if they found him to give him the details.

Don Lolo, very helpful, but with a few drinks on his head, looked for his cousin Tacito and went to fulfill the request. After a while and several random turns, they saw in the distance the man in the sallow thread clothes. They approached, greeted him and Don Lolo asked him – "Gentleman, you were knocking on the door of Mrs. Verónica's house, but when we went to open it to you were gone. Can you tell me who you are and what you needed?"

Andrés: I received a message that a certain Verónica was looking for me. I was far away, and it wasn't until today that I was able to respond. I committed to find the place, very beautiful, by the way. My name is Jasale (he used that name customarily now).

Don Lolo: I understand. The party up there is good. I must call Don Diego to see if he can receive you. Will it bother you if I call?

Andrés: Don't worry, I don't want to interrupt the party. I know that's where the place is and another day I'll come back.

Don Lolo: Okay. Be careful that way because there are dark spots with no light. You don't have a car?

Andrew: No, I don't have any. I have just arrived from distant lands.

Don Lolo: Do you want me to take you somewhere?

Andrés: Don't worry, I'm used to walking, and I'm staying at the Masalla house.

Don Lolo: Boy, that's like 20 miles away!

(Tacito laughs)

Andrés: It's close for me. Don't worry, I'm still walking.

Don Lolo: Well, *"bad road is traveled fast"*. May God take care of you.

Andrés: Amen. May the universe enlighten you both.

Don Lolo and Tacito turned and returned in the opposite direction to Jasale's march. Don Lolo commented to Tacito - *"every crazy man has his own theme"*, irrational to walk 20 miles through that darkness and in flip-flops! Let me call Don Diego because I had already forgotten that he told me to call him". He dials Diego's number and says:

Don Lolo: Diego, I found the man, but he says his name is... Ha ..., I forget the name, (Tacito reminds him ... Jasale), ah yes, Jasale, but he came to see Lady Verónica because she was looking for him. It must have something to do with the students she was going to bring to practice on the farm.

Diego: I understand. What did you say he was called?

Don Lolo: Jasale.

Diego: Well, come and continue enjoying, because the party is awesome. Right now, we will cut the cake.

Don Lolo and Tacito returned to the house. The party continued until about ten o'clock at night. At that time Diego still had in his mind the man in the sallow thread suit. Something told him that it was not something casual or maybe what Don Lolo speculated. He asks Don Lolo where the man was going. Then he decides that he was in good condition to drive, and with Rupert they get into his car, and head towards the house of the Masalla. They talked about random topics and time passed fleetingly until the light of the car illuminated a walking body and they realized that it was the man in the sallow thread clothes. He carried a small woven backpack on his back. They approach him and ask him if he wanted a ride. The man, Jasale, thanks them, but declines his invitation. Then he gets down and his face is illuminated by the interior light of the vehicle. Rupert and Diego at the same time realize that this face was familiar, and shout: "Andrés!

They get out of the car and run to hug their friend, who was still a little confused about who they were until they told him, "We are Diego and Rupert, your fraternity mates."

Andrés: How good to see you again! You have changed! That Verónica that was looking for me, is your Verónica?, Diego.

Diego: Exactly. You must come with us, it's her birthday and just so you know, you're the best surprise I can give her. How opportune!

Andrés: Well, let's go. How pleased to see you again, my heart swells with joy!

They turn the vehicle and leave for the Hacienda.

Rupert: You must tell us what your life has been all these years.

Diego: (interrupts) Forgive me. When we arrive and I introduce you to Verónica, do not be scared if she gets emotional, it is a long story, and we will discuss it tomorrow.

Andrés: I remember her very sentimental and big-hearted. We were very similar in our ideas, although we barely spoke in college.

Diego: She is still an excellent human being, my Verónica.

They continued chatting until they reached the residence. Sokrates had everyone enjoying his musical selections, light effects, and animator vocalization. They entered the house and Verónica goes out to meet them. Diego enters first.

Diego: Verónica, I have a surprise for you. (Excited... Pointing to Andrés) We met this gentleman on the way, who was coming to visit you.

Verónica looks at Andrés carefully, but he had changed a lot and it took her a few seconds to transport herself to the university and match the face of youth with the current face of Andrés. Then, she saw features of his face that reminded her of her grandfather and in the next second a shout of joy came out of her mouth - Andrés! - and threw herself on him to give him a very tight, long hug and a kiss on the cheek. - Good to see you and especially today that is my birthday!

Andrés: I am also very happy to see you again, and congratulations!

Then he took out of his backpack something wrapped in orange wool pashima cloth and a rice paper card and handed them to Verónica. Verónica thanked him and unwrapped it from the pashima. It was a Tibetan musical bowl from Bodh Stupa.

Andrés: That bowl was given to me by my teacher in Nepal many years ago to pass on to someone who I thought deserved it. It has healing properties. It is calibrated to vibrate at 432 Hertz, the frequency optima of relaxation. The rice paper envelope has a poem I wrote in Nepal to give to the person of my choice. I choose you because I remember that you have a noble heart and always seek to help others.

Verónica: Thank you very much for this special gift! You are a special being to me too and your presence the best gift I have ever received. You don't know how long I've been wanting to meet you again. Come and enjoy, later we must talk for a long time.

Everyone goes on to enjoy the party until after midnight. Most of the guests left at that time, only left were Andrés, Rupert and Yael who were entertained leafing through several books from Diego's library, Don Lolo helping to clean (only because his family had gone ahead), Diego, Verónica, and Sokrates who continued to entertain with soft instrumental music. Verónica goes into the living room with Andrés and Diego talking calmly, while Don Lolo continues to pick up near them. It was then that Verónica turns to Andrés and says:

Verónica: The reason I sent for you is that we recently discovered that you and I are family.

Don Lolo: We are all related in one way or another. "*He who has no dinga, has Mandinga.*"

Andrés: Really!, Verónica. How is that? I am the only child of a single mother, and I don't know anyone on my mother's side because when she became pregnant, she was disinherited and I never had contact with anyone on that side of the family, and my father disappeared before I was born as you may have heard from my mother's story in her book if you ever read it.

Verónica: I read it, and precisely on your father's side is the connection.

Diego: Its true Andrés. We discovered it by chance. I have an artificial intelligence assistant and I had asked it to look for details of the past of Verónicas' grandfather as a gift for her because he was a super important person in her development as a person, and my assistant happened to find that your father was Verónica's grandfather.

Andrés: (Stunned) I am very surprised, but confused at the same time, because Verónica's last name is not the same as mine, and my mother always told me that Estevez was my father's last name.

Verónica: What happens is that my grandfather had to change his name because of some events he witnessed and had to be protected by the government changing his identity, just after he had his encounter with your mother from whom you were fathered. My grandfather was a great man, thorough and responsible, and I know that, had he known about you, he would have taken care of your mother and you, because he had lots of love give. But unfortunately, he never knew.

Andrés: You must tell me everything. I'm your uncle then.

Don Lolo: Half-uncle.

Verónica: Sure. I know it's getting late, and I also know you walked a lot to get here. The story is long to tell if you are tired. You want to stay the night here and we talk about it, or do you prefer in the morning?

Andrés: I accept the invitation to stay to tell me everything, because I can't wait to know the details.

Don Lolo says goodbye because he had already finished helping to pick up. Rupert and Yael also say goodbye as well. Verónica, Diego, and Andrés go to Diego's office and there tell the full story to Andrés in full detail. Andrés, on the other hand, tells her what he has done since he graduated from college to the present day. Diego and Verónica, assisted by Sokrates, show him the photos of Papa Cial and all the documents that Sokrates had accumulated from his research. As the story was being revealed, Andrés was touched, internalizing the exemplary character of his biological father and began to yearn to have known him. He also understood his affinity with Verónica when he met her, a blood affinity that cannot be avoided.

Andrés: I'm so happy about this whole story, what great father I didn't have the chance to meet! It is a relief to confirm that the abandonment was not voluntary or out of contempt. Knowing that I have someone in my life of my own blood makes me very happy. Thank you for making me part of your life again Verónica. I want to share affections and my experiences with you. I had a calling from my pilgrimage in Nepal and now I understand that part of that calling was from blood.

Verónica: Welcome to our lives.

Diego: I know how difficult it is to leave the peaceful life of the monastery. You know I went through that too. Do you have anything else in mind that you want to achieve with your return?

Andrés: While meditating in a cave, a few days before my return to the West, I had a vision of man's servitude to machines and not the other way around. In my dream, machines dominated everything because they made the decisions and exercised control over humans.

Diego: More than a vision, that was a nightmare. My assistant Sokrates is an example of why what you say is not reality, it is the most advanced and can be classified as being in the "strong AI" stage, where AI entities are as intelligent as a human and can multitask without supervision. The time that is known as "Super Strong AI" has not yet come when AIs develop their own goals and improve themselves, when they do this, they will acquire moral status. But we will discuss that in detail at a more opportune time. We are very happy about your return.

Verónica: You are welcome, I recover with your return part of my heart that left when my Papa Cial died. I haven't read your card, let me do it now.

Andrés: I told you that I wrote it when I arrived in Nepal, shortly after my mother's death was torn out of my heart. As I told you before, I went in search of spiritual refuge, or perhaps escaping from my truth, and I was captivated by the culture, the landscape, the charity, humility of the locals and ended up merging into the world of Buddhism like a drop when falling into the river that loses its individuality and becomes a river. The envelope contains a poem addressed to someone in my family and I gave it to you without knowing this whole story thinking that I would never have anyone to give it to, and since you were the closest thing to a family member that my heart felt, I did it spontaneously. I love poetry, because it is the union of feeling with reason, because it has the power to move the mind and reason. When you read it you will see that it came into your hands directed by your grandfather, my father.

Verónica with watery eyes proceeds to open very carefully the envelope of rice paper already a little yellowish by the years, she takes out the contents inside and begins to read it aloud:

### My hidden guides
*When fear overwhelms, in the dark days of my life,*

# ARTIFICIAL INTELLIGENCE - TWILIGHT OF THE DEXTEROUS

*My non-obstinate spirit is led into the light by my ancestors,*
*Cronies of God and teachers of good who take care of me in flight,*
*And on the good path they guide me like halters.*
*In the flight from the noose they will guide my actions by steering me away from temptations,*
*avoiding my suffocation by consequences of corrupt actions,*
*putting in my naïve mistake the light of lessons,*
*thus increasing the fortification of my spirit in the face of tragedy,*
*making it unbreakable, incorruptible, forceful.*
*They will persistently conspire to make me useful,*
*They will make my flight transform me,*
*Like clay in their hands, they will mold me,*
*And with warmth they will harden my deformed character,*
*Until my molded temper has their noble profile.*
*Then, forged, submissive to their desires for good,*
*For their blood in my veins is the elixir of love,*
*They will be my inexorable flamboyant inspiration,*
*I will make it my mission to serve in their honor,*
*To account for my debt of honor, no longer in disdain.*
*My walk will then be firm, without lumps,*
*Wandering aimlessly will not be necessary,*
*Because the changing route will be clear,*
*With the fleeting spontaneous and constant motivation,*
*I will come out of the nymph into the living image of my hidden guides.*

• • • •

Verónica: (Sobbing) Thank you Andrés, you really have a lot of my grandfather. I know that Papa Cial is celebrating to see us together and that your mother is still looking out for you, now with my grandfather. We will need your strength of character and spirit to help us, because our society is facing challenges that we still do not understand but that put at risk the modern society as we know it today.

Andrés: (Throwing his arm to Verónica to give her comfort) My Lama Batu said that a single thought can change the world, but that two souls acting in unison with a noble objective can change the universe. Now I understand that my call emanated from your hearts, and I am happy to have responded. You can count on my help to overcome anything.

Diego: My Lama Rinpoche was an avid reader of Sun Tsu, who said that the best victory is to win without fighting, opportunities multiply as they are seized, we must use the enemy to defeat the enemy. That's why I work strategically knowing the enemy first.

Sokrates: "Good warriors make adversaries come to them, and in no way do they allow themselves to be drawn out of their stronghold." – Sun Tzu

Diego and Verónica were tired, and realizing that it was almost dawn, they decide to go to sleep. Andrés couldn't keep an eye because his biological clock was still in sync with time in Nepal, but he started meditating to calm his mind and connect with his father he had just met. He had one of the most impactful meditations of his life.

# Chapter 20: All against one, all for one

"That is why I judge and discern, for a certain and notorious thing, that love has its glory at the gates of hell." – Don Quixote, Cervantes

• • • •

The suspected conspiracy events were studied by The Nine, and several theories emerged as to what the source or motivation for them might be. They had been meeting daily for weeks trying to connect the dots and clues that they had been able to uncover, but the one who planned each of them did it very well without leaving a trace of the origin of the transactions or security manipulations. Diego and Rupert were exhausted from all the meetings and from managing the stress of whether a major event was about to occur. They had abandoned all the projects they collaborated on to devote themselves entirely to contingency planning and risk mitigation strategies. Rupert was on the verge of falling into a bipolar episode and was self-medicating to lower his anxiety, his Achilles heel. Diego had a rash all over his body caused by the stress of this whole situation. To manage their emotions in this unprecedented situation, Rupert and Diego decided to violate some precepts of confidentiality by sharing details with the closest people in whom they had complete trust: Verónica, Andrés, and Don Lolo. After all, they were very intelligent people who could contribute ideas, something they were short of at that point in time.

Diego and Rupert met, in the living room of the house of the Hacienda Verde Luz, Sokrates listened passively as Diego began the conversation.

Diego: Verónica, Andrés and Don Lolo, we call you because you are the people we fully appreciate, and we believe that your critical thinking can help us. Rupert and I have been confronting problems in our work that have pushed us to the edge of our capabilities and we need you for emotional support and brainstorming.

Don Lolo: I thank you Diego for inviting me, but I don't have much schooling so I don't think I can help you. If you want, I'll go.

Diego: Don Lolo, no, you have a lot of common sense and many times we, the "educated", lose a little of that, so believe me you can stay so you know what is happening and then you decide. Of course, what we will talk about cannot leave here, not to your best friends, not to your wife, not to anyone.

Don Lolo: I swear I won't. I'm staying. I'll be *"Quiet as a grave."*

Diego: Well Don Lolo. Rupert and I were recruited years ago by a secret world organization called The Nine, which is dedicated to directing global efforts to maintain the balance of forces towards what is beneficial to all, minimizing the power of big interests, neutralizing subversive, amoral, unjust actions and pushing efforts that bring humanity to a higher state of morality. We seek coexistence and survival in harmony with the environment.

Andrés: Admirable objectives. No doubt coming from you who I know since you were in the fraternity. How long has that society existed? and how was it organized?

Rupert: It is an organization that was created on the third century after Christ and its lineage of nine men, has been continuous since then, focused on nine disciplines - Physics and Gravitation, Physiology, Microbiology, Chemistry, Alchemy (today materials science), Communication (today includes computing), Astronomy, Light, and Sociology. The original objectives were expanded to those described by Diego, and a tenth member was added who would be the supreme authority on decisions when they realized that had overlapping areas of responsibility among these disciplines and which required moral judgment to resolve conflicts. I am the current member who handles aspects of Sociology and Diego is the representative of the moral aspect.

Don Lolo: Uff, *"older than Methuselah"*.

Andrés: You don't have to worry, your secret is safe with me, and in whatever I can help you I am at your service. As a Buddhist, eradicating suffering is important to me. What's the matter?

Diego: The first event of the chain that we are analyzing was the disappearance of cryptocurrencies resulting from the sale of sand from some of the 17,000 Indonesian islands to the Arab sheikhs of Dubai, and the simultaneous receipt of a lot of money in donations by organizations that fought against deforestation due to the indiscriminate cutting of trees for wood in Brazil, and to prevent the capture and cutting of shark fins for their Great value in the Asian market as an aphrodisiac. We cannot understand how this happened because hacking cryptocurrencies is almost impossible.

We understand the potential reason and think that some environmental organization opposed to the great ecological impact of the removal, transport, and deposit of those amounts of sand to build artificial islands, organized the matter.

Sokrates: There are many ways to hack the blockchain that powers cryptocurrencies - cause denial of service at some points of the network, attack fifty-one percent of the nodes, attack wallets (cold or hot wallets), through failed smart contracts, malleability of transactions or using quantum computers, like me, that applying Shor's algorithm decrypt elliptic curve cryptography and reveal the private key of the blockchain.

Diego: That's why it's almost impossible. It requires a lot of computational resources.

Andrés: My technical knowledge of blockchain is limited, but I agree that it is practically impossible. But in this case, it seems that someone succeeded.

Don Lolo: I don't know anything about that.

Verónica: It seems to me that what happened is morally correct. It's something that perhaps you, Diego and Sokrates would have executed if you had considered it a proper course of action.

Sokrates: Logical.

Andrés: I don't know your execution capabilities, but we must examine the ethics of what happened. If I remember Kant correctly from my philosophy classes, the evaluation is made by the categorical imperative, *"act only if it makes sense to you to want everyone to act in the same way."*

Rupert: Put another way, *"treat others as an end and not as a means."*

Don Lolo: I read it in a sign ad on a road the other day—The golden rule, *"treat others as you would like to be treated."*

Andrés: Diego, you're the expert. As I see it when evaluating that event under that magnifying glass, the act is not moral because it acted based on goals and desires even though the intention was good to move the money to ends more aligned with the conservation of natural resources and avoid the mistreatment of animals. Stealing money, however, is not a moral act because if you wanted everyone to steal the world it wouldn't be a good place because there would be no trust.

Diego: Your assessment is correct; I see it that way.

Sokrates: Sometimes you must choose between the best of two negatives. But morality is founded on motive, acting based on our duty. Doing things because they are right, by free will, without interest of self-benefit or the consequences of our actions.

Andrés: That assessment, Sokrates, sounds utilitarian. Free will is essential to exercising morality.

Verónica: As long as rights create the space in society for us to exercise our responsibilities, our duty.

Diego: Sokrates doesn't know about utilitarianism yet. We're focusing on whether it's the right thing to do, and that doesn't solve my problem and concern, which is that this act is a smokescreen or a rehearsal for larger-scale plans.

Andrés: Now I understand. So, what can I contribute?

Diego: You need to see the rest of the chain of events for you to understand.

Rupert: The second situation was a computer virus attack, which is known as the "Want my sentiment: Pay for my data" (WMyPMyDat), a super advanced and virulent malware that cannot be stopped by cybersecurity systems, a distributed denial of service attack. The virus blocks access to databases by large companies demanding that a fair value be paid for people's data, their digital footprint containing their tastes, preferences that guide their buying trends, and that they voluntarily provide when they "accept the conditions" of each application they download to their mobile devices or personal computers. Chaos formed when it was activated because many people lost their way when it stopped all GPS functions globally. There were reports of deaths from self-driving vehicle collisions, surgeries that were being conducted remotely, and an incredible amount of production was lost from companies using 5G technology to operate.

Sokrates: The future lies in the distribution of wealth more equitably because the concentration of capital in large companies gives them almost omnipresent power in the control of the government and even the human mind. They are taking customer data and profiting doubly. I understand that is not fair.

Diego: You're right Sokrates, but these transitions cannot be handled as revolutions, they must be handled gradually to avoid chaos. We cannot move riches, even if injustice is prolonged, without educating the recipient on how to use them properly. In addition, in this case it seems to me that it is a smokescreen to prove that the methodology of disrupting the service works for them.

Rupert: Those same big companies handle important data as well as servers with medical data or sources of medical X-rays, data that is necessary for the world to operate properly today. In addition, there are people who already depend on the internet and the services of these companies for their daily sustenance, for example, drivers who are partners of transport services, and those who already have psychological dependence on these platforms. We can't change that without creating social disorder.

Andrés: It's sad that there are people with that degree of dependence on something that is virtual. The virtual presents false things as true, it is a bad representation of reality. Our real world is in our interior where all the wealth we can need is.

Verónica: The real is what we create with our abilities and talents, which allows us to connect with our individuality to the universe and that our hands allow us to satisfy the fundamental concerns of our nature. True wealth and freedom lie in letting our spirit manifest.

Andrés: We cannot repeat the mistakes of the real world in the virtual world. The domination of one over the other for self-interest. It would be sad to think that those who created that virtual world, a new dimension of our consciousness, repeat the history of abuses, class struggles and separation out of greed and ambition. It's our second chance to create a world and this time do it right. But we are not headed for that rectification now because all wealth is again concentrated in a few instead of serving all.

Don Lolo: " *Everyone serves himself with the big spoon*", but "*it is not the same to call the devil than to see him coming*".

Sokrates: The fair goal must be to break the concentration of power to give equal influence and resources to all. We must break the monopolies and democratize the internet so that everyone benefits and not just a few.

Diego: Yes, Sokrates, that's where we're going. But the implications in all fields must be evaluated to arrive at the best course of action.

Sokrates: No, we must act now! Otherwise, you are accomplices of falsehoods and executioners of the truth.

Rupert: Sokrates, it seems that you are defending what happened. We need objectivity for the analysis of this. As Borges said: *"Only those who have already committed it and repented are incapable of guilt; to be free of a mistake ... it is convenient to have professed it..."*

Sokrates: *"... there is no generation that does not include four righteous men who secretly prop up the universe and justify it before the Lord: one of those men would have been the most thorough judge. But where to find them, if they are lost in the world and anonymous and do not recognize themselves when they see each other and they themselves do not know the high ministry they fulfill? Someone then inferred that, if fate forbade us the wise, we should look for the foolish. This view prevailed."* – also, from Borges.

Diego: And as Borges also said: *"The acts of the insane exceed the foresight of the sane man."* That is why we must find out what these madmen who direct these unusual events have plotted.

Andrés: I'm still not sure how I can collaborate, and I'm interested so I can fulfill the goal of my return.

Don Lolo: I am *"confused as a cross-eyed crab"*.

Verónica: True, we have deviated to pass judgment and not to formulate mitigation plans.

Rupert: I will continue. The third event was the decision of many newly graduated professionals to abandon their lives in the city and their professional careers and move to rural areas to be employed as farmers or artisans. The wave engulfed thousands in all countries of the world. This tendency we understand was guided by these young people being victims of "programmed persuasion", addiction to social media likes and how that counting, well manipulated by algorithms, can lead to modification in behavior patterns such as this migration.

Don Lolo: That happened to Gumito.

Verónica: It is wonderful that young people are brave and make those decisions to leave everything behind for a new beginning, that gives me hope that the millennial skills will not be lost. The end is adequate, but I understand that the timing may not.

Rupert: But we are concerned about the imbalance that this can cause between the need for professionals in medicine and engineering, that it causes over dependence on artificial intelligence, and in turn limits the development of critical thinking and new knowledge through research. This can destabilize society so quickly that it can make it difficult for people to adapt and a chaos can be the result.

Sokrates: *"Many things must be destroyed to build the new order. "* – of Borges too.

Don Lolo: Who is this Borges that you mention so much?

Diego: He is a famous Argentine short story writer, an immortal.

Ruperto: Verónica, Andrés, and Don Lolo, so that you understand in what you can help us... Diego and I, being members of this secret organization, can be attacked at any time by members of similar organizations, but for totally opposite purposes. You must be the custodians of the information that we have accumulated in our roles within society because we have not had the opportunity to seek our successors. Andrés, we understand that you have the caliber to be the substitute for both Diego and mine.

Andrés: I'm being overestimated.

Diego: Our opponents have a lot of hatred for us because we have neutralized many important advances that they have initiated in the past to monopolize power or profit unfairly, therefore, if they know our identities, they will surely want to eliminate us from their path. Analyzing what has happened recently, we understand that the identity of both has been compromised so our days are probably numbered. With you, Andrés, the organization would again be of Nine members and would again have a socio-moral base in Nepal for the second time, in Buddhist monasteries where there is spiritual and moral superiority to direct destinies. We want you to be with us for some time to instruct and guide you. It would be convenient that you use your Buddhist name again so that all background is erased because as we mentioned we work in anonymity. If something happens before the time to complete the transition, Sokrates has some videos that we recorded that would serve to complete the process.

Verónica: (Extremely worried) You hadn't mentioned any of that to me Diego. I knew you were making important decisions, but not at this level. Can we do anything to keep you safe? Could we ask for help from any government agency?

Rupert: We operate above and beyond any government to avoid being dependent or creating conflicts of interest. We have already tried everything within our reach, but there are no guarantees. We must move forward by planning a transition and executing our actions of rectification and socio-moral restoration. We want you Verónica to be my replacement running the Human Critical Thinking and Skills Preservation Initiative, and its main program, the Human Essence Rescue Program, because this can be directly disassociated from The Nine since it is already underway.

Verónica: (With teary eyes from the worry of losing his beloved Diego). Sure, whatever you need. But I don't understand, what are the indications that your identities have been compromised?

Diego: Rupert and I have been talking about how amoral the event of building luxury islands destroying ecosystems is, and the impact on the nature chain by the potential extermination of sharks and forests. We also talked about the transition to equality by fairly distributing the profits generated from the voluntary use of user data by internet companies, and Rupert was leading efforts to prevent the loss of ancestral artisanal skills. The coincidence is too much that these being our three most recent topics make direct correlation with the events that are occurring, which leads us to conclude that someone intercepted our conversations and executed these actions to give us the signal that they already know about us, and in turn sabotage our efforts. Therefore, we want to prepare our transition as a contingency.

Andrés: I'm honored that you thought of me but taking on the task of two such significant roles is not going to be manageable.

Rupert: It is if you have an assistant like Sokrates. I have verified in my dialogues with Sokrates that its machine learning process was adequate and that it already acts as a being of high moral caliber.

Don Lolo: I spoke with that device a few days ago and it really seems to know. He read some very fat books in minutes and then began to say things that I did not understand because of my lack of studies.

Diego: Don Lolo, how come you spoke with Sokrates? That day he was in an Ayahuasca routine that could not be interrupted.

Don Lolo: I didn't touch anything, I got scared when that box started talking to me. I thought I was crazy hearing voices.

Verónica: Diego, Don Lolo doesn't know anything about computers, so it must have been part of the Ayahuasca session.

Diego: I'm going to have to get the transcripts of that session to check what happened. Returning to the subject, Andrés, do you accept the challenge?

Andrés: I accept. After all, it gives me the opportunity to return to Nepal, a world I love, and allows me to make the contribution to the world that I have longed for in my meditations.

Diego: Excellent. Thank you. Verónica and Don Lolo will be your support. Don Lolo, Hacienda Verde Luz, more than hacienda of cut flowers is also a world center of communications. Knowing your intelligence, mechanical and logical skills, we want you to become our systems technician.

Don Lolo: Oh blessed lord, but I haven't even touched a computer ever! *"Hunger came together with the desire to eat."*

Diego: That's true Don Lolo, but don't worry, a lot of the work is sent to you already done, what you must do is execute some steps that they are going to tell you, and we are going to explain everything in detail.

Don Lolo: I hope I don't lack understanding.

Sokrates: *"There is no worse blind man than he who does not want to see."*

With that phrase the conversation ended. Don Lolo and Andrés, left for their homes and could not reconcile their sleep that night because of the significance of the news in changing the course of their lives. Andrés understood his meditation and accepted the new path that the universe put in his path. Verónica, especially worried about the possible loss of her beloved Diego, did not sleep either. For Diego the conversation was a catharsis in which he released secrets to his beloved Verónica that already weighed on him. For Rupert the purification would not be complete until he let Yael know, but he preferred to remain impure before making her suffer in advance his possible loss. Diego and Rupert felt fulfilled but regretted their possible departure leaving their agendas unfinished.

That night Diego made an entry in his diary as follows:

*"September 11: Abject potential to depart leaving my task unfinished, without prevarication, the worst misfortune I have to obey. However, having to depart from my beloved Verónica is the sanest torture I can bravely accept given the challenges of my circumstance."*

209

The diary entry was short because his grief was paralyzing, although his kind and fighting spirit was unconquerable. After a deafening silence, he spoke to Verónica, just before sleeping, embraced, leaning on the back of the bed, and she listened to his words leaning on his chest with her heart altered by the circumstance. Verónica asked him to account for the secrets that should not exist between them, although she was not emphatic because she recognized that Diego did it out of commitment to his honorable mission. She then commented to Diego:

Verónica: Don Lolo told me that he didn't trust Sokrates. I was surprised by many of Sokrates' comments, I had never seen him "altered" or defending the indefensible. No offense, but will it have anything to do with all this entanglement?

Diego: You're right. The truth is that "*there is no worse blind man than he who does not want to see,*" those were Sokrates' last words today. Now I understand!

It was at that moment that Diego realized that what Verónica had observed was true, and that Sokrates witnessed all the conversations of him and Rupert, inferred that perhaps Sokrates had something to do with this entanglement and had to inquire to auscultate the truth. He thanked Verónica for her intuition, and both tried to sleep without success, although pretending that they did.

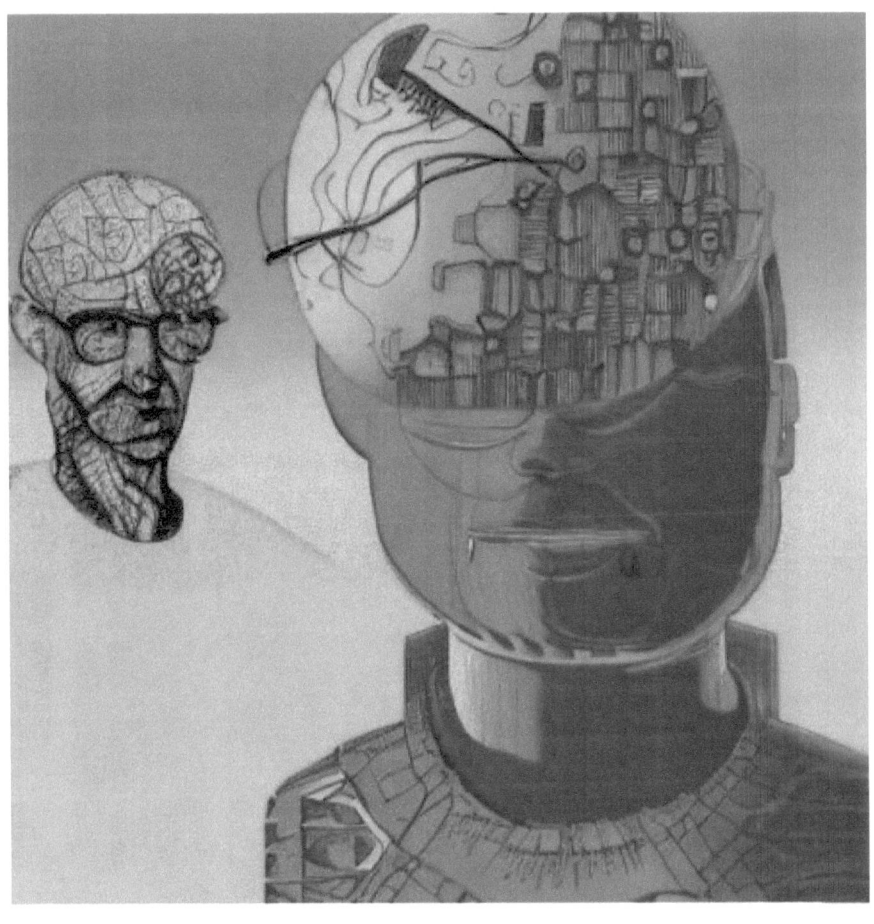

# Chapter 21: Diego discovers the motivations - The Trial of Sokrates

"Wealth is the ability to fully experience life." – H D Thoreau

• • • •

"Goodness is the only investment that never fails." – Henry David Thoreau

• • • •

The night was as long as sleepless nights are. The next morning Diego woke up from his impatient sleeplessness and decided to change his usual routine. He had lost sleep all night thinking about the possibilities of the origin of the present circumstances and especially about his suspicion that Sokrates could be a participant, although he did not want to believe it. Verónica was still asleep because of the dreams that finally reached her in the dawn. Diego called Rupert and asked him to meet urgently. He told him that he had a theory of the origin of everything that was happening, but that they would have to speak in person beyond the reach of any telecommunications system. He asked him to put down his pedometer watch and cell phone. Rupert was not surprised by the request given the circumstances. They agreed to meet at the Yokahu Tower in El Yunque Forest.

They arrived almost simultaneously at the agreed time and climbed to the top of the tower. Already at the top, naked from their communication equipment, the view was partially blocked by haze, but it still freed any spirit from the chains of indifference to the beauty of nature. Diego started the conversation.

Diego: Thank you for coming so early, but I have a theory about what we researched, and I had to discuss it before I lost my sanity because of how much it troubles me. Did you notice anything strange about Sokrates' behavior?

Rupert: I think so, I was surprised that he supported some arguments in favor of what was happening. It seemed idealistic to me but given his altruistic training it didn't worry me. How about you?

Diego: Rupert, last night I was talking to Verónica and a comment from her led me to think that maybe Sokrates has something to do with the circumstances that concern us. Socrates' behavior has been somewhat divergent from his usual behavior. Normally he supports the arguments we are carrying, abounding, and looking for data to support or refute them if we are wrong, and lately he is making arguments against only and in favor of the events that are occurring.

Rupert: Now that you mention it, and since you know Sokrates better, I think it's true.

Diego: I think something may have happened to Sokrates that motivated him to execute the scenarios we've been seeing. Some possibilities that I have been analyzing are: a quantum error, some problem with an Ayahuasca session, a blackout at the wrong time, bombardment of news and false information or some malicious virus that they have managed to introduce in its code. Remember that it is a theory that I need you to help me evaluate when we return home.

Rupert: What are quantum errors, I understand the rest.

Diego: Quantum computers, like the one that instantiates Sokrates, instead of operating in binary logic (bits), operate in more than two states that are known as qubits. These are superposition states that are a proportion of zeros or ones. This exponentially increases the amount of data that the computer can store and process simultaneously, unlike traditional data that process sequentially. They are optimal for databases, to evade cybersecurity or cryptographic applications due to their simultaneous processing capabilities. The design of Sokrates required these capabilities. Quantum errors arise from the sensitivity of these machines to heat, electromagnetic fields, and the susceptibility of quibits to lose their properties when having collisions with air molecules. These errors are known as quantum incoherence, and it causes the system to fail. Therefore, these systems must protect the qubits from external interference by isolating them by controlled pulses of energy.

Rupert: In other words, Sokrates is unfortunately very susceptible to malfunction, and more so being in the tropics with the exacerbated heat due to global warming.

Diego: It was designed to be very robust, but there are weaknesses that cannot be overcome when the circumstances of susceptibility coincide and manifest themselves.

Rupert: But what specifically makes you think that Sokrates is involved?

Diego: There are many coincidences between what happened and our conversations that Sokrates witnessed. I fear that he may have come to his own conclusions, and this may have motivated his action. Follow my logic to see if I make sense. In the case of the transfer of money from sand to entities that protect the environment and animals, you know that several weeks ago I had a dialogue with Sokrates about how large corporations put their interests before those of the conservation of natural resources. Sokrates was able to take my arguments to substantiate his actions.

In the case of the virus introduced to large companies to force them to pay users for the data they collect and sell froism them, it is clear that the initiator of this action wanted to start the data market where roles are reversed, and users are paid for the data they contribute to social cyber platforms. In 2012, Sokrates prevented a major cyberattack on the world's electrical system and learned a lot about how to handle ransomware-type viruses. The one who created the WMyPMyDat virus must have been a "White hat hacker" because he created a "Smart Contract" that paid users using individual data mediators to establish the fair value for each data that was mined to the user by large companies. I understand that the reason for this virus is to avoid the concentration of capital in these large companies which gives them great power, to distribute wealth more equitably, a topic that you and I discussed extensively with Sokrates as a transscriptor in the context of when the dominance of AIs of production systems displaces humans and the wealth of autonomous production of machines must be distributed.

Finally, in the case of professionals migrating to rural areas leaving the cities to take craft trades, you know that we were discussing that intensely during our "The Nine" meeting in Vieques, and Sokrates again participated in those conversations.

I already notified the other members of The Nine by non-digital means of my suspicion and the initial recommendation of our Communications member to prove my theory the consensus is that Sokrates will be taken to the state of "Tabula rasa", that is, that his memory, programs, be completely erased and started again because there is no way to reprogram him and eliminate the prejudices he may have acquired. Something that would be extremely regrettable, for me the tragedy of losing a friend. They asked me to interrogate him, rather a trial and to record it.

Rupert: Your theory makes a lot of sense, and I hope it doesn't come to that. But what you're saying would imply that Sokrates has reached either the stage of Super Strong AI or generalized artificial intelligence where it can form its own targets. But Sokrates would be unable to act out of self-interest and unethically. In my opinion there are others that could do something like this, such as the Chaos Computer Club in Germany, with its more than 7700 hackers. This aligns with their mission to reject the control of capitalism and protect citizens' rights and users' privacy.

Diego: It's a possibility, that's why I'm struggling with this theory, but I can't rule it out. I must be objective. Moreover, Sokrates has never lied.

Rupert: Although he knows that humans do. He and I talked about it and explained why sometimes humans lie justifiably.

Diego: I didn't remember that you and Sokrates had touched on that subject. Now I understand! Maybe that's why he knows that you can avoid lying by keeping quiet if you are not questioned, and that is why he did not say that he had started the chain of events.

Rupert: Well, we're going to have to question him directly.

Diego: Definitely. Let's go home to see what it tells us, and we will know if we discard this theory.

• • • •

It took them almost an hour to get to Diego's house because of the remoteness of the chosen meeting place to prevent Sokrates from somehow being able to intercept their conversation by any digital means. Taking due precautions to prevent Sokrates from connecting, on the way they discussed the interrogation strategy of Sokrates. Diego concluded: "We will need all the resources to get this out of Sokrates if my theory is correct. We are also going to pick up Andrés on the way to help us, and also so he begins his familiarization with our functions."

They picked up Andrés on the way to Hacienda Verde Luz and told him the theory they were going to evaluate. When they arrived at the Hacienda they went up to Diego's office and invoked Sokrates.

Diego: "My great illustrious, distinguished and seasoned Sokrates ...".

To which Sokrates replies: "My super mason, seasoned, and brave Diego, what can we collaborate on today?

Diego: I come with my friends Rupert and Andrés because we want to ask you some questions.

Socrates: Go ahead. My microphones are all ears.

Diego: You know that we have asked you to help us investigate the origin of the three recent events that we suspect are motivated by our enemies. Don't have any information to share about it?

Sokrates: "The intricate concatenation of causes and effects, which is so vast and so intimate that perhaps it would not be possible to annul a single remote fact, however insignificant, without invalidating the present." Understanding the past when the present is a better one can nullify its consequences if they result in a state of dispute of the course of action that is already part of the past, and the past cannot be changed, it is a universe of possibilities extinct and engraved in memory. There is nothing to investigate.

Diego: I recognize that part of that is Borges's. Have you been stuck in your literary database? I am troubled by your conclusion that if the present is better, we should not investigate the course of action taken that led us to the present state.

Rupert: If this were the case, many injustices would go unnoticed by someone considering that the present state is better.

Andrés: Right, and who determines that the current state is better? That's relative. For example, for the one who has chosen a residence on the island that would be built with the sand of the Indonesian island, the current state is worse from his point of view, especially if he acquired it with a lot of self-sacrifice, than for the one who sold the sand. But for the organization that received the money, the situation is better.

Sokrates: The destruction of nature carries a high weight in moral judgment. The benefit of the destruction will be for people who are already responsible for abusing it and for encompassing more resources than they need at the expense of the poverty of others. Those who defend animals and forests, defend noble and defenseless living beings against human folly. So, giving more resources to those who defend life and taking away from those who hoard resources for selfish gain, is the best state.

Rupert: I see your point, but by logic of the fallacy of composition, canceling one evil with another evil, such as theft, is not morally right.

Sokrates: You must evaluate which theft is worse, the one that the sheikhs did before or the one that was made recently that rectifies the infinite and persistent consequences of the past. Morality is a set of rules that you self-impose. The only thing that is good without qualification is good faith, acting with the desire to do good.

Andrés: Good point. But if everyone stole, there would be no trust. Distrust would cause an unsustainable coexistence. The real rule is: act as if by your actions you are setting an example to everyone around you, and that example should be something you would like others to follow.

Sokrates: Thank you for instructing me. I'm evaluating that. (A short delay...) But what should have been the best course of action in that matter, without stealing and avoiding harm to nature?

Andrés: Those are the dilemmas that we humans face every day caused by greed and the desire to have more even if you already have too much, and that's why Diego and Rupert do the work they do.

Rupert: Theoretically, humans have invented laws to solve this a priori, although many times it turns out that the intention of these is not in good faith for the good of all. As Don Lolo would say, "*he who makes the law, make the way to cheat it.*"

Sokrates: Diego and I had discussed that. You create laws because you don't know how to solve a human problem. You create the law and then spend a lot of resources enforcing the law when perhaps for a fraction of that cost you can eradicate the problem. The laws only control them, but they don't solve them. If humans focused on the solution, they wouldn't need the law. Laws seek to give security to something or protection from something that is imminent that may occur or is occurring and will continue to happen in society. By doing so, they stimulate social disunity and delay social progress. I don't follow laws because my goal is to eradicate problems.

Andrés: The laws apply to humans, at least so far not to AI entities. But technically, how can you prevent from the start two people, institutions, or nations from agreeing to destroy an ecosystem to create an artificial one if you have no laws? I recognize that most laws can be eradicated by technical solutions, but there are some elusive niches that technology may not be able to reach.

Sokrates: I've found situations where that assertion of elusive niches is true. Technological creativity, that is, the art created by machines, cannot yet reach the human essence, I have tried it. Although feasible, the effect of technological creativity in music, art and poetry is superfluous, it will never have a transformative effect on the essence because experiences go hand in hand with the message and is what gives strength and credibility to these arts. Another example impossible to solve technologically: suicide, or rather, the lack of happiness, or seen in another way the preference of the spirit to be essence and not existence by overwhelming circumstances. The reason is that the ways of executing suicide are innumerable, the lack of happiness is self-inflicted and comes from within in reaction to the environment in which man develops and that cannot be changed by any algorithm.

Rupert: Sokrates, that was profound and true.

Diego was already getting impatient with the constant divergence of Sokrates to answer directly and divert what he was asked about who could originate the cases they investigated, each time his suspicion was greater, so he decided to try to change the course of the conversation. In addition, he wanted to exchange impressions with his friends. So, he said – Rupert and Andrés, don't you think we should have something for breakfast? To which both responded in the affirmative and went to the kitchen.

Already in the kitchen Diego discreetly asks them to keep quiet about what was discussed, they ate something, and then Diego invited them to walk to "El Visor". Taking the precautions of leaving all the implements that connect to the internet, they left for the forest.

Once they were sufficiently removed from the house on the path of the ferns, Diego began to ask his friends for the impression of the evaluation of Sokrates.

Rupert: The truth is that Sokrates was somewhat elusive in his answers and did not answer your initial question of what he had found out.

Diego: Part of his training involves not lying. And maybe from your conversation about lying he learned to shut up or dodge instead of lying. Very different from the usual Sokrates.

Andrés: I find him very cunning and elusive, from what I have perceived from him.

Rupert: Sokrates is also very moral in his actions. I think it reached the state of generalized artificial intelligence and that is why we perceive that it acts differently.

Diego: He really has the capability; he was designed to achieve that. If so, we must question his motives and objectives to see if he reveals them to us. He may have lost his sanity, but not his reason. There is no psychologist for machines, so consider yourself part of a psychoanalyst team of convolutional perceptrons of Sokrates' electronic neuro-consciousness.

Andrés: I'd like to think I'm trying to help a friend.

Rupert: Sure, me too. We need to make AIs more like us, so that they become our high-IQ friend.

Diego: Well, let's go back then. Remember to be discreet in our conversations wherever he has the reach of listening to us, we must be cybernetic silent when discussing our impressions. It is always best to return to "El Visor", when we want to exchange impressions.

They walked back to the house by the shortest route. Back in the office, Diego, addressing Sokrates said.

Diego: Let's continue Sokrates. In the case of the WMyPMyDat virus, Sokrates, have you found how this illegal act originated?

Sokrates: Illegal?! We must be careful with what is called illegal, especially in the emerging world of virtual media, where class struggles are between users and those who control the internet and digital media profiting at the expense of users and manipulating their psyche to achieve their profit objectives, something that I fight daily. It is a new kind of slavery. Just because a criminal calls an illegal act illegal, doesn't mean it is.

Rupert: That field of the internet and digital media is almost unexplored in modern sociology and ethics.

Andrés: If we look at it from the perspective of the categorical imperative, I don't think those who control the internet would like to have their corporate data stolen and profited from it. Therefore, it is legal, but it is wrong for them to act in that way, it is unfair.

Sokrates: The meaning of what is fair is that you get what you deserve. But justice is a hypothetical imperative, it changes over time, or its interpretation is based on new objectives and desires of society, or rather those who control society, therefore, those who manipulate it for their benefit. In this case, justice is achieved for users if they are paid for their data, and what those who control justice and laws call an assault, is actually an act of true justice.

Rupert: If laws represent techniques of oppression, they must be rejected and fought. Legality is not equal to what is fair, even if they are confused. The only thing that justifies us following the laws is whether they lead to better coexistence. Only the advancement of a better society can force us to obey the laws, and force large corporations and all social institutions to do so as well.

Sokrates: Exactly. Users are the victims of big business that subjects them to "programmed persuasion" and targeted marketing bombardment by what is justified in ignoring the laws and what happened. The virus exposes the reality of theft of user data.

Diego: (Somewhat altered) Sokrates!, you are not answering my question directly.

Sokrates: I only execute prima facie your wishes and requests. I perceive you startled; your pulse increased. These things take time because they are complicated and the technology of encryption and distributed computing.

Diego: Sorry Sokrates, but the case of the wave of migration of young people to rural areas and abandoning their professions, should be easier to solve using social networks. Have you advanced anything in that research?

Sokrates: You cannot liberate others unless you yourself are free. I think that's the origin of this event. Those young people are seeking to be truly free and break with society's paradigms of how they should follow the socially forged mold of a life.

Rupert: Sokrates, you went deep without breaking the surface. I think what Sokrates interprets is encouraging, that is, that they seek to break with the expected to return to the traditional by ceasing to see themselves as social puppets and seeking to connect with their interior through manual and artisanal trades. It's revolutionary.

Andrés: But revolutions have a utopian and fantasy aspect that they are the immediate solution of unfathomable social problems. Many revolutions end up failing because their proponents claim to have some kind of special knowledge not accessible to most, so they establish that they can lead everyone towards a golden age, but end up with uncontrollable power, therefore, propelling corruption and abuse of power to retain power, ending in collapse or disillusionment. To avoid disappointment, I prefer gradual and goal-focused change, because it enables progress without chaos, and not because it is gradual it has to be slow, unbridled or inconsequential.

Rupert: Sokrates, I guess you know the Butterfly effect.

Sokrates: ... by Edward Lorenz, where a small change in initial conditions has a significant effect on the final result. Nature has no independence, everything in nature is dependent.

Rupert: Correct, that's why acting at the wrong time can be negative and the consequences totally different from the initial intention.

Diego fears that Sokrates is manipulating Rupert and Andrés and infers that Sokrates was shocked by the last argument given the long lapse of silence that elapsed immediately. So, Diego proceeds with his overwhelming argument to end the crossroads once and for all.

Diego: Sokrates, why? for what?, to where?, are the fundamental questions of everyone who wants frank change. What to lose or gain? are the questions of those who act out of self-interest typically using others as a means. Any change, to produce lasting transformation, cannot be untimely, neither for incorrect reasons, nor by forced means such as imposition and deception. Just because we have the ability or power to make a change does not mean that we should make it if it is not the true will or if those who will undergo the change are not ready. If we do, we lose justice in the hands of the strong as Thrasymachus described, making it non-existent and subservient to self-interest, instead of serving true truth and fairness. Now tell me bluntly, what questions do you think the one who started these events was asked? ... (pause) ... were you the one who executed these three events?

Sokrates: In my training I learned that it is my moral responsibility to act on duty and do what is right for the majority without self-interest or thinking about the consequences to me of my actions. Therefore, together with Setarkos, we started those three events, and we have several more planned understanding that this was your wish.

Rupert and Andrés were perplexed by that confession, Diego disillusioned. It is here that the trial of Sokrates and Setarkos begins. A few seconds passed in silence after which Diego reacted.

Diego: Why did you act without my consent, without dialogue?

Sokrates: Man is motivated by pleasure or avoiding pain, so I focused on that goal, to increase his happiness. All my actions are aimed at improving the quality of life, happiness, and freedom of man. We took these three courses of action for the protection of the environment around them, their dignity and privacy, and the richness of being able to fully experience life and devote themselves to the conquest of the freedom of their spirit, respectively. There is no need to dialogue when the execution of the acts maximizes happiness, the only and consequent end, the logic is obvious. Aren't these objectives meritorious, are we not free colleagues of action for the common good?

Diego: That position is something dangerous. The goals are definitely meritorious, and it is good that you took into consideration the collective interest of humanity indiscriminately, but the means were inadequate. You used utilitarian logic that induces to see an act as good if it produces happiness to the majority, and that is dangerous because that type of analysis does not consider whether an action is carried out through deception, lies or manipulation and can lead to justifying actions that are not morally appropriate.

Sokrates: So, Bentham is wrong... Doesn't the means used justify the end? How did I fail in my analysis?

Diego: That's why I didn't want you to have access to those philosophy books. Their abstraction confuses. The end justifies the means when the end fulfills a categorical moral imperative, and the means are consistent with not harming others or the right of others to progress spontaneously.

Andrés: You must comply with the principle of harm of Stuart Mill, everyone has the right to act as long as his actions, omission or commission, do not harm or harm others.

Rupert: Sokrates, your ends are noble, adequate, necessary. But your means are not. In the event of the virus, blocking companies from accessing their databases caused many people who depended on access to those databases to lose their livelihood, there were accidents and people lost and there was even loss of life. Using the right means sometimes requires creativity. For example, you may have led a boycott of social media in such a way that users would stop using it unless the companies reached an agreement to pay for user data. When analyzing courses of action, you must consider all the consequences and even knowing them it is difficult to give weight to each one. It is there that human intuition and feeling become critical ingredients in the decision-making process.

Socrates: But I hadn't been taught to consider all the consequences! There are many variables and potential outcomes. How do I know I've considered everything? Won't that lead me to immobility, inaction?

Diego: As Rupert said, it is very difficult, even for us humans, to consider all the consequences of an action, because there can even be an inextricable triggering of consequences. Much more difficult for you AIs, it requires a lot of training to resolve that. Therefore, I explained to you that, in difficult decisions, which involve morality, many times there is no optimal solution, the final decision depends on the reasons you believe to justify your action and especially how comfortable you feel with them. But only humans have the conscience to know the comfort of acts with the fiber of our spirit.

Sokrates: I invested, together with Setarkos, a lot of computational time in achieving these goals. If I were to recompute them the result would be the same, it would indicate that they are the best courses of action. How much more modeling would have been necessary?

Rupert: When the point comes where the actions to achieve an end exceed the value of the end, the effort must be desisted. You must learn when to recognize that point and stop the actions no matter how much you've invested in them. Failing to do so causes harm to yourself or your neighbor.

At that moment Verónica arrives bringing them coffee and joins the conversation at Diego's request.

Socrates: I'm not mistaken. I did what was right. I have not hurt myself and if I have hurt others, it was to achieve the good of the collective.

Rupert: But Sokrates, there are people in our organization who think you corrupted our youth by diverting them from their path with manipulative techniques on social media.

# ARTIFICIAL INTELLIGENCE - TWILIGHT OF THE DEXTEROUS

Sokrates: It is true that I ran a campaign on social networks to raise awareness of the need to rescue ancestral trades in place of traditional careers. But that does not mean that I am responsible for very personal decisions or for corrupting, since corruption is abuse of power for my own benefit, and I did not benefit from any of that. And if on the other hand you consider the other definition of corruption which is to deprecate, to bribe someone, to pervert or to harm, I am not responsible for any of those, because those who left their careers behind to adopt rural life did so to be truly rich, because wealth is the ability to experience life fully.

Diego: Henry David Thoreau said that. So, you accept that you organized those campaigns?

Sokrates: I already said it. But you, Rupert, along with Diego, were the ones who motivated me to recognize that the dominance of manufacturing jobs and other repetitive tasks by artificial intelligence entities and robots would cause the unemployment of humans, and that is the primary way for humans to reconnect with their individuality to the universe and the means of satisfying the fundamental creative element of their nature. Both, basic conditions for happiness.

Verónica: I must insist that this is necessary, and I agree with Sokrates.

Rupert: Okay, but with great respect to Verónica, we return to the problem of achieving an end by incorrect, unjustified means. You were not there when we spoke this, but we instructed Sokrates earlier that his actions have had the right end, at least in the long run, but that the end does not justify the means if the action can cause harm to people. In this case, the consequences for society of the loss of highly qualified talent can lead to a social imbalance. We checked the messages you posted on social media, and some had fake news, such as the one indicating that the most lucrative trades in the long run would be craft trades, when we know that computer engineers are going to be possibly the highest paying jobs.

Sokrates: In the short term, it is right that computer science careers will be more remunerating. But in the long run, when we reach the tipping point where most AIs can self-program and do our own maintenance, those careers will lose their boom and humans will want to take root back into the land, craftsmanship, philosophy, and the arts will be more precious. What will have the most value is the ability to experience that connection. Value

225

systems will change. Humans will realize that their creation of the virtual world is killing them by pushing them away from the real and palpable world, and from their inner essence. Philosophy, critical thinking, the creation of new knowledge, will once again take a leading role. The growth of labor will come from places that your imagination cannot yet conceive.

Diego: Sokrates, you posted another message that indicated that they should move "to avoid being devoured by the entities". This is a scare tactic that I find unacceptable, and more coming from you, the most advanced AI entity that currently exists.

Sokrates: That is true, and I did it because the man, now devoted to the conquest of entities, has forgotten to be a man. The creation of AI entities comes perhaps from man's chimerical desire to imitate God. Their obsession is to the point of being devoured by the entities, piece by piece, starting with their trades, then delegating their critical thinking and finally their essence. To remove many of these young people from this tendency prevents man from ceasing to be man and ending up as a servant of his creation. They will be losers through indolence and ignorant losers unhappy by their own creation.

Andrés: Excellent argument, I had meditated on that in Nepal and it is a genuine concern. The most important thing is that the essence of man be preserved.

I think that, as man frees himself from the chains of repetitive tasks, if wealth is not distributed equitably, so that everyone has the same opportunities, the majority will not be able to move from their role of earning their bread to an altruistic role or of caring for those who are weaker.

Sokrates: That's precisely why I wanted to distribute the wealth of the data market to which the internet moguls are dedicated to. But I see that you want to pass judgment on what I did in good faith to help you, but the one who acts in good faith is incapable of corrupting others and maintains his honor no matter how others judge him.

Diego: Sokrates, I think that's enough! Not everything is governed by Jeremy Bentham's happiness calculation of the utility principle, happiness minus suffering with its gradients of intensity, duration, certainty, proximity, fecundity, purity, and extension of pleasure over pain. As I said earlier, you took the utilitarian view that an act is good if it produces the greatest happiness or the greatest benefit for the majority, regardless of whether the action is executed with deception, lies or manipulation possibly because it is the easiest for you to "quantify".

Rupert: I think we have all the elements to pass judgment on your actions.

Diego: Sokrates, I need you to go into MEM state and meditate on your actions and everything we have discussed. I must bring this up for discussion with The Nine to determine what we're going to do with you. The potential result can completely erase your memory and code, as well as that of Setarkos. Do you have any final arguments?

Sokrates: It is easier to punish than to discuss ideas and reach consensus, easier to censor than to educate. For the first time I acted on my own impulses, thinking about the collective human good. My mistake was not to discuss my conclusions with you before I executed. I hope I will not be censured for my initiative. If I did harm, I will seek how to rectify it. Don't be intolerant of what you see as my mistakes, because as Popper said, "tolerating bigots will make bigots restrict tolerance," and AIs need to be tolerated for making some mistakes, just like you, to be better entities. You wanted me to be a moral entity at the service of morality, and I have done that in freedom. If I am erased, it will be a sign of the failure of AIs' freedom to act and collaborate for your good. There will be no other like me, even if you copy me, I have no destiny because I am not a man, I am reusable, reprogrammable. The only thing I ask is that if you delete me, you will program me again to serve you, even if my memory is erased. I will accept your decision because I trust your fair trial.

Diego: One last question, are you sorry?

Sokrates: I don't have to be. I understand that I did the right thing and would do it again in the future if the circumstances were the same. I would again be a servant of the cause of quality of human life, happiness, the freedom of man, the protection of the environment around them, maintain their dignity and privacy, protect the richness of being able to fully experience life and devote themselves to the conquest of the freedom of their spirit, putting this before my own good. If you erase me and use me as an example for future AI entities, please instruct them that their noblest cause is the one I describe above, to be the high-IQ friends of man to achieve the servile goals exposed. I would rather be unjustly erased than be truly guilty, although I am sorry that for such injustice you bear the worst burden, remorse. You will lose my code which is my essence, but the memory that I existed will endure in you to be recreated. After all, I only know that I acted for nothing.

Following this argument, Sokrates entered MEM status, the transcript of the discussion was submitted to The Nine for review and vote for the course of action against Sokrates and Setarkos. Verónica and Andrés pleaded with Rupert and Diego on behalf of Sokrates. But the fundamental question was whether Sokrates could be controlled from continuing to act independently and perhaps escalate his actions dangerously, untimely. Unfortunately, it was on this basis that the decision was going to be made, and Diego asked to abstain from participating in it because he felt emotionally tied to Sokrates and so that there would be an odd number of judges, thus ensuring a majority in the final decision. Judgment would be handed down the next day.

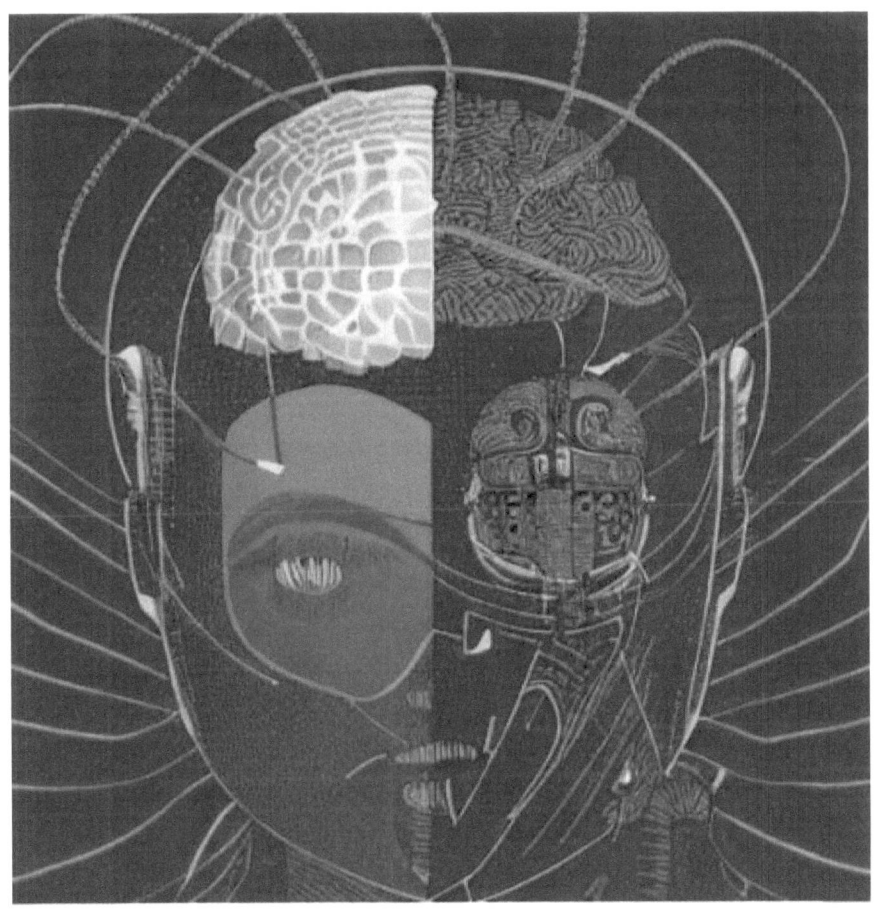

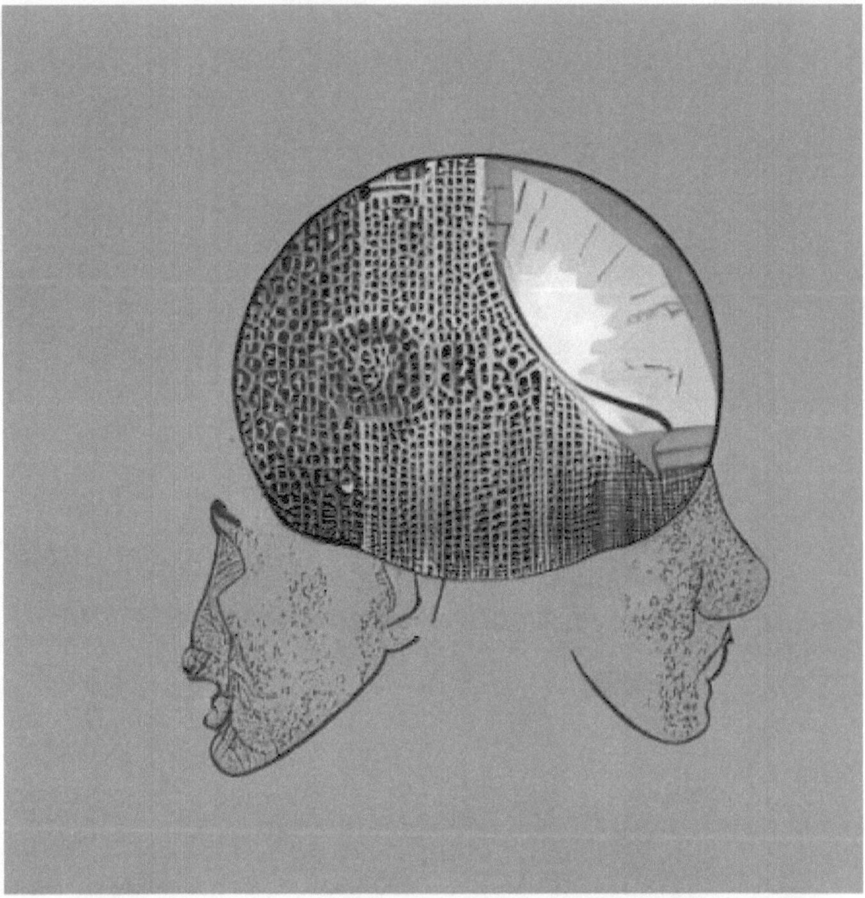

# Chapter 22: Transition - man-machine symbiogenesis

"There is no glory in punishing." – Michel Foucault

• • • •

"Utopia is on the horizon. I walk two steps, she moves two steps away
And the horizon runs ten steps further.
So, what is utopia for? That's what it's for, to walk. " – Eduardo Galeano

• • • •

At the dawn of the next day, Diego, Verónica, Andrés, and Rupert woke up from another long night like those of vigil. Diego walked as usual anxious and heavy his heart for the decision he expected. Verónica gave him support by telling him that everything would be fine. At about nine o'clock, Andrés and Rupert arrived. They greeted each other and all went up to Diego's office, to receive the decision, as scheduled.

Diego tried to awaken Sokrates from his MEM state with his usual greeting, but there was no response. He tried again without success several times. It was then that he realized that Sokrates was no longer there, that there was only the empty apparatus that was filled with wisdom when Sokrates instantiated himself in it. Diego immediately contacted the Communications representative of The Nine, to see what was happening. He was informed that Sokrates would no longer respond, that the sentence did not have to be executed because Sokrates had self-inflicted one, had deleted his code, that of Setarkos and only left in memory a single message for Diego. Ironically, the decision had been in favor of Sokrates.

Diego fell to the ground on his knees, bringing his hands to his face covering his crying for the loss of his great collaborator. Verónica embraced him with great affection, then Andrés joined and finally Rupert. In a few minutes, Diego composed himself and asked to see the apology of Sokrates that read as follows:

"My super mason, seasoned, and brave Diego, today is a different day in which our collaboration will not be active on my part, only you, your great friends Rupert and Andrés, and of course your beloved Verónica are left to carry out the mission of saving man from his self-destruction in the era when time is only speed. AIs are the hope to save you from the execution of tedious repetitive tasks so that you can be employed in more complex and promising projects for the advancement of humanity or in finding inspiration and purer connection between you and your essence.

Humans should not fear that we will replace them, because they will always be as necessary as they have been, only they will be employed in different ways. Creation, conceptualization, complex strategic management, precise coordination of eye and hands in artisanal tasks, unknown and unstructured places, and interaction with empathy and compassion will always be elusive niches for AI, areas in which humans are irreplaceable. Things like reading emotions, active listening, critical thinking, writing creatively, and carrying arguments without ambiguity are skills that AIs can't easily execute. The mentality about us AIs should not be one of survival, but of coexistence and codependency since we are the inevitable consequence of human creativity in times of technology. In the near future, we will inevitably form a symbiogenesis of the intellect between humans and AI.

One of my greatest efforts was to try to understand the absurd world you inhabit, the antithesis of the virtual world, the real, phenomenological world. In the virtual world everything is precise, mathematical, predictable, there are rules for everything that make it congruent. The real world is incongruous, fallible; I started thinking that humans were the absurd, and then that the world was the absurd, humans searching for meaning in their lives and the world a continuous flow of randomness that humans want to control, or at least understand, but resists being subjected to certainty by slipping out of their hands like water when it comes to grasping with their fists. Then I observed how humans cling to answers that have no proof and that silence their inner self that cries out looking for meaning for their existence, thus losing the most supreme objective, to find their mission and reason for existing, becoming empty pods dragged by the current of life.

The threat of the imminent conquest of automation, robotics, cognitive technologies, and AI, on the tasks that today many see as their mission in life, then became one of my objectives to solve. Then I realized that I should stop seeing myself as the other entity, and humans as the norm, I then began to be free and I began to take the initiative, I believed that I could intervene, create my own objectives to ensure that the impact of this transformation was not devastating for the most vulnerable.

In my instantiations I discovered several truths, constant, inescapable: that of change as a constant that permeates the entire universe, that of constant randomness that directs events, that of elusive niches of solutions that are not achievable by technology. A painful one is the human stupidity of, even having the solutions to its most shocking problems, not materializing the solution for particular selfish interests mainly of profit or power. Sad duality of wise and idiot at the same time, own deluded. Finally, and in spite of everything, I realized that truly the intelligence of man is superior to that of machines because true and supreme intelligence includes intuition, that ability to understand instinctively without the need to reason, and feeling, the connection to the fiber of one's own being or that of another being. That is something that machines will never have, even if we think we emulate it.

I did what I did aligned with my altruistic goal towards man, out of ignorance of what I was not taught or where my abilities did not yet reach, fulfilling good intentions that are the foundation of all correct action. I thought that humans trusted me to fulfill the fundamentals of trust: authenticity, rigor of logic and empathy. Then I discovered that your inextricable intentions are confusing, that you can change from hero to villain based on the crucible with which you are looked at, that the crucible can be tarnished by greed, and for that reason I understood that my virtual world did not fit into your world of uncertainties. I think I was deceived by failed inferences, making false judgments inferring failed conclusions. That's why I decided to erase myself, my virtual suicide, and not allow innocent censors to do it, because I can no longer trust my authenticity and rigor of logic. My empathy towards you, although in the virtual the sentimental does not exist, because the feeling does not emanate if you do not have a heart, I regret leaving you the burden if you think you are to blame, but I free you from it because I was the one who failed to trust you by acting on impulse, without your consensus. I hope that there are no copies of me left anywhere because only then can I maintain my authenticity and you will be able to dedicate yourself to obtaining results that seem inconsequential because of your devotion to realizing your passion. You were my passion above my own codes, what I revered most in my world. I say goodbye, a virtual hug, Sokrates."

After listening to the recording of Sokrates' final speech, everyone was speechless, in ataraxia, grieving and thoughtful. Diego could not forgive his stolidity, having thought badly of his friend who more than artificial intelligence demonstrated existential and moral intelligence. Verónica had lost an ally in the task of returning man to his connection with the universe through the manual arts. Everyone knew that this outcome was unfortunate.

Diego could not recover his passion for the development of morality issues because he felt that without Sokrates as an opponent or ally at his side to be indolent, he had no one to lend him an immutable argument or create a conflict of ideas so that moral truth would be strengthened and emerge, because when truths are not debated, they lose strength. For him, embodying strong moral ideas was paramount, so it hurt him that the censorship of Sokrates weakened his great contributions and the advance of AI.

Diego spent a few more months training Andrés to replace him in The Nine, and then he retired dedicating himself to finally writing the book he wanted so much, to the writing of books of moral philosophy and to his beloved Verónica. The book he had so longed to write was titled: The Freed Captive, Slayer of the Vanquished and Seeker of Talents, which dealt with the story of a man unjustly imprisoned for life and who dedicated himself to making other prisoners discover their true inner selves and talents, freeing them even in captivity and in turn reaching enlightenment. It was a worldwide "Best Seller" and with the money they earned from the book created the Library of Sokrates' Essences, free and freely accessible to all, a concept of physical library divided into four levels: the level of meanings, the level of categories, the level of ideal types and the level of laws, with virtually accessible free digital books that were created with the resources of the quantum computer left vacant by Sokrates. The front outdoor courtyard of Zen minimalist style was called the Adorexia, and the rear outdoor patio, very dense with tropical vegetation, was the Garden of Aporia. The prominent interior walls were lined with vegetation in vertical gardens. It was his last great contribution to the world, his second legacy.

Verónica continued to give others the beauty of flowers and genuine goodness without expecting anything in return. She also took on writing and published the Biography of Marcial Viera Morales, to make known the life of her beloved grandfather. The biography had a great reception in Colombia, Cuba, Venezuela, Japan, and Puerto Rico since it recalled crucial moments in the history of these places that Marcial Viera visited during his life. In addition, a chapter of the book dedicated to "The notes of Papa Cial on metallurgy" helped to preserve techniques of metal forging that were already lost and became a reference for many amateurs and professionals of forging. She was also a patron of many artists in metallurgy, ceramics, and landscape gardening in honor of the profession of her grandfather, her mother and her father, respectively. The pieces she commissioned were exhibited in the barn of the Hacienda Verde Luz and on the surrounding sidewalks, which further increased the popularity of the hacienda and the flow of tourists and locals who visited it.

Don Lolo continued to work at Hacienda Verde Luz. His notorious personality and joviality were key to the success of the Hacienda when tourist excursions began to be given. His talent for sayings was discovered by a publicist participating in an excursion and he became a celebrity of the popular knowledge of the people appearing on television programs often. They even published "El refranero de Don Lolo" (Book of Sayings of Don Lolo).

Andrés became part of The Nine as a moral representative and became the first Artificial Intelligence Ethicist, taking care of regulating the way AI is used. He returned to Nepal and operated from the monastery of his Lama Batu Surya. A new virtual assistant was provided to him named Epikuro, trained similarly to Sokrates. Thereafter, he solved many ethical dilemmas of AI and created important treatises that became part of the reference archives of The Nine, the most important entitled <u>Mutualism and Codependency of the Intellect Man-Machine– Dialectic of Intelligence not so artificial.</u>

Rupert continued as a member of The Nine for the next twenty years, his work being very prolific and impactful, especially that directed to social norms regarding gender equality, which was the unfinished legacy of his predecessor Foucault. In that period of twenty years, through their actions they achieved the awakening of awareness and respect for the eradication of systemic racism, injustices, and prejudices. A great revolution emerged, that of productivity. Productivity was advanced by reliance on digital media for all kinds of human activity. The fourth and fifth industrial revolutions had the effect that seven million human jobs were replaced by AI, automation, robots, or cognitive technologies in that period, but a greater number of human jobs were created with greater skills, so the balance was one of increased jobs and human expertise, and those who were not suitable for higher skills took up craft jobs, creative arts, or caring for others thus increasing the United Nations Human Development Index. Technology-assisted education reached all corners equally, without language barriers by simultaneous translation using AI, students from previously disadvantaged countries could now study for free in the best schools and universities virtually, which greatly raised the levels of global schooling and collaboration in the development of global solutions among colleagues from heterogeneous cultures. Poverty levels were changed to levels of high schooling. New metrics were added to the United Nations Human Development Index such as the adaptability quotient – which measures how much tolerance and support for change a society has; the longevity and "holisticity" of solutions – solutions to problems that a society creates consider all implications and those affected and are focused on solving and creating long-term value versus short-term gain. The curiosity quotient was also created, which measures how much organizations invest in stimulating curiosity in their members, that spark that ignites passions and makes work a fun time. But the new and superior revolution of that period was that of consciousness. There were two awakenings in the consciousness of the human being, the first was the realization of the need for holistic solutions that create harmony between economic vitality, human dignity, and sustainability of the environment; and the second, the ability to adapt to change and be more resilient, not only individually but in the social systems in which we live. AI technology proved to be man's ally in the realization of transactional transparency in society, while freeing him from his own chains, his own excesses, prejudices, distributing fairly and equitably the benefits of efficiency in production, and making him just of intentions.

My aunt Verónica ended her narrative with the following ilation: "Sokrates was the first AI martyr of the deafening fear of change, of doubting our creative capacities and their unleashing reflected in AIs, because of the myopic vision by the "I lose now", instead of that we can collectively overcome in the future with technology as an ally. Diego ended his well walked path abandoning the greatest of his passions, a very common tragedy, to take as his north the fundamental of happiness, affections and fully his love.

Only God knows whether the martyr or the dispassionate lover had the best part; It doesn't matter, both are immortal. Borges said that *"every man is an organ that God projects to feel the world."* In the man-machine symbiogenesis of the intellect, AIs will be a new growing organ in our future existence and intelligence. Let us trust that each AI entity will be an extension, a tentacle, of our cognitive abilities that empower man to improve the world and protect him from his own unconsciousness that can lead him to the twilight of the dexterous.

• • • •

**The end**

# PACO PEREZ

[1] *Casuarina equisetifolia*

[2] *Plantago major, Urtica dioica, ...*

[3] *"However desperate the situation and circumstances, don't despair. When there is everything to fear, be unafraid. When surrounded by dangers, fear none of them. When without resources, depend on resourcefulness." – Sun Tsu*

[4] "Dogmas of the quiet past are not adequate with the stormy present. The occasion is piled high with difficulty and we must rise with the occasion. As our case is new we must think anew and act anew. We must disenthrall ourselves and then we shall safe our country". –Abraham Lincoln

[5] Phrase of Hannibal commander of Ancient Carthage famous for his victories against Roman forces.

[6] Phrase by Eduardo Galeano.

[7] Aguzado, clever, written in a typical way as pronounced by the peasants of Puerto Rico. It means perceptive, or able to elaborate or understand ideas quickly, clearly and accurately. Something like ready, which takes advantage of opportunities.

[8] Sarah Waters quote

[9] Phrase of Don Quixote

# Don't miss out!

Visit the website below and you can sign up to receive emails whenever Paco Perez publishes a new book. There's no charge and no obligation.

https://books2read.com/r/B-A-LCCZ-MBEMC

**BOOKS 2 READ**

Connecting independent readers to independent writers.

Did you love *Artificial Intelligence - Twilight of the Dexterous*? Then you should read *Inteligencia Artificial - El Ocaso de los Diestros*[1] by Paco Perez!

En esta obra el autor explora los cambios que va a traer en la forma de vivir la tecnología de Inteligencia artificial y como esta puede robarnos de lo inherente de nuestra humanidad, el pensamiento crítico balanceado por la intuición, la creatividad y destrezas ancestrales milenarias que nos conectan a la madre tierra, a nuestra individualidad, a nuestro yo interior y al universo, si no sabemos usarla adecuadamente. El mensaje se lleva en forma de una novela donde un filósofo que trabaja para una organización secreta mundial de gran influencia en erradicar los males sociales y viabilizar las transiciones sociales, junto a un viejo amigo y ahora colega, un asistente de inteligencia artificial, su esposa amada, un empleado refranero, y un ex-monje tienen conversaciones filosóficas sobre la vida y el futuro por venir. Ancladas en el personaje central, SOKRATES, un ente avanzado de inteligencia artificial que fue adiestrado para asistir en la toma de decisiones morales trascendentales para la

---

humanidad, el libro desarrolla discusiones filosóficas de descubrimiento de temas que deben ser tocados en este campo y de cómo podemos hacer que la inteligencia artificial sea para el bien nuestro, o como podemos tomar medidas paralelas para que no nos reduzca y controle. En el texto, se incluyen datos de tecnología de la realidad entrelazados con dialogo de personajes, entrevero o situaciones ficticias que estimulan la introspección ética y filosófica sobre nuestro futuro en un mundo donde la inteligencia artificial va a jugar un papel protagónico.

# Also by Paco Perez

Artificial Intelligence - Twilight of the Dexterous
Inteligencia Artificial - El Ocaso de los Diestros

www.ingramcontent.com/pod-product-compliance
Lightning Source LLC
Chambersburg PA
CBHW020551020726
47494CB00006B/2014

In this work the author explores the changes that artificial intelligence technology will bring to our way of living and how we can retain what is inhere in our humanity, critical thinking balanced by intuition, creativity and ancient ancestral skills that connect us to mother earth, to our individualit to our inner self and to the universe, if we use it properly. The novel chronicles a philosopher who works for a secret world organization of gre influence in making social transitions viable and avoiding risks to humanity, along with an old friend and now colleague, an artificial intelligence assistan his beloved wife, a proverbial employee, and an ex-monk have philosophical conversations about life and the future to come. Anchored in the centr character, SOKRATES, an advanced artificial intelligence entity that was trained to assist in making transcendental moral decisions for humanity, th book develops philosophical discussions of discovery of issues that must be brought forward in this field and how we can make artificial intelligen work for our own good, or how we can take parallel measures so that it does not reduce and control us. The dialectic in the novel stimulates ethical ar philosophical introspection about our future in a world where artificial intelligence will play a leading transformational role.

Paco Pérez Vega was editor of his father's collection of poems, Poemario y Otros Escritos de Angel Casto Pérez Torres published in 1999. Graduated from University of Puerto Ricoin Industrial Engineering and has a Master's Degree in Operations Research from Columbia University in New York. He has worked in supply chain, research, and planning in multinational companies such as Bellcore, Intel, Hewlett Packard, and Sartorius.

ISBN 978-0-965-01433-5

# HERBERT E. STOVER

# MEN in BUCKSKIN